NECRONOTE

NOTES OF NECROSOPH 1

AL K. LINE

Copyright © 2021 Al K. Line

A Warning

I write dark characters, but always with a lighter side too. This time things are a little different. Or maybe I should say a little more extreme. I've upped the snark, the banter, the bad jokes (trust me, they are the worst), but most importantly of all, hence this introduction and warning, the absolutely foul language and the violence. The swears are there from page 1, the violence too. The brutality, and the descriptive nature, grows towards the latter third of the book. Please bear that in mind. Ugh, makes me shudder!

At its core, the Necroverse—and the many stories I hope to populate it with—is about people. Family, human interaction. Everyday struggles like discovering who ate the last biscuit, and why do tumble dryers have to beep so damn much? The normal conversations we all have, and the way we act often under the direst of circumstances. But there is a deep and undeniable underlying tone of violence, verging on madness, in the Necroverse. It's at the heart of everyone's lives.

We have magic, all manner of supernatural creatures, and an awesome world to explore and discover together. But rather than fight scenes that go on for chapter after chapter, the violence is usually brief, very brutal, and as grounded in reality as I can make it without ever having been stabbed in the heart or blasted by a freaky looking witch. The true heroes of this world are the myriad misfits—human, animal, and everything in-between—who inhabit a universe that may seem all-too-familiar. One we can all imagine as possible in the not-too-distant future. Especially after recent worldwide events, and the ever-present threat of climate change and the problems this will undoubtedly bring. Let's be honest, they're already here.

It's not about preaching, though. Don't ask me how to solve the world's problems. I find it hard enough to figure out what socks to wear, and I have two styles of pants (I'm British so I mean underwear) to choose from now, which causes issues, but we can all picture a future something like the one presented in the Necroverse.

Soph, our hero, but let's get real and call him an anti-hero of the truest kind, is a bad man in many ways. And no, he is not a wizard, at least according to him. He has no fireballs to sling, but he has his own gifts, which you will discover as we go. Soph loves his family, and when you peel back the protective layers of sometimes unhinged violence, his heart's in the right place. But this is warts-and-all, so expect to get annoyed with him. He's making his way through best he can, but he's got a lot of issues, and more than his fair share to deal with.

There is too much larking about for this first-in-series to be classed as Grimdark, but there is a darkness, albeit often hidden under the light of Soph saying stupid stuff and cats called Mr. Wonderful (wouldn't they all be called that if you gave them the option?).

Please enjoy the first in the Notes of Necrosoph series. I think it can take us all somewhere special. As the books unfold, we'll learn more about this world together, watch it change, see characters we have learned to love deal with untold problems, maybe lose some too, and if you want to get new release notifications then please sign up for news of new notes.

The plan, if enough people read and I can justify continuing this series over the long term, which I hope will happen, is to see everyone grow and change over many years in the Necroverse, and we might even get some spin-off series. Drop me a line if you want to suggest anything; I'm always open to reader's ideas.

This first book has already been my most challenging work to-date—I really need a wiki already—but I think this world might be something just that little bit special. I hope you will join me for the ride.

Don't forget—swears aplenty (and I mean a lot), violence to make you squirm, jokes that are even worse, and really fucking stupid unicorns.

Stay jiggy,

Al

p.s. There's a dragon too. You gotta have a dragon.

Note

"For crying out loud, Mr. Wonderful, how many times have I told you not to bring your, and I'm definitely doing air quotes here, your scumbag, 'prizes' into the damn house?"

Mr. Wonderful dropped his "prize" and glared at me in the way only a cat can. Full of utter contempt, enviously secure in the knowledge he was far superior to any other living creature, me in particular.

"Maybe you should actually look at the 'prize' I just brought you," he said in his slow Southern drawl, although he was from Essex. Somehow, he managed to do air quotes without making any kind of effort.

I stared down at what he'd dumped on my rug, his usual place to leave the bloody, headless corpses of unfortunate creatures he'd tormented before decapitating.

Sighing, I rocked my awesome, tatty brown recliner forward and stared at the stained rug, scene of countless crimes against nature.

"A piece of paper? Well, beats a dead bat." My head swam, my guts churned, the old ticker beat ten times faster, and I broke into a sickly sweat, but I went along with the game we'd played way too many times before.

"Hey, I told you that was an accident. Bats are weird to eat. It's not a piece of paper, it's a note."

"A note?" I tried to act surprised, but my heart really wasn't in it.

Mr. Wonderful vibed me.

I waited. He waited. He would win, so I said, "And?"

"And what? It's for you."

"How'd you know that?" I asked, feigning suspicion.

"Got your name on it, numnuts. See?" He pointed with a perfectly manicured claw at the note. I squinted and tried to read it, but it was just a blur. I grabbed my glasses then continued the charade.

"Necrosoph."

"Yep."

"Where'd you get it? What's it say inside?"

"How should I know?" he grumbled. "I'm a cat. I can't read."

"I know that," I snapped. "But you knew it had my name on it." I was getting carried away here, so was he. Why did we continue this idiocy?

"I may not be able to read, but I'm not stupid."

I let it go; sometimes he was like that.

Against my better judgment, and still without answers as to provenance, I heaved out of my chair with a groan and several creaks, and reached for the paper. It was still crisp-looking, folded neatly in half, and incredibly white. Almost beyond white.

I hesitated, almost sat back down, and then that's exactly what I did because I knew this was nothing good.

"Why do we continue with this stupid game?" I asked my companion of fifty-three years.

"We thought it would be a good idea. Lighten the mood. Make it less stressy. Remember?"

"Well, it isn't," I told the perfectly preened pure white cat as he licked a paw then used it to rub his face. "I am the epitome of stress, and this isn't helping."

"Suit yourself." He continued to clean himself, not caring either way what I felt or thought.

The paper shifted on an impossible breeze, then snapped at my face and covered my mouth and nose, sealing my airways.

I tore at it, but it was stuck fast like Duct tape. Bastard notes. I hated them more than anything. This was because I didn't open it immediately. A reminder. Soon I was on the floor, gasping, as I clawed at the paper, but to no avail.

I rolled my eyes, pleading with Mr. Wonderful to help. He shrugged, then reluctantly swiped at the paper. It dropped to the rug in front of me and unfolded.

After getting my breath back, I retrieved my glasses then got onto all fours and read the psychotic note. "Twinkled. Wizards. Ugh, it's that fucking app thing now, isn't it? Where's my phone?" I tapped the screen, pulled up the Necronotes app, then signed in. I typed in the two random words and waited. And waited. And waited. "What's the point of there being an app? We never used to need apps? Just an address or a coordinate, that's all you need. Bloody stupid," I grumbled. I grumble a lot. It's one of the few consistent things about me. Got to have something that keeps you going through the ages. "It's just going around in circles, this little wheel. It isn't working. It isn't loading! Crap."

"It's so they can keep..." slurp, slurp, "...track of you. They're watching." Mr. Wonderful, and no I did not name him that, he chose it himself, rolled his eyes and stuck out his little pink tongue.

"Will you stop licking your balls when you're talking to me?" I shouted. "And I don't want to be tracked or watched, or anything. I want to sit in my chair and chill. I want to eat a biscuit, not use a bloody app to confirm I have a nightmare looming that will make my stomach hurt for weeks after. If I even survive."

I studied the screen again. There it was, the location highlighted on a satellite image.

"Oh no, could this day get any worse? Look, it's bloody miles away. Out of my zone. And I need a new bike. I'll never make it. It's all, you know...?

"Tiring?" slurped Mr. Wonderful. Apparently clean, he jumped onto the windowsill to admire his reflection.

"Exactly!" This was getting worse by the minute. I lived a stone's throw from the Welsh border, but it was still England, and my duties encompassed both countries, but never so far as to encroach on another Necro's territory. That wasn't how it worked. The only answer was that several others had died and so my patch had grown. Joy.

CRASH!

I readied for the threat as my head snapped to the shattered window. A familiar long white horn protruded five feet into the room, stuck dead center on the stupid looking head of what you might otherwise mistake for a horse. Everyone else does, as horses don't have massive horns, now do they?

The animal was grinning, a wide smile with teeth as white and perfect as the sparkly horn. Nearly as white as Mr. Wonderful.

"Oh, for fuck's sake, Bernard! I've told you over and over again. It's a window, not a hole. This isn't your bloody stable."

"Oops," said Bernard.

"And look what you did to Mr. Wonderful."

Bernard checked the room then shook his head, glass shards flying. "I don't see him."

"Man, he's so dumb," I muttered. I pointed at his horn. Blood trickled down, pooling on Bernard's forehead. "On your horn, you numpty. You killed Mr. Wonderful."

"Oh no, not again. He's gonna be so mad." There was true terror in Bernard's pale eyes.

"Oh yeah, and then some," I agreed, perking up a little.

Mr. Wonderful's limp body trembled. Blood defied gravity and trickled up the horn into his body. The lifeless form of the nasty cat slid off the shimmering spike as Bernard lowered his head, then landed on the carpet on all fours. Mr. Wonderful's eyes snapped open; he glowered at Bernard with utter menace. His claws nicked out as the feline fucker swished a paw through the air.

"I just finished getting clean," he hissed. Bernard backed away slowly.

"Time for a cup of tea, methinks," I said hurriedly, then scarpered into the kitchen as all hell was let loose in my living room. Bernard would be a bloody mess within seconds. Luckily, my kettle was crap and made a right racket. Not loud enough, but it helped disguise the screams. Trust me, you ain't heard nothing until you hear a unicorn scream.

I attempted to drown out the promises of vengeance and pleads for mercy of my "pets" by humming as I stared at the kettle. Don't ever let them know I used that word. They're funny like that. All, "Animals have rights," and "We're our own person," nonsense, when I don't see them doing the shopping or paying the bills. Um, not that I do either. But I think about it, so that counts.

The dented old kettle boiled, and boiled, and kept on boiling. Why wasn't it switching off? The steam built in the room, and the heat began to intensify. WTF? Can

I say that as a three-hundred and forty-year-old man? Is it still cool? Hard to keep track. I even tried a LOL once, but it plain didn't feel right.

Steam billowed at the ceiling. Damn, and it had just been replastered too. At least I'd used apparently wipeable paint, although that never used to be a thing mere decades ago. Soon, I became lost to the swirling patterns. So pretty. Hypnotic.

A hand reached down through the fog and grabbed me by the throat. Ethereal, but real enough to my neck. A body soon followed, until I was suspended in the air by a bloody daemon of the most unfriendly kind.

I sighed. This kind of crap was always happening. At least once every decade or two if I was on a spell away from the spells, haha. You just never could tell what would come with the yearly Necronote.

At least I was a fucking menace with a blade.

I snapped the popper on my knife sheath, pulled out an old favorite—ebony handle, damascus blade— and stabbed the bugger right in his eye then sliced off his nuts. Damn daemons did like to wave their bits about. The ball-sack dropped with a gross squelch and the daemon howled as he grabbed at his crotch with both hands.

I was getting into the swing of things now, and I snarled as the rage and all-encompassing blood-lust took me over as it so often had before. Just like the Hulk, you really don't want to see me mad.

Never one to ask too many questions—I'm not inquisitive by nature when it comes to other-worldly entities ruining my cup of tea—I sliced his neck deep and fast. His head lolled back and the gaping wound spat out not one but three of the beasties, each bigger and badder than the last. Like Russian dolls in reverse. My kitchen was soon as cramped as a Mini full of clowns.

"A little help in here, guys," I shouted to the fools in the living room, but they were busy.

I glanced at my watch nervously. My insides spasmed and I came close to tears. Damn, almost quarter to four. Where had the day gone?

"Okay, what do you want? Make it quick. I'm in deep trouble if you guys are around in the next, oh, one minute." I was already sweating; I was so screwed it wasn't even funny.

"The Necronote," said the biggest, baddest daemon of them all. He held out his hand. It tore through the air and snapped into his palm then danced around before settling. He handed it to me.

"Well, that was utterly pointless," I told him. Just because I was annoyed, I launched at him, clung to his body like a limpet, and stabbed him repeatedly in the chest until leathery red skin shredded and inside bits became outside bits. He wasn't bothered; he liked it. Laughed and moaned. You can't win with these guys; they don't play fair. I got bored and jumped off, watching as guts and whatnot plopped to the tiles.

"And if I don't do what it says to do? Go where it says? You bunch of twisted fucks," I asked. Utterly pointless, but I liked to test the waters now and then, see if there was a change in policy.

"We know where you live." I shrugged. "We know why you are so afraid."

"Well, you are kinda big. And the red skin looks good on you, sure, but it's somewhat intimidating."

"No, we know all about you, Necrosoph, and your darling daugh—"

"Hi, honey, we're home," shouted my beautiful wife, Phage, from the hallway. I heard the front door shut behind her.

"Hello, Daddy. It's me... Jen."

"And Woofer," came an excited voice.

"Of course it is. Um, be right there. Love you both. You too, Woofer. Don't come into the—"

The daemons vanished, and thankfully so did the mess. The note snapped into my hand so I pocketed it and turned, wiping at my brow and straightening damp hair that hung limp past my shoulders, peppered with silver the same way it had been for nigh on three centuries.

I realized I was brandishing a vicious knife so quickly sheathed it and turned back around, beaming. Innocent as the day Jen was born seven years ago.

"Hey." My heart melted with love as I spread my arms and Jen launched at me, utterly confident Daddy would catch her. Panicked, I grabbed her before she slid on the goopy bits. But of course, they were gone, being the supernatural boogers that they were.

Woofer ran circles around us, shouting, "It's so exciting, it's so exciting. What are we excited about? It's great to be home. Haven't seen you for... Um, a while.

Hooray!"

"You okay?" asked Phage with concern, looking almost as stressed as me, having just waited for our daughter outside primary school. Jen was adorable but she gave her mum the runaround and then some.

"Fine. Perfect. Why do you ask?" I took in the scent of our daughter, all peaches and apples mixed in with maybe a little bit of sick from being at school all day. Wonderful. The smell of innocence.

"You seem a little jittery. And you had a massive knife in your hands whilst hugging our daughter."

"Did not! I put it away," I protested.

Jen stared with longing at the sheath fixed to my belt. "Can I hold it, Daddy? Can I?"

I kissed the top of her head then put her down. "No, honey. Remember what happened last time you stole Daddy's knife?"

"That was an accident, and the tail grew back. Like magic."

"I know, little apple, but Daddy had to do a lot of very unpleasant things to make up for that." I shuddered at the memory of having to be nice to Mr. Wonderful for a whole week as penance. "Now, promise you won't play with knives?" I held up my hand for a high-five.

"I promise." We slapped palms.

Jen skipped off with Woofer right behind her. I smiled as I watched her go, then shouted in a panic, "Don't go into the living room."

"Why not?" asked Phage.

I slid close and hugged her. "Love you."

"Love you too, but what gives?"

"Tell you later. First, you need to shout at me while I make us a cuppa and Jen a snack. How was she?"

Her face brightened. "Amazing. No tantrums, no 'mishaps' at school. The perfect day."

"Great."

"Naughty cat. Naughty horsie," shouted Jen from the living room.

"Bad cat," shouted Woofer, joining in. "Woofer never bleed on rug. Never break window. Bad Bernard."

"Quiet, Woofer," I shouted.

"What did Woofer say?" asked Phage. Luckily, she didn't have to listen to him constantly like I did. She just got the barking; I got the gibberish.

"Nothing. Want another hug?" I held out my arms and smiled.

Phage glanced at me then frowned as she went to see what had happened.

I felt the note in my pocket squirm with impatience.

Just another day in the life of a regular old guy and his family. Plus a "pet" or two.

I Need a Drink

"It's five o'clock somewhere," I grumbled, as I unlocked then opened the door under the stairs and
pulled the cord for the basement light. I needed a drink.
I had several bottles of that 1890 vintage homemade el-
derflower wine still left, and I intended to make a damn
good dent in the stash. Such a fine year. It felt like the
sun would never stop shining in the long summer days,
and the nights had just enough rain to ensure everything grew tall and wondrous.

Ah, sweet, sweet summer. Sweet, sweet wine. I
licked my lips as I pulled my basement boots on then
clomped down the stairs. Thick rubber soles were the
order of business, necessary for my kind of basement.

"Oi, turn off the light. It hurts my eyes," grumbled
just about the grumpiest grumbler grumbleland has
ever known. He even beat me, and I've got a medal.

I sighed deeply, and not even for the hundredth time, before taking a very deep breath. It stank. Stale, fetid. Like if you'd buried a pair of socks you'd worn for several weeks in a small wooden box, then it rained, then you dug up the box, opened the lid, and took a lungful.

"Why do I always do that? I wondered out loud.

"You talkin' to me, Soph?" boomed the basement-dweller.

"No, I was not."

"But you are now, right?"

"What? Yes, of course I am now. We're having a conversation, aren't we?" I reached the bottom of the rickety wooden steps and kicked aside a golden crown and felled a teetering stack of impossibly valuable gold coins. They tinkled as they landed amongst all the other gold stuff.

"Hey, careful with the coins, old man. Took me ages to stack 'em up."

"And I will ask you yet again. Why bother?" I glanced around my basement. Everywhere you looked there were towers of coins of all shapes and sizes. Well, I guess they were mostly round, but not all. Some stacks reached the low ceiling I always banged my head on, others were just beginning to grow like stalagmites. As if they were organic. Alive. I wouldn't be surprised if some were. They were from strange places, mostly far underground, never to see the light of day.

Dwarf gold.

Speaking of which.

"Hey, hey." I was tugged by my hanging shirt-tails. I looked down and smiled none-too-fondly at my very annoying freeloader of a lodger.

"What? Hands off the shirt please."

"Can you turn the light off? It hurts my eyes."

"No, I won't be able to see then. And I need to see so I know what I'm looking at."

"What you lookin' at?" What can best be described as a four-foot bundle of hair wearing thick leather armor and chainmail, squinted around the room, pretty much unable to see a bloody thing.

"Put your damn glasses on. How many times do I have to tell you?"

"You bin sayin' it this past sixty years or so. At least," Shey Redgold of Oxten griped, as he reached into the folds of his ample girth and fumbled about. Finally, he found his glasses and put them on. "Ah, that's better." He peered up at me and almost smiled. The thick lenses made his eyes cartoonishly large.

"It hasn't been that long, has it? Anyway, I've only been in this house nine years. That's when I got you the new pair."

"Yeah, an' a bugger of a job I 'ad findin' you. I mean, it was almost like you didn't want me to come live with you. Haha. Took me days of tunneling to get the right place. I'm still recoverin' from it now." He arched his back until it cricked, as if to prove his point.

Did I mention I hated dwarves? Cause I do. This one, anyway. Actually lots of them are rather nice. In small doses anyway. Haha. No, I'm not sizeist, some of my best friends would be short if I had any friends at all.

"I told you before, many times, I left a note. You must have missed it. If you didn't leave all this crap lying about, you would have seen it." I hadn't left a note, I wanted my basement back. So I moved. That and the neighbors were getting a bit funny, what with them all getting old and wrinkly and me just staying wrinkly and a bit old, but always the same. It happened way too often, but what else could I do?

"After all we've bin through." He tutted and shook his head. "I remember when we first met, how I saved you from the Clan of Doomy. They was ready to chop you up into itty bitty pieces an' feed you to their dragons."

"Yeah, yeah. That was all a misunderstanding. And if I recall correctly, which I do, it was to our mutual benefit to save each other. You were in big trouble for nicking their stash, some of it anyway, and happened to free me as you ran past screaming, swinging your axe about."

"You remember it your way, I'll remember it mine." He waved my words away with a sweep of his meaty hand. "But we've bin together ever since. A team, right?" He peered at me with hope in his dilated eyes.

"Yeah, a team." I would have gone back to get him after I moved, promise. I just wanted a few days of basement peace to sort out the shelves before he ruined it. He's a nice dwarf really. "Anyway. I have a new note, and everyone's home, so I need wine for dinner. You better not have drunk it all," I warned.

"That piss water. No thank you. I drink proper booze. Mead for me."

"Good. Keep it that way." I kicked through the shin-high piles of gold coins, crowns, armor, battle axes, spears, golden eggs, golden bows, golden spoons, and anything else you can think of that can be made out of gold and thus rendered utterly impractical, like a knife or a cup, and reached the rows of shelves I'd placed up high on the wall. High for him, low for me.

He'd still managed to chuck a load of crowns up around several dusty bottles, but everything was still intact, so there was that. I checked the labels until I found what I wanted and grabbed two bottles. One for me, the other for me.

"Right, well, see you," I said as I turned and waded to the steps.

"Aargh, argh. Stop! Soph, stop," he shouted in an utter panic.

"What?"

"Your boot. There's a coin there. Bring it back, put it down. Don't split the collection. You know what will happen if you do."

I did as I was told, and stared at him for a moment. "You have issues, my friend. Real problems."

"I can't help it," he whined. "You know that. It's in the DNA, in the genes. Dwarves cannot, must not, ever, lose their gold. Once it's ours it stays ours, otherwise that way lies madness."

"How could I ever forget?" It was true. Dwarves, and Shey Redgold in particular, had an utterly schizo-phrenic, maniacal obsession with keeping their hoard intact. Once they acquired even a single coin, they saw it as theirs for life. An extension of their own being. And in a way it was. It became part of their very essence, of who they were. Their identity. The more gold, the more powerful they became. Not just in the eyes of others, but in strength, mental capacity, skill, sexual prowess—although I didn't want to think about that too much—and every other way.

Steal a dwarf's gold, even a gold pin, and they lose a little of themselves. It's like chopping bits off them. It went even further than that though. They genuinely lost their mental faculties. Many a dwarf had been driven utterly insane by losing even a meager stash. They would descend into a funk, turn into utter rage, and be-come utterly obsessed with tracking down the lost coins until they went completely mad or were defeated by those who had claimed the gold as their own.

Let's just say they spent a lot of time either fight-ing, going nuts, or counting their stash in a way so mind-bogglingly obsessively it was amazing they weren't all utterly gaga anyway.

I peeled the coin from my boot and flipped it into a pile. Shey Redgold sighed with relief.

"Don't forget the light," he called after me.

I got to the top step, turned out the light, and with him sighing in the dark I closed then locked the door and headed to the kitchen muttering, "Bloody dwarves."

Remarkable Zoo

"Can I ride horsie?" squealed Jen as she skipped about in her cute pink wellies, fairy tutu, and princess tiara.

"Sure thing, honey. Horsie would love to give you a ride. Wouldn't you horsie?" I emphasized the horse bit, just to piss off Bernard.

"Do I have to?" he whined, or should I say whinnied. "You know how it makes me feel. Like I'm nothing but an animal. It's degrading. And please, teach her I'm not a horse."

"Are a horse," insisted Jen. "Daddy said so."

Phage and I, glasses in hand, wine going down nicely, did a double-take at Jen. So soon? No, surely not? She was way too young. By about a decade and a half. A lifetime if I had my way.

I crouched beside her amongst the straw and the "horse" shit and took her hands. "Listen, Jen, this is very serious. I want to ask you a question, okay?"

"Okay." Jen put on her serious face, and all I wanted to do was pick her up and cuddle her tight. She was the most perfect child a father could ever wish for.

"Did you hear the horse talk just then? Did you hear words or did you just imagine what he would say?"

"All animals talk," she replied, like it was nothing.

"Yes, honey, but so does Mr. Squiggles, and Fat Dinosaur, and Funny Bear."

"That's only pretend. Horses, and cats and dogs and silly birds and ants and all things, they talk. Poor fish. Why has Bernard got a sparkly horn on his head?" Her face brightened, cheeks crimson. "It's true! I knew Daddy told fibs. Bernard is a unicorn! Horsie is a unicorn." Jen danced around the stall, arms waving, her little limbs manic. She reached up and Bernard obligingly lowered his head. She stroked his horn.

"Wow, it's real. Sparkly and shimmering, like my disco light. Where did it come from?"

I felt rotten to the core, like I could puke, but I kept a smile on my face and nodded. "Yes, well, this is a big secret. You must never tell anyone you hear animals talk. Most people can't hear them. Not even Mummy. And you must certainly never say you have a unicorn. So, the time has come," I said as I turned to Phage. She just stood there, motionless, arms limp by her side. Crying.

"Why not?" Jen asked suspiciously.

"Because they aren't gifted like us. Like you. I think you can see Bernard's horn now because you know he's something special." I patted her on the head then stood up, swung her up high, and cuddled her tight. "Love you, Jen."

"Love you too, Daddy." She squealed as I tickled her, then we turned to Bernard and asked, "How about a ride?" He nodded morosely. Jen laughed with delight.

I placed her on his back and reminded her to hold on tight to his mane. Bernard left the stall and headed to the paddock.

Reaching for Phage's hand, I said, "We knew it would happen."

"We hoped it wouldn't." She sniffed, then wiped her eyes.

"If she's hearing them, and now starting to see what we see, then she's developing fast. Watch her carefully. We don't want her saying the wrong thing to anyone. We want her in regular school as long as possible. You know what happens to some kids."

Phage nodded, too emotional to speak. We followed them outside and watched Bernard trot around the paddock glumly. Jen squealed gleefully.

"I'll see you later," said Phage as she waved to Jen then headed for the house.

After Jen had a couple more laps of the paddock, she grew bored so I took her back inside and she ran off to her room to play.

Phage was in the kitchen listening to the radio and drinking wine, like it was just another normal day.

She began to cry the moment she saw me. I comforted her, held her tight, neither of us speaking for a while.

We sat opposite each other after we'd both recovered, had a talk about things we'd avoided for years.

"Did we do the right thing?" she asked.

"Of course. She's beautiful, kind, utterly adorable, and alive. If we'd decided not to have kids, then we wouldn't have her."

"But think what she's got to go through, what we all do. It isn't fair. Poor thing. Time goes so fast. She'll be twenty-one before we know it, and then what?"

"We both know what then. She'll get her first note same as the rest of us, and she'll continue to get one for as long as they, whoever they are, believe she's still fit and able enough to carry out the work. We went over it a million times already. We knew the deal. We made a choice."

"But is it fair? Maybe it was a mistake?"

"Don't ever say that again," I whispered, checking the door for little eavesdroppers. "Our daughter is not a mistake. She is perfect. We will protect her, we will train her, make sure she's strong and ready. This life is incredible, full of wonder and magic and things hardly anyone else in the entire world ever gets to see. We pay the price, but it's more than worth it."

"I know, and sorry. You know I didn't mean it was a mistake like that. I love her so much, both of you, but I can't bear to think of what she will go through, what will happen. What else do you think she can do? Other gifts?"

"Hopefully none. But if she's already taken after me, you can bet your ass she'll inherit your gifts too."

That silenced us both.

Eventually Phage stood, and with a sadness so deep it broke my heart, she said, "Then may God forgive us both," before she left the room.

"Amen," I whispered, wondering if He would. Not that I was a believer, but it never hurts to hedge your bets.

A Sentinel

"You should get rid of that bloody sculpture," shouted Mrs. O'Donnell, a hard-ass sweet old lady who'd lived here for seventy-odd years but still retained a little Irish twang.

"Hey, Mrs. O'Donnell, how are you today?" I stopped the mower and wandered over to the garden hedge. My neighbor's head of shocking curly white hair was just about visible, but then her head and shoulders peeked over the hawthorn as she climbed up the steps she kept handy to be nosy and have a chat now and then.

"Mustn't grumble. You know me, Soph, don't like to complain. Look at that bloody thing." She pointed at the nine foot "statue" of a man made of rocks, fully six feet wide, taking pride of place in the middle of the lawn. I kept the grass tidy for Jen to play on, or adults to sit out with a cuppa by day, booze by night. "It's so ugly. Look at his head! And those fingers, so clumsy. Who in their right mind would make such a thing? Let alone have it in their garden?"

"Jen loves it, you know that," I told her. "I can't go upsetting my little girl, now can I?"

"Hmm," she grumbled. "S'pose not. What was all that smashing and banging yesterday? Scared the bejesus out of me. I almost came over, thought maybe there were burglars, then I saw Phage and Jen and assumed everything was alright."

"Oh, just a problem with the horse. Got into the garden again. Smashed a window. Nothing to worry about. So, you need anything? Everything okay over there? You have a lot to look after. You coping?" Mrs. O'Donnell had several acres to manage, and she was no spring chicken, but she pottered about, one of her sons came now and then to keep the weeds in check, and she'd long ago given up on animals apart from chickens and geese.

"It better not get into my cabbage patch," she warned.

"Oh, he won't. We had a good long chat. He knows to behave from now on."

"Good lad. How's the girl? She doing well?"

"Great, thanks. Are you coming to the party tomorrow? We'll have balloons and cake and games, and it seems like the weather will be nice so we can do it outdoors. I've got a marquee and everything." I winked at her and she laughed.

"How could I refuse? Not that the weather is anything but nice now. My, how it's changed so much. Never rains. Always hot and dry in the summer. That's not English. It's not right. I'm burning up and it's only eight. But listen to me complaining. I got Jen a lovely present. What's she now? Eight is it?"

"Haha, nope, my little girl was seven on Monday. But we're doing her party tomorrow. Parties are best on Saturday. You already told her happy birthday, remember?"

"Course I do," she said dubiously. "Such a lovely child. Takes after her mother, doesn't she?"

"Haha, you bet she does. Her looks and charm, my knobbly knees. Well, gotta get this lawn mowed, then head out and check the animals are behaving. You don't want a horse, do you?"

"Oh, you daft lad, haha. You keep your silly horse. See you tomorrow, Soph, and get rid of that bloody thing." She gave the statue daggers then clambered down off her steps, swearing as she went.

She cursed at the geese as she wandered away back to her cottage.

She was a sweet lady, put up with us for a start, but it wasn't easy having neighbors when you lived lives like ours. But that was all part of the plan, of trying to live a normal life, let Jen experience a regular childhood before it went to shit when she was older.

I winked at the towering troll. Slowly, like watching a glacier move, the eyelid closed then opened again. Damn, he was frisky today. Hadn't sen him move that much in over a year.

"You excited about the party too, eh? Be warned, there will be kids all over you tomorrow." I yanked the cord on the mower, swore as it refused to start, and after plenty more choice words, a sweat building, the thing spluttered to life and I finished mowing the garden area.

I'm sure the troll shuddered. Well, it was his choice, so he had to pay the price.

We all did.

Dastardly Fridge

In some ways our property was a weird set-up, in other ways not so much. Country houses came in all shapes and sizes, the same for land. Although our house was well away from our two neighbors, with lawns and gardens and paddocks between, it didn't mean we never saw or heard them. The properties merged with each other at the boundaries, fences or no.

I was often out looking after the animals, Mrs. O'Donnell loved to wander about, tend her veg, swear at the geese, kick a chicken, so we inevitably crossed paths. Meaning, we shouted at each other over hedges, rotten fences, or sometimes from trees. She was to the right of the rear of our property, my other neighbor off on the left, but his land backed up to the side of ours, so kind of leftish, kinda.

It was a good job too, because like me, he wasn't exactly a normal guy. I knew it the moment I set eyes on him, and he read me the same way. We all have that look. Not quite haunted and broken, but a hardness, a way about us. You get it over the years, if you survive.

Most don't. Most succumb long before me. Necronotes destroy the faint of heart in the first few years if not on the first ever job. It's the way of it. It's the fear I have for my family. One that will never end.

Job, full name Necrojob, with it pronounced Jobe, was my other neighbor. He was an old guy just like me. Appeared to be late-fifties but was well over the four-hundred mark in reality. He was a hard man, took no crap from anyone, and a right bloody pain in the arse.

He was one of those farmer types who never threw anything away. His place was littered with rusting cars, rotting caravans, decrepit tractors, and a worrying number of baths. He didn't even have cattle to use them for water troughs, just loads of empty baths piled up about the place.

He had over fifteen acres that was left to its own devices, long ago having given up any pretense of farming. Didn't blame him, there was no money in it any more, not unless you went down the farm shop route and opened up the place to visitors. Job was not that kind of a dude. He didn't like people and they didn't like him. Perfect for the yearly Necronote, not so good the rest of the time.

After mowing the lawn and tidying up the garden ready for the next day, I strolled down to the animal enclosures, what I liked to call the zoo, and before doing my chores and checking on everyone I took a deep breath, told myself to stay calm, and wandered over to the scrappy hedge that bordered the corner of our land and a field of his.

Woofer ran around being as mental as usual. Shouting about rabbits and could he eat one if he caught one. Which he never did. I let him go first, then hopped over a wonky bit of stock-proof fencing and made a mental note to replace it, then waded through the pretty weeds over to Job's barn. Job was always in there tinkering with something or other, but he never seemed to produce anything.

No thanks to his efforts, his land was achingly beautiful. Before he took over, much of the soil health had been eroded by intensive farming, creating a perfect environment for all manner of wild flowers. The recent increase in temperature and lack of rainfall made it perfect for certain species. Poppies, daisies, other stuff I didn't know the name of, it was a vibrant mat of pinks and reds, blues and yellows, and I could almost relax as I wandered over to the open barn where he was swearing like the bastard he was at what seemed to be a very upset fridge.

"What you doing?" I asked, keeping well back as he had a tendency to wave tools about and whack things when he got cross.

"Shouting at the fucking fridge, what does it look like I'm doing? I'm not prancing in a meadow looking at the lovely bastard flowers, am I?"

"Um, no. What's up with it?"

"How the fuck should I know? If I knew, I'd fix it, but the shitty thing is holding out on me. Aren't you, you useless lump of bastard scrap?" The fridge remained silent, because you know, it was a fridge.

"So, yeah, we're having a party tomorrow for Jen. Did you get the invite?"

"Dunno. Never open my mail, do I?"

"You open one, that's for sure."

Job looked up at me and asked, "You trying to be funny? Course I open the Necronote. I'd be a fool if I didn't. A dead fool. But no invite, didn't read it."

"Okay, well, it's her birthday party. You are invited. She likes you."

"Why?" he asked suspiciously.

"No idea. You're awful."

Job cackled and spat on the ground, something black and gross. "I know. That her Necroname is it? Jen?"

"Don't be daft. She's bloody seven. She gets that when she's twenty-one, you know that."

"Course I bleedin' do, but I don't know how old she is, do I?"

"She's a little girl. She likes horses and tiaras," I said, exasperated.

"Whatever." He waved it away with a grimy hand, the nails chipped and foul. "What you celebrating her birthday for? They're nothing but trouble as we both know." He peered at me through bushy yellow eyebrows. Damn, but his brown eyes were intense.

"Because she's a kid, and much as I detest birthdays, like the rest of us, she's got years of innocence and doesn't know a thing about what will happen when she's older. When the time comes we'll explain, and then she can wish she never had to have another birthday. Until then we make life normal. Do parties. You know the deal."

"Fucking birthdays. God, I'm weary of this shit, aren't you? Every bloody year I do my job, always beat the buggers. It's sickening."

"Tell me about it," I sighed, feeling the same way.

"I can't celebrate birthdays, not now. I wish there was no such thing."

"Me too. But don't you ever wonder, if you had the choice to lead a normal life, die at a regular age, or get the notes, do as you're told, what choice would you make?"

"I know the choice I'd make. If I'd been given the choice when I was young, then I'd pick the notes, as who doesn't want to live for-fucking ever? But if I was asked now? After all I've done. All I've seen. I'd tell them to shove it up their arse and die laughing at the bastards. Whoever they are."

"Yeah, whoever they are." There was a silence for several seconds as we both thought about a topic we'd undoubtedly ruminated on thousands of times before.

"Sausages?" asked Woofer. "Walk? Play ball with Woofer?" He stared up at me hopefully with those sad puppy-dog eyes, then less certainly at Job.

"Dogs are so stupid," noted Job.

"They have their moments. Woofer's a real smart boy, aren't you? Tinged with magic, able to talk to all other creatures." I rubbed his head and his tail wagged.

"Woofer super-smart."

"You are not," said Job, as he bent to stare into Woofer's eyes. Woofer hid behind my legs. "How many fingers am I holding up?" He held up three.

"Hey, come on, he's only young, not even grown-up yet. He has a lot to learn," I protested, with a wink to Job. Poor Woofer; I didn't want to hurt his feelings.

"Two fingers," said Woofer.

"See," said Job, standing, his back creaking, and looking immensely pleased with himself. "Daft as a fucking brush. Anyway, thanks for the invite, but I can't come, won't come, don't want to come. You go for it, make as much noise as you want, but I've got things to do."

"What you got going on?"

"You mean you didn't see it?

"Um, no. More tinkering in your shed?"

"Tinkering be bollocksed! That's quality work I do in there. But no, that." Job pointed at the small copse of trees that was once a hedge, now a proper little grove. I put my hand up to shield my eyes and stared. It did look a little different, come to think of it. Planks and odd struts sticking out at weird angles.

"A treehouse?" I ventured. "Bit old for that, aren't you?"

"Not a treehouse, no. Something utterly ground-breaking, never seen before, fucking A class balltastic."

"So what is it then?"

Job tapped his nose. "All in good time, neighbor, all in good time. Anyway, it's your birthday too, isn't it? Yesterday, right? Or the day before. Got your note?"

"Yes," I said glumly. "But I have a week, so I'm waiting until after Jen's party tomorrow. Then I'll sort it."

"I wouldn't wait. Best to get it done soon as. These things hang over you, and what if you need the time?"

"Yeah, I know, but what can I do? I have to be here for her when she's little. It'll be a rush job, but I've done it before. "

"I'm sure you have, me too, but it ups the ante, makes you all stressed. Ugh, these goddamn notes!" Job chucked a spanner at the fridge, denting it. Sparks jumped from the filthy extension lead and the fridge whirred to life then hummed pleasantly. "Ha, you fucker, I knew you liked it rough." Job smiled, satisfied. I nodded and left him to his cackling.

Before I hopped back over the fence, I stared at the group of trees, wondering what the old bugger was up to.

Right, time to check on the fizzy drink supplies. Knowing the kids, there would never be enough, but I had to at least try.

Necropub

"I'm off to the pub, love," I called optimistically, trying to sound all casual and like it was as important as mowing the lawn or taking Jen to a playdate.

"Oh, haha, you are so funny for such an old man. If you think you're going to the pub then you better think again."

Goddammit! I was a grown man, a very old grown man. I had seen the ends of hell, broken bread with creatures of the night, stolen gold from mighty dwarves, and even had a pint with a man with pink hair, if you can believe such a thing. And some of that is even true! Nobody told me what I could do. "Aw, that's not fair," I whined.

"Gotcha," said Phage, as she poked her head out of the back door and smiled at me.

"You're so beautiful. What did I do to deserve you?" I grabbed my luscious wife around the waist and squeezed her tightly. She smelled of shampoo and these new woman creams that were all the rage. I kissed her lips; they tasted like cherries.

"You kidnapped me, remember?"

"Hey, we've been over that before. It was not a kidnapping per se, it was a removal of a beautiful woman from distress and danger. I call it a rescue, not a kidnap."

"Does that mean I am free to go now?" she asked with that dangerous twinkle in her eyes.

"Never. Absolutely never. You're stuck with me until the end of time."

"And you're stuck with me forever too," she purred, making me go all tingly in all the right places. "So, you gonna buy me a pint too? Jen will take an age to get ready, and I told her where we'd be."

"Of course! Although, in my day, ladies drank halves." Damn, that was a relief. I needed a quick beer before the madness began. "Let's go to the pub!"

We wandered down the garden, holding hands. The tang of freshly cut grass, perfumed roses, and assorted flowers a real heady mix. Birds sang, bees buzzed, my idiot neighbor banged his bits of wood and swore loudly. All was perfect in the world.

Apart from the job I had to do, whatever that might be.

Trying to keep my spirits light, I pushed the thoughts away and focused on the now. We got to the edge of the garden, opened the gate, and went through into the rougher ground beyond. There was a path before you could get to the paddocks and animal houses, but instead of turning that way, we took a right, then stopped a few moments later outside a rickety, wany-edge oak-clad shed large enough to fit a family of four comfortably.

"Well, here we are." I grinned at my wife.

She shook her head in mock-despair. "Men."

"What? It's awesome."

"The building's nice, all weathered and full of history. What isn't so awesome is that." She pointed at the sign I'd lovingly carved and placed above the rotting door.

"Took me ages. I think it's perfect."

"Necropub? Bit of a bad joke, don't you think?"

"The Necropub is the perfect name for a man's own pub in his back garden. It's apt. The name fits."

"But it's so sinister," she told me, not for the first time. "It's like calling it Death Pub."

"And that's exactly what it is. A place to kill off all those evil brain cells that are forcing you to think about all the horrible things you'll have to do, are currently doing, or have done. See, it's perfect." I opened the door and breathed deeply as stale beer molecules rushed to escape the dark interior.

I stepped aside and ushered my one and only guest inside. I followed in behind, flipped the light switch, and closed the door.

"Ah, nothing like going to the pub on a Saturday evening," I sighed, as I took in the polished bar top, the brass rail, the gleaming beer taps, all three of them.

Rows of bottles reflected back at me from the mirror behind the bar. The only thing missing was a till. No paying guests here; everyone drank on the house.

"It's morning."

"Oh, yeah, right."

"And it's ten in the morning."

"Oh, is it? Well, that's why we're here. A quick break. Sorry, I'm all out-of-sorts, what with the party and whatnot. Jen's freaking me out. I can't stop worrying about her. I've never felt as stressed in my life. Every day there's something else."

"I know." Phage put a hand to my shoulder and smiled, warming my heart. Her straight chestnut hair hung long and low, tickling the back of my hand. "Now, bartender, give me a half of your finest beer if you'd be so kind."

"Right you are, love. Sure you don't want a pint? I was just kidding."

"At ten in the morning?"

"I'm having one." I walked around to the other side of the bar, flipped a clean white tea towel over my shoulder, grabbed two gleaming glasses, then pumped the tap a few times to get things going. I poured the perfect half for Phage and a crisp pint for me.

"Cheers." We clinked glasses and took a wary sip of the delicious-looking liquid.

"Wow, that's actually good," I sighed, relieved.

"It is." Phage took anther sip and said "Yum."

"Think it's okay to drink? Remember last time?"

"I do not remember last time, and that's the point. But this tastes proper, like beer should. Nothing weird about it."

"Wonder what he made this time?" I mused, looking at the cellar door.

"Go ask him," teased my lovely wife.

"You go bloody ask him. I'm not going down there today. I need to stay relaxed. If it tastes good, then we should be fine. I do not want to get all trippy and be off my head for a kid's birthday party."

"It took me a week before I felt normal after last time," agreed Phage. "Ugh, my head hurts even thinking about it."

"Mine too. I just wish he'd stop experimenting," I whispered, just in case the thing in the cellar could hear.

"Where's the fun in that?"

"The fun is in drinking lots of normal pints and getting tipsy. Not wondering if you'll wake up a day later after half a pint, with someone else's clothes on, and twenty grand in a rucksack you're using as a pillow."

"I wonder where that money did come from?"

"We shall never know."

We drank our drinks; the Brewer remained silent below.

"Woofer feel lonely," came a shout from outside the door. He scratched away and whined like he'd been on his own his whole life. Phage smiled and went to let him in.

"Hello, Woofer. How you doing, boy?" asked Phage as she bent and rubbed his back. Woofer's tail spun so fast he was liable to take off.

"Woofer so lonely. All alone in the house. Jen in her room getting ready for party. Woofer so excited about party. Lots of children want to play with Woofer. So fun." Woofer licked Phage's face and scampered over to the bar and jumped up so his front legs were on the counter. "Pint please, Soph." His tongue lolled out and he smiled at me.

I patted our idiot dog, although in my experience all dogs are really rather dim, then told him, "No pint for you. You aren't old enough to drink. You're only three. Oh, sorry, Phage. Woofer said he was lonely, but he's looking forward to the party. He also wanted a pint."

"No pint. Soph's right. You're too young," said Phage.

His ears went flat against the side of his head. Poor guy was crestfallen. "But in dog years three is..." He tried to do the math but gave up in a millisecond. "It's older than seven," he said triumphantly.

"It is," I agreed. "But you still can't drink beer."

Woofer sulked and hopped down then curled up on a rug in the corner by the dart board, content to be near us. He loved to sleep there, always dragged his bed over. Can't beat the risk of being impaled by small arrows while you doze to make life more interesting.

As Woofer snored happily, we drank our beer. A melancholy fell over us even though it was a day of celebration.

"What do you think will become of her?" asked Phage.

"Not today, okay? Let's not do this today. Not now, not yet. We have time, plenty of time. Let's just enjoy the party, be nice to everyone, and be normal."

Phage nodded. Her shoulders slumped. I moved around the bar to hold her.

Tears mingled with beer while our dog snored in the corner.

Garden Party

"C'mon, Soph," Francis laughed, his words slightly slurred from too many beers. "You never join in."

I kept my fake smile plastered on my face, but I'd never liked Francis. He was too eager to please a crowd, never had any depth to his conversations, and small talk killed me inside a little more each time I had to endure it.

"I'll pass. Don't want to get soaked, but you go enjoy."

"Just take off your shirt, the others have. Come on. It's boiling hot. This damn climate change is a killer." He flexed his chest muscles then did a double biceps like it would impress me.

He was showing off, trying to make the others feel insecure, as though he was the alpha male here. He knew I knew it was all bravado, that he was weak, afraid, so he hid behind this front. The others were a little intimidated by him. God knows what they thought of me, but I never tried to act the hard man in front of any of them. Kept it cool and friendly, made them feel at ease. At least I think I did.

"No, Francis. Honestly, I'm not comfortable taking my shirt off. You go flaunt your muscles, play with the kids in the paddling pool, I'll just watch."

It was stifling, the air heavy and still, but there was no way in hell I was taking off my shirt in company.

Phage came over when she realized I was struggling. "Everything okay here, boys?"

"Fine," I told her.

"I was trying to persuade your husband to come join us, but he's being stubborn. Come on, Soph, what's wrong with you?"

This guy, he was really getting on my nerves.

Phage raised an eyebrow at me. I nodded that I was fine, under control, so she gave me a peck on the cheek and left me to it.

Francis downed his beer and began on another as a few more of the guys and several women gathered around to see what the fuss was about.

Some men had tops off, others, the overweight, the less than proud of their dad bods, kept their shirts or tees on. Everyone was sweating, the marquee as hot as everywhere else.

"Are you shy?" asked his wife, Mary, a despicable woman with fake tan, fake smile, and fake tits. "I bet you've got a lovely body, haven't you? So slim. I can tell you have hard muscles."

"Hey, what about me?" slurred Francis, his face reddening, his anger rising.

"Of course you do, love," said Mary, but she gave me a look, and he saw it.

"Come on then, Soph, let's see what you've got."

Before I knew what was happening, and trust me, this would not happen if I wasn't at my daughter's birthday party, he'd wobbled close, then grabbed my shirt and ripped it clean off my back.

Nobody said a word. It was obvious why.

Children laughed and shouted in the background, but the adults remained silent.

Mary slapped Francis across the cheek, leaving a red mark. He put his hand to his face, anger bubbling, but the look on her face told everyone exactly who was in charge.

"I'm... Sorry, Soph, I got carried away. I didn't mean to embarrass you." Francis' ego was deflated, all bravado gone. He was a pathetic, drunk man, way out of his depth.

"You poor man," said Mary, full of insincerity. She was just curious, couldn't take her eyes off me, off my body. Off my scars. "It must hurt so much. Francis is just drunk, he didn't mean to shame you."

"Shame me? I'm not ashamed," I told her. Told everyone. "I cover up because nobody wants to see this. This is me, who I am." I turned three-sixty, just to get this over with, to show these clowns, and the nice people, that I was not a man who was ashamed of his body no matter what it looked like.

And anyway, lots of it was great. I was firm, defined, slim enough that veins wriggled like worms over my arms, even had a bit of a defined stomach, but that's not what people were gawping at, even though they tried to be polite and hide their stares.

It was the scars.

Lots, and lots of scars.

Wrapped around my right-hand side from just below trouser line to my chest I had a nasty slab of scar tissue, like a canyon seen from space. Thick, gnarly, the result of a nasty burn by a very capable warlock who was handy with the old blasting cane.

Across my lower chest was a red welt where I'd been sliced deeply by a magic-infused blade wielded by a batty ancient man with a collection of artifacts so large he had a five-level bunker.

My abdomen was a patchwork of small burn scars, stab wounds, surgeries, and even a couple of gunshot wounds. I was a radiologist's worst nightmare.

My back, well, I never got to see it much, but I knew the tales it told. Shootings, slicings, and another burn mark from the same mage who'd almost got the better of me. I'd taken months to recover enough to even wear clothes without bandages, and it was tight to this day. Still gave me trouble now and then.

I was a battlefield made real. The result of hundreds of fights, so many killings, and they weren't always easy. I paid my dues, I took the injuries, and I damn well owned it.

"How... how did all of this happen?" asked Pete, a nice guy with cute kids who I always got along with.

"Pete, I don't want to get into it. It's why I stay covered, to avoid questions like that. It was all a long time ago, and I'd rather it stayed in the past, okay?"

"Sure thing. Don't sweat it."

"Haha, well, we can safely say Soph beats the rest of us both in the muscle department and the scar department," laughed Francis, trying to lighten the mood he'd caused to darken. "Damn, Soph, you got some definition. What's the secret?"

"Push ups, and pull ups, every single day for years and years." I didn't tell him over three hundred years, but that was exactly the case.

"How many?" he practically drooled, thinking I had the secret to improving his already ballooning muscles.

"Hundreds. Every morning."

"Oh."

"Man, c'mon. You telling me it actually takes work to build a cool body?" sighed Pete. Then he laughed, and the rest did too, trying their best to take the edge off, believing, even though I told them I wasn't, that I was uncomfortable with the state of my body.

"'Fraid so," I told them, then I turned as Phage handed me a new shirt and picked up the old one from where it still lay.

"Thanks, honey." I kissed Phage then buttoned up my shirt. I saw the look Mary gave her. Jealousy.

"Francis, I think you've had enough," Phage told him, and she took the beer right out of his hands, smiling sweetly, but I knew she wanted to kick his ass as much as I did. She could do it in a heartbeat. Dude got off lightly. Very lightly indeed.

"Yeah, sure. Sorry." His wife scowled at him, embarrassed for the tables being turned and her husband's actions reflecting badly on her.

"Shall I kill him?" Phage purred, loud enough for everyone to hear.

They all laughed.

"Maybe not today, honey. It is a celebration, after all." I winked at her, then put my lips to her ear and whispered, "Don't kill him. He's just a dick, but harmless."

"Okay, sweetie." Phage slapped my arse then went to check on the kids.

I saw Job standing alone over by an apple tree, watching closely. I gave everyone my excuses, knowing they'd be talking about this for bloody years, which was exactly the opposite of what I wanted, and wandered over to see my surprise guest.

"You gonna kill him?" he asked smoothly.

"Nope, but Phage offered."

"You should take her up on it."

"He's just a regular guy who had too much to drink and wanted to act the alpha. It's a lesson for him. I'll let it slide."

"Suit yourself." He shrugged; it was no skin off his nose. "You got some mighty fine battle scars there, Soph. Shows you're no spring chicken."

"Yeah, most are from centuries ago. You learn as you get older to be a bit more careful. Haven't been properly injured for decades. Just a few scrapes and whatnot."

"I remember when I was just a kid, going after my marks all gung-ho. I got my arse kicked and then some. Never let the bastards beat me. I was tough as old boots even back then, but I got close to being dead so many times it makes me shake even thinking about it."

"Ha, I hear that. You don't get wiser as you get older, but you do get more careful."

"Wish I could go back, but there's no point dwelling on the past. We are the men we are today because of the men we were yesterday."

"That's quite profound," I told him, impressed.

"Hmm, maybe I read it somewhere," he said gruffly. I think I embarrassed him.

He checked nobody was looking then lifted up his grubby checked shirt, revealing a still tight midriff.

I whistled. "And I thought I had it bad." There was little skin that wasn't scarred. Still red and raw after who knew how many years.

He lowered his shirt. "Like I said, I was gung-ho back in the old days. Anyway, I only came to give Jen her present."

I grinned at him. "Thought you didn't do birthdays?"

"Yeah, well, it's Jen, isn't it?"

"What, the girl you didn't know the age of? That you forgot the name of?" I smiled at his discomfort; I knew he loved her really.

"Haha, you got me. Where is she?"

I pointed and he nodded then wandered over to give her the gift. Silly old sod, he was a good guy really, just liked to hide it behind a protective layer. We all had our own ways of disguising who we really were, to make it through this world the best way we could. Some drank and acted tough like Francis, others pushed people away by being grumpy bastards. We were all more similar than we liked to think when you got down to our true selves.

Scared, worried, holding it together the only way we knew how.

I returned to the party, but I avoided Francis. Didn't want to kill the guy by accident or anything.

Reminiscing

I was drunk, no denying it. Not hammered, but buzzing. I liked it. What I didn't like was being up in the attic. No, there were no vampires or bogeymen, just memories, and that's a damn sight scarier.

Nevertheless, after the revelations concerning Jen, I was in one of those kinds of moods. It happened now and then. Something would trigger this—usually getting a new note.

This was just another job, yet I had a real bad feeling about it. Maybe I'd come for solace? No, to dwell, to try to make sense of it all like I had countless times before.

I swiped at cobwebs and smiled at bats, and wondered why we stored so much crap when it hadn't been touched since we moved here. Spitting dust, I rummaged until I found an ancient wooden chest which was probably worth a fortune now it was an antique, even though I'd bought it new direct from the maker.

After searching the rafters, I finally found the key I'd stashed there, and sat on the dusty floorboards as I unlocked my entire history of madness.

There they were. Three hundred and eighteen notes. Some so brittle they could disintegrate at any moment, others as crisp as the day I received them.

I pulled out the stack carefully, wondering why I kept them, why I cared, when all I wanted was to have never seen one in my life. Because this was my life, why I was the man I had become. Angry, bitter, full of love, even a little hope, but hard, dangerous. Cruel too.

Would I have been like this regardless? I would never know. But something deep inside told me I was the same, that I was chosen because of who I was, what I was.

The bottom note was the one I was after. Necronote number one. The day my life changed for good. It was still folded in half, still pristine. I didn't open it, didn't need to. I remembered every detail inside, and all that had ensued. What I'd done, what I saw, the things I never knew I was capable of but had carried through because it was him or me, his life or mine.

But that wasn't why I was here. It was to remember something that was becoming harder to recall. Some days I couldn't think of the name at all. Other days, it sprang into my head the moment I awoke. Today was a blank day. So here I was, buzzing on beer and wine, sick with worry and stress about what lay ahead, and utterly freaked about my daughter's future.

"Andrew Blaine."

The name sounded unfamiliar, like it was made up, when I read it aloud. As though it belonged to someone else. But it didn't. It was my name, my birth name. This was who I had been until I turned twenty-one and my world was turned upside down. I held the note almost reverentially, when it deserved nothing but contempt. There was a line through my old name. Necrosoph was written in large, untidy calligraphy beneath.

A day later, several other documents arrived, but back then life was different, not like it is now. I'd heard how it worked these days. Poor kids would be bombarded. All manner of mail arriving with the friendly whistling postman. A driver's license with the new name, bank cards, library cards, new National Insurance card, you name it. Anything that had the old name on it was replaced with the new one. The old surname was kept, just because it was needed for identification, but that wasn't who you were. You had one name, your Necroname. God knows what they did with social media. I'd have to find out.

I was Soph.

I laughed, remembering how I looked up the meaning once I could track down a book—we weren't big on books back in the day. But I went to see an old man, older than I am now, and he showed me a book. I still recall his gnarled finger underlining the entry for Soph.

It meant wise in ancient Greek.

It was funny even now. So that was it, I was Soph to the wider world. Nothing more, nothing less. But for those like me, those who had their lives ripped apart, and to those behind the Necronotes, I was Necrosoph.

Dead wise. Or a wise corpse. Maybe wise in death? I certainly wasn't in life.

But goddammit, I would not die. I had made it this far, and now Jen needed me more than ever. I would do as I was instructed because I liked being alive, even dealing with the things I did, and no way in hell would I see my little girl grow up without Daddy.

"Farewell, Andrew Blaine."

I stacked the notes back up, locked the lid, hid the key, battled spiders, then went back downstairs.

Woofer was snoring halfway up the stairs like the utter fool he was. I smiled as I tiptoed past him, but he was wise in some ways and his eye opened. His tail thumped against the carpet. I stroked his head, then said goodnight, and headed down into the living room to watch mindless TV before bed.

I knew Phage was upset and would be awake, but I hadn't even told her about the note yet, and honestly, I was too dog-tired to have that conversation. Part of me was being mean, too. She should have remembered. My birthday was three days after Jen's. Same as it had been since she was born. I knew Phage was beyond worried, had been getting worse for months now as Jen showed signs of inheriting our abilities, but still.

Ugh, would we get through this?

Yes, we'd have to. There was no escaping a Necronote.

Rev Her Up

Phage stared at me in utter horror, hair still mussed from sleep. I'd been awake for hours, lying there, dreading the day ahead.

"Oh my god. Oh my god. Soph, I am so sorry. I haven't been keeping track of the days. Your birthday, it was days ago. What the hell is wrong with me?" Phage began to cry. Then I started. She had never missed a birthday. Not that we made a big deal out of ours, but they were so sickeningly significant that it was kinda impossible to forget. She wasn't right, that was clear.

"It's because of Jen," I said, putting my arm around her. "I get it. And besides, after you've had three hundred and forty of the buggers, they kind of lose their impact. I'd rather it never happened."

"Don't we all? Imagine if there were no birthdays. No notes. Just us. Just regular life."

"Now, let's not get carried away. I doubt it would ever be what others call regular."

"No, but it would be to us. Did you get your note?"

I looked at my wife. "Of course. The other day, when you came home from school. I was in the kitchen. Looking stressed."

Phage groaned. "What is wrong with me? You didn't say. When are you going? Oh, right. Today. You waited until after Jen's party. You're such a good man. I'm such a bad wife."

"No, you aren't. I get it. I figured best to not mention it. Didn't want to spoil the mood. And you had enough on your plate sorting the party and everything."

"I don't deserve you. I didn't even do your special thing," she groaned.

"Maybe there's time now?" I asked optimistically.

Jen banged about in her bedroom, readying for the seven-year-old onslaught that was Sunday morning.

"Maybe when you get back?" Phage wiped her eyes and smiled. She groaned again. This time not because of sadness, but from a hardcore horniness that took us both over as we thought about the birthday tradition.

"It's a date."

One thing about having a wife named after a bacteria that can replicate itself, and is so named for good reason, is that you can get seriously fruity in the bedroom. Only twice a year though. It took so much out of the poor thing that she needed days to recover. So did I.

"When this is all over, I will give you a night you will never forget," she promised.

"I'll be there." I put my arm around her and we lay like that for a while, just us.

"Come on, I'm going. Sunday morning action stations," I called up the stairs, before heading out front with my heavy pack and Woofer getting under my feet.

Jen and Phage arrive together. Jen looked happy, Phage looked stressed.

"Brrm, brrm." I made the sound of a car as I twisted the handlebars of my bike left to right like I was holding a steering wheel. Jen clapped with delight and did a little jig; her tutu bounced like a jellyfish on a choppy sea. Her white tights were grubby at the knees, I was pleased to see, so she was still a tomboy at heart.

All my arrangements were made, meaning I'd packed up my gear and grabbed as much food as I could manage. Now it was time for "Daddy's work trip."

"Love you," I told Phage as I kissed her.

"Love you too. And sorry."

"Don't be."

Jen got in on the action, hugging our legs, so I bent and picked up my little girl. "Listen, I want you to be a good girl for Mummy, okay? Be on your best behavior and do what she asks. Did you have a great party yesterday?"

"The best!"

I kissed Jen, then gave Phage another kiss and patted a forlorn Woofer on the head. I'd already had a long discussion with him about why he couldn't come, but the poor fella was heartbroken. He really, really wanted to come with me.

I finalized my pack and then pushed off down the track away from my life, and into the yearly nightmare.

"Don't forget to walk Woofer," I called over my shoulder. They both waved back.

I had seventy miles or thereabouts to cover, so it would be Monday before I got to kill a guy. In the meantime, it was just me and the open road. The quiet, almost deserted, open road. I was headed deep into the heart of England, past my usual border by a long way, but it wasn't like I had anyone to complain to about it. The app gave the exact location, so there was no risk of confusion. Final destination, a small village on the outskirts of Derby in the East Midlands. A hard six-hour ride, or an easy day-long trip with plenty of stops and shouting at my bike. I chose the latter.

First, I had to pass through our local town, Shrewsbury. A beautiful place in the West Midlands nestled around the river Severn. Full of leaning, half-timbered Tudor houses right out of a picture postcard. Every now and then I'd pass a place of sanctuary for ones like me. Necrosleep—it was a hotel. Necropub—bastards stole my idea. Necrosweets—which was pushing it. And Necrogrub—my kind of place. Everyone thought they were chains with an edgy name, but they were independents set up by people so they could serve our community, and so nobody felt quite so alone.

Necrogrub had been there for ever. And I mean that almost literally. I'd visited even before I was Soph, but it became a yearly haunt for a long time once I was of age. The food had gone downhill though, so I skipped it today.

One place I absolutely wouldn't even consider bypassing, and would visit even if I was headed in another direction, was Necrosmoke. I came to a squeaky halt outside and parked up along with several equally crap looking bikes and surprisingly, an Audi. You didn't see many cars, and I liked it. Reminded me of the good old days when everything smelled of horse-shit, and the cobbled streets, if you were lucky, ran with dirty washing water, wee, and faeces. They knew how to assault the olfactory senses in those days.

Already my nostril hairs were standing to attention, ready to be bombarded with nicotine. My mouth was dry, my tongue poked out, as I anticipated the nasty tang of dark, rich tobacco. I rubbed at my pipe in my breast pocket—older than me and twice as gnarly.

My legs were knackered, and I hadn't even left the town yet. For a moment, I regretted not riding Bernard, then I recalled what had happened last time and shuddered. He was weaker than a kitten and moaned more than both my neighbors combined. I'd used horses for centuries, even a camel once, but cars had been awesome. So easy. So comfortable. So much room for gear, food, and weapons. But that came to an end almost as soon as it began, and after a few trials back to using horses, I soon came to realize that the best bet was a bike. As long as you had a pump, a repair kit, and a spare inner tube, you didn't have to worry. Modern bikes were awesome, nothing like the bone-shakers of the past. Animals needed food, they talked too much, and they were so damn uncomfortable.

A carriage was too much hassle when traveling alone, plus it was slower, cars would get you arrested before you got ten miles as it was for the twats in charge and haulage only these days, so a bike it was.

Still, there was always tobacco.

Feeling chipper, I turned to the window display and nearly choked on my tongue.

I barged inside, the bell above the door about the only familiar thing. "Pam, what the fuck!? What's all that shit in the window? Where's the bear smoking a pipe? I liked that dead bear, poor guy. Where's the Zippos, the pouches, the random crap ornaments you can never sell? What's going on?" I sniffed the air. "It smells clean! What the actual fuck?"

It was only then I realized I wasn't standing in a room I knew. Gone were the dark oak cabinets brimming with brooding tobaccos waiting to poison you. The stained mahogany counter had vanished, replaced with some plastic crap. The usually manky floor covered in sawdust had vinyl planks if you can believe such a thing, and the shelves full of jars of dark delight, the dusty lights, the whole damn lot was gone. All of it.

Instead there were glass cabinets full of brightly colored metal boxes and little plastic bottles of liquid.

"Pam, why are you selling little stupid drinks? What gives?" I turned at the snickers from a group of men with beards and tattoos. They blew clouds of smoke at me and laughed.

I sniffed. "What's that? Smells like melons and apples. Are you guys smoking fruit?" I couldn't believe it, they were.

"Where you been, gramps? Under a rock?"

"Gramps? My daughter's seven."

"Yeah, seven hundred, haha." They high-fived each other and laughed.

"Oh, yes, good one, twat-face. Now, run home to mummy and ask her if you can have another slice of melon for being," and I got right up in his face for this bit as it would be so awesome, "such a fucking moron." I turned away, looking for Pam, as I knew none of them would move.

You don't react, do you? Most people don't, anyway. Maybe they knew what I was. Doubtful, but some knew, more every year. Rumors spread. As technology went nuts, it was harder and harder to stop weird shit being seen around the globe. But they didn't know, they just thought they knew. If only.

Pam came bursting from the back with a shotgun and locked and loaded it for the visual effect. "What the fuck's going on?" she bellowed, looking so sweet with her pigtails, her tight vest, her ample bosom, and her snarl.

"Ah," I relaxed. "At least some things haven't changed. Pam, what's with the drinks and the twats smoking fruit?" I turned and glared at them. "Not a word, if you value your nuts," I warned.

"Soph, it's been so long." Pam lowered the shotgun but kept hold of it.

"It's been a year, Pam, same as always. Where's the bear? Where's my goddamn tobacco? Look, I brought my pipe and everything." I pulled it out and showed it to her, like it would make everything alright.

Pam shrugged. Pam did the most awesome shrugs. The guys behind me sighed; I didn't blame them. People came not only for the smokes, but for Pam. A sight for sore eyes in a world where beauty wasn't so easy to come by.

"Gotta roll with the times, Soph. Everyone's into health these days." She leaned closer and whispered, "Makes me sick, and it's not as though the likes of us have to worry about it killing us, but what's a gal to do?"

"But it's fruit!"

"It's flavorings. It still has nicotine. They call it 'the juice.' You put the liquid in a small device and it makes vapor. You should try it."

"No thank you very bloody much. What about the electric? You can't tell me that's a good thing. We're all limited. How come this is a thing?"

"It uses hardly anything. You won't notice much difference to your quota." Again, Pam leaned in close. "Not that you have to worry, eh?"

People got funny if they thought you had more power than most folks were rationed. Nevermind it was because you built your own bloody arrays and used wind and water so you could have an extra freezer. They still got angry about it.

"No, I don't. But that's not the point. Let's have a go then." I took the offered black box and sucked on the tip. A lungful of melon hit me. The hit wasn't bad, but it wasn't the same, nowhere near it. "I'll pass. Hey, who's got the Audi? Don't see many of them. Don't see many cars full stop. It's like things are getting better. Back to the good old days.

"What would you know about the good old days?" asked a man who appeared from out the back and came to stand beside Pam.

"I've been around," I said suspiciously.

He appraised me, then nodded. "So I see. Well, so have I, and ain't nothing good about cars being rare. I remember when everyone had a car, maybe even two."

"Yeah, so do I. Everywhere stank and people spent their lives traveling to and from work. It was carnage out there."

"So you saying it's better that everyone works from home and only the blessed get to drive? You want everyone to stay rationed for fuel, making it impossible to travel?"

"No, it sucks. The country is for shit and it's getting worse. No travel, can't get hold of half the things you used to be able to, but you can't tell me you miss the cities and towns stinking, the office blocks lit up like Christmas trees every night of the year."

"All that's fine, good even, but it's the underlying cause that's the issue, isn't it?"

"I'm not arguing." I told him.

"Yeah, yeah," interrupted Pam. "You're like two ancient fools moaning about the good ol' days. No speech today, fellas. We've all heard it before."

"Have not," grumbled the Audi owner.

"Have too. It goes something like this." Pam smiled, took a deep breath, which was nice, then blurted, "Universal electric vehicles are a joke, especially now nuclear is banned. Hydrogen caused so many deaths it was vilified, and all that remained was dirty fuel from the ground. The good old combustion engine. Solar, wind, and ocean-derived energy are ace and getting there, but it will never allow for clean transport for all. Am I getting it right so far?" she asked the man, with a wicked grin.

"I don't talk like that," he said gruffly.

Pam continued, warming to her role. "But with the cost of oil escalating to astronomical highs thanks to the worldwide limit on production, and the subsequent banning of all motor vehicles apart from haulage, other necessary transport needs, and the twats in power, the world suddenly became a much brighter and cleaner place. Apart from the fact everyone is cold at night, as you can't use much electric, oil is strictly rationed for heating, gas the same, and burning wood is banned anywhere but the countryside. Did I miss anything?"

"That's not how I talk," he repeated. "But it's right, isn't it?"

"It's better now," said Pam. "Sure, things take longer, but everyone's more relaxed. We have to think of the climate. It's fucking burning up out there."

"Language," the man warned. What was with these two?

"Sorry. But come on, at least something's being done. Finally. We left it too late, but at least everyone's trying now."

"Amen," said one of the dipshits behind me. I turned and glowered at him.

"I know the climate's a mess! But they're using it as an excuse. They give us all this nonsense about the need for fuel and energy rationing, but it's an excuse, I tell you. They want to keep us under control. They want us to be sheep. Kept in our own little fields so they can milk us dry."

"That's cows," said Pam.

"You know what I mean," he growled.

The old dude was growing on me. So much was different now, so much. Used to be you saw vehicles everywhere. Now it was only trucks, bigwigs, delivery drivers, that kid of thing. It got slower every day. Every country in the world was the same. Everything was rationed, like we were going backwards in time. Much of it was good, the air was certainly cleaner, the sky at night darker, but it meant there was a general air of decay to the country. Less was fixed, more left to rot or break down slowly.

"So, who are you?" I asked the old man.

"He's my dad, Soph."

"Oh, right. Pleased to meet you."

"Dover. Pleased to meet you too. A fellow traveler, I see." He meant more than he said. It was the eyes. Hard as our taskmasters.

"So, how come you're driving?"

"Yeah, old-timer, what gives?" one of the young-sters bravely called. "We gotta ride these crappy bikes, but you're driving a fucking Audi. You a politician, is that it?"

"Do I look like a politician, kid? Listen up, young fools. I've saved up my allowance for years. I haven't sat behind that wheel for over a decade. This is my swan song. I'm done. What better way than to go out in an Audi?"

"That dude's crazy. What's he on about?" the youngster muttered to his mates. They all got up and shuffled out the door. The bell rang.

"You giving up?" I asked him, my eyes darting be-tween him and Pam.

"He is," said Pam.

"I'm not giving up," he snapped. "Sorry. Soph, how long you been around? Three hundred is my guess."

"You aren't far off."

"I've been at it for over four hundred years. I've sired countless children, killed so many people. I've watched the world change over and over again. But this is different. This time and place we find ourselves in, it's so wrong. We have the greatest technology ever, and it's getting better, but nobody is allowed to go anywhere. Do anything. We're prisoners. But that's not the reason. It's the notes, Soph, it's the goddamn bloody notes." A single tear fell but he sniffled and wiped it from his lined face. He was beaten, had enough. Plain and simple.

"I get it, I really do. But is it that bad, really?" asked Pam as she put an arm around her father's shoulders.

"Yes. I cannot, I will not, kill another person. Four hundred years, Pam." He stepped away then turned to his daughter. "You have to understand. In all this time, I have never found out a thing. I can't find who sends the notes, how they decided who is to be dealt with, what their motives are, none of it. I can't stand the not knowing. I can't stand the heat. I can't stand myself a moment longer. So I'm doing the rounds, saying goodbye to the kids, the grandkids, the great-grandkids, and on it goes. Even the wives, the ones that will talk to me. Then I'm done."

I nodded. It wasn't like I hadn't thought about it. Like it was a novel idea. I'd lost count of the number of Necros who had offed themselves over the years. Not that it was always that simple. After all, it wasn't unusual for a Necro to receive a note to kill another. Happened an awful lot. I knew that from personal experience.

"Good luck, fellow traveler. Go out with a bang."

"Oh, I intend to." He smiled. We shook, and he retreated to the back.

"Sorry about that, Pam. You guys close?"

"Kinda. Don't see him that often, but he's a good man. Good as he can be. Good as any of us can be."

"Yeah, I hear that. Now, where's the fucking good stuff?"

Pam smiled and beckoned me closer with a crook of the finger. "That's what I like in a man. Someone who isn't afraid to stink of cancerous chemicals."

"You know it."

Pam got me sorted out with a nice large stash. As she handed it over and I offered money which she refused same as always, she said, "Don't forget that thing. You can call any time and come over to get it, you know."

"Oh, er..."

"Not that, you dolt. The collection. You said you would take her."

"I will, I promise. Just haven't had the time. You sure it's okay?"

"Yes, she's pining, Soph. Needs the company. Make it soon, okay?"

"I will. Promise."

Ten minutes later, I was sorted with enough tobacco for a week. My yearly ration. Just to keep me grounded. I hopped on my bike and rode through the town, passing people going about their business—shopping, shouting, some even smiling. Half the storefronts were boarded up, the other half were struggling to fill the shelves. Most had a single light on inside, some none. It was almost like the government wanted them all to shut down, wanted everyone to stay at home. Stare at screens and not cause any bother.

I rode on. I had more important things to worry about than whether you could still buy bits of plastic crap.

I had someone to kill.

Camping

By early evening I was exhausted. I made a mental note to keep up the cycling all year; I was getting unfit in my dotage. Fuck that! I'd live with the aches once a year. The town had turned to village, then to nothing much of anything. Just farmhouses dotted about on either side of the roads, sheep in the fields, cows munching on grass, the flies buzzing everywhere, and the relentless heat. It was almost unbearable. I was so damn hot and the water never lasted. I spent more time sneaking up to people's outside taps than I did traveling. How long would such a luxury last? Already, there was a permanent hosepipe ban. When would drinking water be rationed too? And I was almost out of sunscreen. We never had enough, even though everyone got monthly deliveries. It was more important for Jen than us, so we hardly ever used it.

But hell, it was hot. Rain, what I wouldn't give for rain.

"Why don't you rain, you bastard?" I shouted at the sky, shaking my fist. The sky remained silent; not a bloody word. I wobbled and nearly fell off my bike. Time to rest up for the night. Get an early start. With any luck, I'd be at my location tomorrow afternoon and I could get a feel for the place before nightfall.

With plenty of fields to choose from, but access limited, and crops aplenty after the massive drive to make the UK self-sufficient in most produce, I cycled on until I found a sun-baked, wilting field devoid of live-stock. A stream, a beautiful, wondrous, increasingly rare stream meandered along the north side. Cool, and shaded by a small copse of ancient, gnarled oaks. Sentinels guarding what little remained of the world that was.

Weird how I could remember these very fields covered in native species, with deer running freely, rabbits galore, fish in streams and deep, dark forests at every turn. Grass was so green it hurt your eyes, now animals struggled to find sustenance.

It changed so rapidly. Agriculture became big business, and once the machines were available to all, it was as though the world scraped itself bare overnight. Gone were the historic forests, gone were the crofters. In their stead were mono cultures and massive metal beasts chugging along neat rows of crops. Progress. It was still happening, you couldn't get away from it, but chemicals were rare now—we had to be eco these days—and at least the bird and insect populations were recovering. We nearly lost the bees, and that would have been devastating for the entire planet.

I pushed my bike across the field and, distracted, tripped over. My bike went flying.

The carcass of a sheep lay half-hidden in the meadow, stinking to high heaven and buzzing with flies. My guess was it hadn't died of natural causes. Poaching was rife because people wanted meat, so farmers were now very good shots.

Not my business, nothing I could do. But come on people, these are the ones keeping us alive. Don't take advantage. Eat your vegetables.

Suitably sat on my high horse, I righted my bike and continued until I reached the oaks.

Exasperated, sweating like a hipster on a bicycle who refuses to take off his woolly hat, I nevertheless untied my pack from the back of my bike and set it aside carefully. In minutes I had a small fire going and life was as good as it got.

What a wondrous thing it is to lean back against a tree older than you and listen to the gurgling of a crystal-clear stream. The cool air was heaven-sent, the insects only slightly irritating, the ache in my legs already fading.

Ah, lovely clean air—time to put an end to that. I reached for my pipe, unwrapped the package of tobacco Pam had tied with a sweet red ribbon just to take the piss, then loaded up old faithful and lit it with a stick from the fire. I reached over and grabbed my pack, fumbling for tools of the trade no Necro is ever without for long. With gun, blade, and air pistol now at hand if I needed them, I could truly relax for a while.

Next thing I knew, I awoke with a start to a noise from behind. I remained motionless, already feeling the tiny life-force projecting my way.

"Get drink, thirsty," came the voice that was not a voice but was.

A rabbit. The burrow was probably right there behind me; they liked to be close to water sources if the option was there.

I focused on him, reading what I could. No sense of there being a family or mate in the burrow; he was a lone stud.

He hopped down to the shallow edge of the stream and began to sip. Smoothly, slowly, I reached for the air pistol and shot him dead.

"Sorry, little fella, but I couldn't waste the opportunity."

I quickly retrieved him, gutted and skinned him, then added twigs to the fire before I washed the rabbit and myself in the stream.

Once the fire was burning nicely with plenty of coals, I skewered my prize and left it to cook slowly while I went back to relaxing against the tree.

Many times through my life I had sworn off meat —being able to understand and talk to the animals can really put a downer on a bacon sandwich—but I always returned to it eventually. Some minds were incredibly complex, like bloody immortal cats and unicorns—although Bernard was not the best example of that—others were dumb as rocks, like chickens. So I simply chose my meat carefully, always mindful, but I never judged others, as quite simply they didn't know and they were hungry. I would never eat a gifted creature though. Many were smarter than us humans.

Besides, some creatures were so incredibly annoying that frankly they had it coming. Don't get me started on squirrels, the fuckers. They'll nick your nuts and laugh in your face. The bastards.

There was still a pang of guilt as I ate the rabbit even though it tasted marvelous. You cannot beat meat cooked on an open fire. I finished the lot, sucked the bones clean out of respect.

Wondrous night would wrap its infinite shroud over me soon enough, so I got busy setting up camp. Small one-man tent, coffee pot, little Tupperware containers with coffee and even a pint of milk. There was a container with vegetables that Phage always insisted I bring, as she was a stickler for your five-a-day. I ate them begrudgingly, but eat them I did.

After coffee, I settled down in my sleeping bag against the tree and watched the fire dance; orange light flickered on the stream. It was beautiful.

Late into the night, half drunk on strong vintage wine with a definite tang to it, I was lost to the dance of the wood sprites like I had been so many times before. It was a rare treat, but not unheard of, especially for those with a gift or two.

They came cautiously at first, attracted by the fire and the knowledge there was someone a little like them. Someone with a link to this thing humanity called magic but nothing else did. They sensed I was of a like mind. Not good, not bad, just attuned. Their moral compass was like mine, like most Necros. Obtuse to say the least.

The sprites flew high above the fire away from the flames, but enjoyed the heat even though it wasn't exactly a cold night. They danced and sang and swung each other, chattered away in a tongue I had no way of deciphering. That was okay, I didn't need to understand to know they were having fun. They rejoiced in this small spot of natural beauty, and let me join them.

Once thoroughly drunk, I danced along with them, sang some songs of old, even shared a little wine. They turned their noses up at it at first, but soon gave in. We cavorted around the fire, drunk as you like, enjoying the night and each other's company.

They left eventually, and I sank back against the tree, hot and sweaty, happy and tired.

It wasn't long before I began to doze off, but the night hadn't finished with me yet. The cloud cover cleared, leaving the stars to shine cold and uncaring down upon this drunken man beside a tree. The full moon shone through the gaps in the oaks, same as it always had, except now there were bits of metal on it, and a flag, which seemed like yesterday.

"Ugh, full moon." I was instantly sober. "There goes the nice night's sleep."

I put coffee on to brew. It would be a long night.

Full Moon Blues

In many ways, some Necros are lucky. Many can talk to animals, quite a few can read minds, even see the future, all of which may be seen as a blessing. There are many Necros who are undoubtedly cursed.

And as the world changed, so did they. We all belong to the shadows, and as the governments around the world put in place sanctions to stop humanity from obliterating itself and its inhabitants, so the shadows deepened.

Cities were dark at night, which led to astronomical increases in crime. Partly because nobody could see the buggers, but also because food, water, power, transport, all of it, became more rare. Some countries were much more extreme than the UK, were quickly returning to agrarian cultures, even though the tech got better every year.

Without ease of travel, so entire countries appeared empty; everyone stayed close to home now. This gave many Necros a freedom our kind hadn't experienced since I was a lad. It was nice, an easier life, less stressful in many ways. Much more stressful in others as you never knew what you'd encounter when out and about.

I could look after myself, sure, but there were limits, and this damn "gift" meant we could sniff each other out a mile away. It was hard to pinpoint exactly how you knew there was another Necro near, but let's just call it a sixth sense. You knew, you just knew it, like you know when there is something missing from a room you walk into, even if you have no idea what. Something in the air, a twist in your gut, a knocking in your head, whatever it was, we all had it to some degree. And the older you got, the more pronounced it became.

So I slithered from my sleeping bag like a spastic snake and sat with my coffee and my weapons, praying for morning yet knowing it was a long way off yet.

Wispy clouds sailed past the moon, briefly obscuring the cold eye in the sky. But tonight wasn't a night for a cozy blanket of fluffy clouds, tonight planet earth was open to the cosmos.

Some time around two I heard the first howl. Must have been miles away, but that didn't matter. I knew what was coming. At half past it was close enough to give me goosebumps. At quarter to three I was on my feet, gulping coffee like it was the last I'd ever drink. By three, I was up the oak tree with my weapons in hand and feeling jittery as a young girl going on her first date.

A mind came into my perception. A confused, conflicted mind. So sad, so hard to listen to. To attempt communication would have been a bad mistake.

He spoke into the night. "Must hunt. Don't want to hunt. Must eat. Don't want to eat. Must kill. Don't want to kill."

The werewolf loped slowly across the field. The meadow rustled as seeds fell to the ground like hail. Every few seconds the wolf man would stop and sniff, mutter to itself in the schizophrenic way all of its kind do. Never fully wolf, never fully man. It was not a nice way to spend your night once a month.

He was on to me, like I knew he would be, and sure enough he headed straight for camp, moving fast, loping with an easy gait, half running, switching to all fours effortlessly.

He stopped by the fire, unafraid but wary just the same. He sniffed the rabbit carcass I hadn't had the sense to bury deep, then pounced on it and chewed on the dry bones, snarling and constantly searching for any sign of life.

The creature sat on its haunches and stared up into the tree right at me. Such sad eyes, so full of pain. Hunger too. And death. The human's eyes were replaced with those more like a cat than a wolf. Slits that immediately made you think of the creature as cruel. But it wasn't cruel, just a wild animal trapped in a man, or a man trapped in a wild animal. Neither ever won, they just shared an unholy, unhappy alliance.

I remained still, shut down communication links, did my utmost to ensure it couldn't discover that I could communicate with it. I didn't want to hear the insane ramblings I knew were going on, never wanted to be a part of that ever again. It was enough to drive a Necro insane, just contacting a mind so unraveled.

We held each other's gaze for the longest time, but then he edged to the stream, took his fill and was gone.

Poor man, poor creature. He would awake in the morning, lost and alone, and spend the next month trying to recover his wits until the night repeated.

Lycanthropes never made it to old age. They either went insane, killed themselves, or got killed by another Necro. They were high on the Necronote radar—too unruly, too dangerous, too much of a risk. Nobody wanted the general populace to fear the wolf—things were bad enough already.

I still stayed up the tree until morning, just sat there smoking my pipe, enjoying the silence, the solitude. Times like that, sitting in a tree as the sun rose over my beautiful country, well, it almost made this life worthwhile.

Inevitably, the sun continued its ascent uninterrupted by cosmic madness, so I clambered down, joints stiff, mouth dry, lungs tight from the tobacco.

After doing what bears do in the woods best, then brushing my teeth and even braving the cold water to freshen up, I drank coffee and ate a light breakfast of dried fruits, cheese, and some hard-boiled eggs.

Once I was pleased with the tidy-up, the fire doused, all litter collected, all signs of my passing eradicated, I broke camp. I pushed the bike across the meadow then hit the road again.

It was busy this morning, when most people liked to do their traveling if possible. Horses and carts passed me by, lone rangers with broad hats and neckerchiefs right out of westerns from movies of a bygone era. Others were on foot, carrying loads, off to visit, shouldering lightweight tents and sleeping bags. There'd definitely been a boom in outdoor camping gear since the fuel veto—should have bought shares.

I nodded, waved, said a few words to those I passed, but I knew from experience it was best to keep to yourself. People asked too many questions, and I was crap at lying. I always got carried away and ended up losing the thread of my story halfway through, resorting to scowling and storming off. Utterly shady.

Drones passed overhead, keeping an eye on things. One in particular was certainly following me, keeping tabs on events. It had been unusual maybe a decade ago, but now it was commonplace. Not only did the government have eyes everywhere, to keep control of the new laws and monitor traffic, people, just about everything, but the Necrobastards were out there somewhere, watching, ensuring we performed like good puppets.

Word on the street was that since drones and other surveillance tactics had been instated, fewer Necros had attempted going underground to avoid their notes, and business had never been better. Meaning, more folks died.

I ignored the buzzing overhead, focused on my cycling, on not riding through horse shit, and was lost to the heat, the road, and my ever-so-slightly sore head.

Come late morning, I was dog-tired, so hot I could have cooked eggs on my scarred stomach, and ravenous. Time for a break and a doze somewhere shady. There was little in the way of hospitality out here, I'd passed the last village miles ago and there was nothing for hours yet, so I simply took a turn off the road down a small lane, found somewhere out of the way, and set up for a nice rest.

There was no stream, no beautiful ancient trees as gnarly as old Soph, but a weeping willow was even better in many regards. Its branches hung to the ground, it was utterly hidden, it was cool, and the grass was even green and wet underneath its respectful boughs. Perfect.

After sweaty sandwiches and even more sweaty water, I pulled my hat low over my eyes and settled back on the cool wet grass and sighed.

"Hot out there." Ribbit.

I lifted my hat and turned my head. Smiled at the frog. "Hey there. Sure is hot. Stay cool, my friend."

Ribbit. "What you doing?"

"Trying to sleep. You?"

"Hanging out, waiting for flies."

"Oh, right." There was an awkward silence. "That's nice.

Ribbit. "What you doing now?"

"Still trying to sleep."

"Oh, okay." Ribbit.

He took the hint and hopped off somewhere. Frogs can be annoying, especially when it's hot.

Wakey, Wakey

"You took your time," I said as I awoke to a familiar heat on my thigh. No, I hadn't wet myself, although I did need to go. This was the intense heat of one of my best friends in the whole world, apart from Phage and Jen. Plus Woofer. I did love him too.

"It's the drones," said Tyr. "So hard to avoid. And cameras. Makes Tyr lose direction. Sends brain all skewy."

"Well, you're here now, that's what counts." I reached out without looking, knew exactly where he was because of our connection, and rubbed his small bumpy head. The scales were warm as a bath, yet dry as a bone in the desert.

Tyr sighed with contentment, pleased to be back where he belonged, in dire need of a rest and refueling. "Very tired."

I felt his mind slow, his eyes close. He settled, curled his tail around his little body, and sank dangerous claws into my legs. I didn't mind. I had much worse scars than any he'd given me. He was a bugger with the claws when grumpy, went with his nature, his kind, which was probably why we hit it off so well.

I settled back down, pleased he was here at last, and we slept away the heat of the afternoon together.

Waking up to your trousers on fire is never enjoyable, but over the previous seven years I'd grown accustomed to it. Tyr, which we pronounce Teer, full name Tyrant of the Sky as he rightfully was allowed to name himself once old enough to talk and understand the world, was still just a wyrmling, barely past a hatchling really, and not entirely adept as of yet.

"Dude, seriously?" I groaned, patting at my leg, knowing it wasn't really his fault, but c'mon.

Tyr shifted as he awoke, then turned and stood on my leg, looking sheepish. "Sorry, sorry, just a little accident."

"I know, didn't mean to be grumpy. But you need to watch it, you could do some damage. You want to be with Jen when you're older, don't you?" He nodded vigorously. He loved her, even though he'd never met her, just watched her play whilst hiding outside.

"Tell me again, tell me the story again," he pleaded, eyes all soppy and tail thumping on my knee.

"Okay, hop on up," I patted my shoulder. Just like Jen, all kids really, Tyr, he who has battled nothing but a chicken and emerged bruised, and far from victorious, loved to be told of his birth over and over again. About the stuff he did as a hatchling and wyrmling.

My scaly, currently green buddy settled on my shoulder. He stared at me with his intriguing eyes: vertical slit pupil, purple iris, orange sclera. I could stare into them for hours and always see something new. I began my oft-repeated tale.

"Forty-seven years I'd held onto this egg, always wondering if it would hatch one day. A true discovery it was, as rare as rare can be. Pried from the corpse of an evil mage on the other side of the world. I'd tried heat, even baked it in the oven for a whole night. I'd tried cold, and everything in-between. I got nothing. When I moved house, when I was utterly out of ideas and fed up dusting it, I chucked it in the airing cupboard, and promptly forgot about it."

"So mean. How could you forget about Tyrant of the Sky?"

"You weren't called that yet. You were just this heavy egg. Weighed a ton, and hard as a rock. And you really should have chosen something shorter as a name."

"Tyrant of the Sky is perfect name for dragon."

"Is a perfect name for a dragon," I corrected him. He had to learn to speak proper, like what I did.

"See, told you." His tongue flicked out and he hissed, pleased with himself.

"You leave the jokes to me. I'm funny as fuck."

"Language," he warned.

"Sorry. So, where was I? Ah, yes, the airing cupboard. I found the most rare egg in the whole world, an egg I had battled monsters to own. The day—"

"You said it was from a mage," he interrupted.

"Yes, after battling monsters. Where was I? The day Jen arrived, and let me tell you, that was one helluva day, I was running up the stairs, stressed to buggery, when there was a right commotion in the airing cupboard."

"It was me. It was me." He hopped up and down on my shoulder and giggled with glee.

"Haha, it sure was. I needed warm towels for Phage, and in a hurry, so I ripped the door open, forgetting about the egg, and there you were, about as large as a newt, which was weird as the egg was bloody massive. I discovered later that your egg was mostly filled with nutrients that you absorbed as you grew, needing a lotta fuel to develop over what can sometimes be fifty-plus years."

"But I was premature, wasn't I. Couldn't wait to meet you all. Meet Jen."

"Ain't that the truth. Hell, what a day that was. Fires in the airing cupboard. You set her first baby blanket alight too. And the poo, my god the poo. We were overrun with it. It was everywhere."

"I do like to poo," he admitted.

"At least it's hard now, like stones, but it wasn't always like that. All squishy. You flew about and dropped it everywhere until we could get you to settle."

"Phage hated it, didn't she?" he asked, knowing the answer, giggling about poo like kids do.

"She sure did. Oh boy did she. I got a right earful. Anyway, it was Jen that had summoned Tyr, that's you," I said, tickling him under the chin, "into the world, as dragons are incredibly protective and caring creatures. Faithful to the end. So the little fella, that's you again," I poked him gently in his proud chest and he licked my finger, "had heard the commotion of the baby screaming into the world and figured now was as good a time as any."

"I'm a good dragon."

"You sure are. Now how about some food?"

"Yippee." Tyr launched up, smacked his head on a branch, crashed down, ran along the ground to get some steam up, then took off out from under the willow to go see what he could catch to eat.

Jen absolutely did not know any of this yet, as even I knew a little kid and a baby dragon would not end well for anyone. He was still a secret, but with her new-found gifts emerging it was only a matter of time before I had to reveal him. Better to do it soon, let them grow together, before he was full-on massive and deadly in a few more decades.

Slowly, slowly, one day at a time. He was currently about the size of a blackbird, plus the massive tail. In another year or two he'd be twice as big, then on and on, exponentially growing until he reached maturity. Even then it wouldn't be like you saw in the movies. He wasn't about to raze cities to the ground, but he'd certainly be able to cook a house, no problem there.

If the dipshit ever learned how to breathe fire rather than fart it.

"Hey, wait, I forgot," I called. I rummaged around in my backpack and found a zip lock bag for Tyr. I un-sealed it and counted, "One. Two. Th—"

"Mine, all mine," he shouted as he crashed through the trees and smacked into the bag full of dead crickets.

"Haha, easy there, buddy. Take it slow. We don't want you getting any digestion problems. Here, let me help." Before he could rip the bag to shreds, I laid out a handful of crunchy treats on the grass and he got to work. He didn't finish until his stomach was so dis-tended he resembled a balloon with a crocodile face painted on and a tail attached.

With a massive belch, a tiny flame shot out and singed the grass.

"What do we say?"

"Pardon me," he said, then grinned, toppled over sideways, and began snoring.

"That's my boy," I said, with probably more pater-nal pride than I should have. Still, he was a good lad, and I missed him when he wasn't around.

Now, time for me to eat a little snack then get go-ing.

Stakeout

"Tyr, you see that?" I called mentally to the wyrm-ling keeping pace with me high above.

"The drones? Yes, I see them. Tyr hates drones."

"And they don't like you either, buddy. Stay away. You know you send tech all wonky. And no, not the drones, that bird. Over to your right. I think he's follow-ing us. Care to get closer, take a gander?"

"Shall I kill it?"

"Um, not right now, but thanks for the offer." The wyrmling was becoming more violent by the day. Keen to destroy, to hunt, feed the power maturing inside. Shame he was still utterly crap at it. He still needed feeding as he wasn't capable of catching much more than the odd moth, maybe a baby bird if it was newly fledged, but his coordination was still off, his skills lack-ing. This was the problem with dragons.

If you wanted one, and let's face it, who doesn't, you had to have them from birth. You wouldn't stand a chance with an adult or even a juvenile—it would tear your face off if you tried to interfere with it in any way. I shuddered at the thought of Tyr once grown. How would we keep him hidden? Adult dragons were meant to be able to cloak themselves, their chameleon-like characteristics taken to another level, but massive juveniles with all the sense of a teenager? Yeah, good luck with that, Soph.

We were in for a rocky few decades, but I was in no hurry, and Jen was gonna love this in a few years when they were introduced. The wyrmling pined for her every day. Watched her at home from his secret spot, reluctantly obeying my orders.

I stopped the bike and shielded my eyes against the sun as I watched my dragon soar closer to the bird. It looked like a buzzard, but it was no ordinary buzzard. I could feel its mind from here, that it was something other, part of the Necroverse.

It isn't magic, the things some of us Necros can do. It's merely another part of existence. As natural as eating, sleeping, dying. At least, it isn't always magic. I've always had a hard time defining it. Where's the border between magic and simply being? I never have got it straight.

I never tried to hide Tyr from the Necrodrones. I knew those behind the system watched, studied, kept tabs on all of us, so hiding a creature like him was pointless. But damn, I wish I knew who they were, what they were, what the end game was. If there even was one. What was the plan? Why all the killing?

Was it part of the government? Was it a group of ancient demonic entities, witches, warlocks? Fucked if I knew. I'd searched, even studied as best I could in utter secret, but there was only so far a man could push it without risking his life and that of his loved ones. My conclusion?

Nobody knew anything. Drones had been captured, inspected, but they'd burned up before any details were gathered. Same with the notes. They'd been studied in labs, people tried to trace back the route they took to us, and nothing but dead end after dead end.

Pure mystery.

But this bird trailing us was not theirs. I knew it, could taste it on the breeze. This was something else. Someone was working with this entity. Watching. I was uneasy.

"He's not very friendly," said Tyr, sounding worried, poor guy. "Won't talk to me, even say hello. He did try to peck me. Can I kill him now?"

"Try one last time. Ask him why he's following us. Say you mean him no harm. But tell him to leave. We don't like being watched."

I waited while he tried to chat to this sneak, knowing it could understand him the same way all Necros in this world could understand each other. This wasn't just a bird I'd be able to communicate with because of my gift. This was a creature far more complicated, far more dangerous. Who knew what it was capable of?

Tyr cried into my head, freaking me out, as the buzzard attacked, vicious claws hanging low as they snapped at the little guy. He swerved off, then circled back, his anger up despite his juvenile years. Once riled, there was no stopping him. I sighed as he darted at the buzzard, his own claws out, long jaws already strong enough to shatter the bird's neck if he got a good shot. But he didn't. He snapped and missed. I felt the pain as he was caught by the buzzard with a ferocious peck to his underbelly. The bird shook its head manically. Tyr screamed then belched an impressive orange flame at its head and it released him.

As he fell, so I ditched the bike on the empty road and hopped a fence, running to catch him as he tumbled head-over-tail through the emptiness. I dove as he came hurtling down like a dead weight. Dust billowed from freshly plowed earth as I stretched out my hands and caught him.

I sat for a moment with his lifeless, bloody corpse in my hands. His innards spilled out of the nasty gash in his belly, pink and blue. Congealed globs of half-digested insects and grubs coated my fingers with sickly goop.

"Lesson learned, buddy. Never underestimate your prey. Always go for the weak spot. Never expose yours."

Tyr warmed fast. He nodded weakly as the life-force returned to his immortal body. All the goop, the slime, every atom of his body, shone as it returned to its rightful place. I lay him in my hat on the dirt and told him, "Relax, recover, take some deep breaths. And remember what I just said."

He smiled weakly, then cried out in pain. "Never expose your weak spot. Alwa... Always go for theirs."

"That's my boy."

I stared up at the buzzard still circling high above. Resigned, I took a damn deep breath, cursed and blessed my ridiculous classification as Necromorph, then launched skyward as my body dissolved into itty-bitty disparate motes of utter pain. Billions of fragmented shards of Soph, each like a lit nerve, shot up and into the aether. Ash from an angry fire, full of heat and promises of pain. Transmuted, but still me. The energy of Soph. Ravaged, breaking the rules of nature some believed in, but I was breaking no rules for this was who I was, what I was. One of my gifts. May I one day be relieved of them all and live in peace.

I gritted non-existent teeth as my essence shot up at the bird, pushed down on the excruciating rending of my soul. My dark, noxious soul. This was the price to be paid. I hated that something foul buried deep inside reveled in the misery, the pain I inflicted. I deserved this; it was my punishment. I craved it, too. Wanted it. This sense of power, of being indestructible when in this form. Nothing could touch me for I was nothing solid, nothing real. I was the universe, the dark matter that pervaded infinity. Wild. Free. Alone. Full of darkness.

All for a little fucking bird.

I circled it, like a tornado of black jagged ash, faster and faster, delirious with freedom, reveling in the act itself. It had been many years since I had performed such a feat, but the moment I became airborne I felt like it had only been yesterday.

A lover had returned. One I despised with all my being, yet could never bear to be without. I had to be quick; my ability had severe limitations.

"What do you want?" I called on the wind. No words spoken, a purely telepathic act. Often, I never knew if I was talking out loud to animals or communicating this way, and it got me some funny looks at times, but we all have our quirks.

The bird banked hard left.

I dove after her, the strong currents as nothing to me, my incorporeal body not prey to the whims of the air. I went where I wished, did as I pleased, screamed in anguish as I did so.

"What do you want?" I asked again. "There is no escape. Answer or die."

"Merely a watcher," said the bird, a hint of fear in her voice.

"For whom?" I growled, as I circled her repeatedly, forcing her to hover.

"Master. He waits. He knows you come. He is scared."

"Okay. Fair enough. Go, tell him then, but tell him this also. It will make no difference."

"He knows this also. But still, I must do as he asks."

I dove headlong at the parched earth and the little wyrmling only now getting to his feet. It took nerve to plummet headfirst, but the sooner I was back in corporeal form the better. My time was almost up, my threshold reached, and the agony threatened to destroy my mind, so deep did it hurt.

As I reached terra firma, my will, my sense of survival, took over and I changed once again. The motes of Soph spun, spiraled, whipped up in a frenzy until they took on the form of a man once more. Then there I was, human (of sorts) once again, standing unsteadily, every nerve promising an eternity of pain.

I collapsed beside Tyr, crying, screaming, cursing, sweating, and utterly ravenous.

But one thing overrode all sensation.

Oblivion.

With a twisted smile, I sank deep into emptiness, pleased to be reunited with the most callous of all lovers.

"What? Who's there? What's that?" I rubbed my face with dusty hands and surfaced from the grogginess. My head was fit to burst, my stomach growled, my entire body ravaged by wicked pins and needles. I couldn't move my legs.

"Soph okay?" asked Tyr as he nibbled my ear.

"Ugh."

"Your phone's ringing," he said weakly. "Shall I answer it?"

"No!"

But it was too late. He hopped down to where it had fallen and deftly opened the dragon and water-proof case, slid it out, and nudged a button with his snout before I had time to grab it.

"There," he said, pleased. "It might be important."

"Goddammit! I told you never to do that. You'll break it. Or melt it. Back away, back away."

He hung his head then launched back onto my shoulder. I held the phone at arm's length, as far away as possible. His aura would wreak havoc with the phone in no time, so I'd better make this quick.

"Um, hello?" I said, realizing it was a video call.

"Hi, honey. Just checking in," said Phage brightly, but she failed to hide the concern in her eyes. "You didn't make your daily call. We were worried."

"Damn, sorry, got a bit pre-occupied."

"You look awful. Oh, no, you did it, didn't you? What's happening?"

"Nothing to worry about, just some surveillance. What's up? Jen okay? How was school?"

"School was fine, Daddy," shouted Jen. She appeared on the camera, beaming.

"I told you to wait until I said it was okay. Daddy might be busy," warned Phage.

"It's okay," I told her. "Just having a little rest before Daddy continues his trip."

Jen just stared at me, wide-eyed, her mouth agape. She opened and closed it but no words escaped.

"Honey, what's wrong? Phage, I thought you said she was okay."

"She is." Phage's eyes shifted a little, and then she said, "Oh my god. Oops."

"What? What is it?"

"Hello, Phage, and hello, Jen. Tyr finally meets Jen. We'll be best friends when we're all grown up, your Daddy said so."

No. Not now. Not like this. It wasn't time. But there was no putting the genie back in the bottle now.

"Um, Jen, I want you to meet Tyr. He's very excited to see you."

Tyr hopped up and down, farted, singed my shirt, then belched and let out a tiny burp of fire.

"Um, he's a dragon," I said lamely.

"It's a dragon, a real life dragon. I knew it. I knew it," Jen sang shrilly, as she squirmed with glee. Encouraged, Tyr bounced about, bit my ear, all the while joining Jen giggling and bopping, making me dizzy.

"We'll be best friends," Tyr told her.

"We will," said Jen. "You're a dragon. A real dragon. How did you get here? I cannot believe this! A real dragon. Whee! Wow, your eyes are purple. And orange. And your scales. So shiny. And all kinds of green too. Wow, now you're brown. Now, red. Wow! Amazing!"

"All in good time," I told her. "But I promise, you really will be the best of buddies."

"What's he saying? Damn, can she communicate with him already?" asked Phage. "Sorry about this, I should have thought. She's such a pest, sneaking in on Mummy when I told her not to." Phage cuddled Jen and I couldn't help but laugh.

She was just like her old dad, super stealthy when the need arose. Some call me ninja, others call me a fucking dick. Whatever; I know the truth. It's somewhere in-between.

"He's just excited to meet Jen. Now, look, I'm okay, but I have to go. Jen, listen carefully. Dragons can mess with technology, so keep them away from important stuff, okay? And not a word to anyone. Promise?"

"I... I promise. Is he really a dragon? Can he really talk? He's not just an armadillo, is he?"

"An armadillo? Huh?"

"Haha, no, not armadillo. A, you know. A chameleon? Will we really be friends? Hello, Tyr." Jen waved manically. "It's a dragon. A dragon." Jen ran around the room screaming, laughing, and skipping. She was verging on hysterical.

"Bye, love. Have a great afternoon." I blew a kiss to Phage.

"Yeah, thanks for that. Be careful, Soph, and do not morph if you can possibly help it. You know what it does to you. Check the bottom of your pack. I knew you'd need it." With a look behind her at our wild daughter, she sighed, but smiled, and we closed the call.

I put my phone on standby, put it in its shielded case, and hoped Tyr hadn't screwed it up.

"She's lovely," sighed the wyrmling.

"She sure is. Protect her with your life," I told him. "All of your lives. For eternity."

"I will. You can count on me. I am hers, she is mine. We are linked."

"You are. Now, I wonder what's in my pack?"

I delved to the bottom, found a small container, and pulled it out blind.

I lifted the lid of the Tupperware and smiled as the aroma greeted me. Meat tinged with the magic of the woman I loved so much. I recognized the smell of Phage's power anywhere. Cool air tickled my face; they were still cold. Man, she looked after me well.

"Ah, corned beef sandwiches." I took a bite, threw a corner to the giggling dragon dreaming of playing with my little girl, and we sighed with contentment.

"Can't beat a corned beef sandwich after dying or transmuting, am I right?"

"Mmm." Tyr spat crumbs as he agreed.

We ate in silence. Crickets chirruped while the sun beat down on us in a dusty field far from home.

I checked the sky. It was clear as the day the heavens were first created.

Rest and Wait

Neither of us were in the best condition, but we had to get to the location. The day had slipped away from me. I'd hoped to be done and on my way home soon. Never mind that my cover was blown, it had happened many times over the years. The result always the same.

I was never complacent though, never took anything for granted. It was just that I was better. One of the absolute best.

Many marks had much more power than I, knew dark magic, could change into animals, wield fireballs, pop in and out of existence even, and communicate with animals to some degree.

But few had my skills, my edge.

You can have all the magic in the world, but what most people lacked, because it simply wasn't in them, was the ability to become disgustingly violent. Almost everyone, be they the regular person at home watching TV, or the wildest dabbler in all things esoteric, even dark practitioners, are incapable of unleashing violence with utter abandon.

Nobody knew how to actually fight, to let go and become the unthinking animal that lay curled deep down inside the dark of our souls.

I could. I did. And I emerged victorious each and every time. I had the battle scars to prove it. Mental ones too. I wasn't immortal though. I could be killed same as any man, if you held your nerve, had it in you to look me in the eye and kill me. Because you could be sure of one thing—if you paused, even for a second, I'd stab you in the heart.

Even with my latest mark having the ability to communicate with animals, I wasn't any more concerned than usual. Whatever he could do, I was ready.

That wasn't to say I wasn't scared, I was, and it was the fear that made me ever more fearful. I had more to lose than I had for so long because of Phage and Jen. I never believed I would love again the way I did now, and I did not want to lose it. But it made me weak, this love, and I had to push it down, because if I was afraid, I would die.

Death, life, it was the same thing. I knew this, but I wanted to see my daughter grow up, regardless. That was it. Use that. Make it the reason. Not merely survival of this mean-spirited man, but to guide Jen, to nurture her. Teach her how to grow, even thrive in this new world I found myself in.

My mind spun like this as we traveled ten miles through the early evening until we were close enough to make the morning an easy stroll for an hour or so and arrive. Any closer wasn't worth the risk, it would make us too easy a target, so we holed up in one of the increasing number of abandoned farm cottages. So many people had left to become part of a more communal lifestyle, as most simply couldn't make it alone nowadays.

I knew it was empty by the state of the land around it and the lack of signs of life. Still, I was cautious, moved through the undergrowth, did a spot of spying, then snuck up to the back door and peered through a grimy window into a kitchen that hadn't been updated for decades. True farmhouse style.

The back door wasn't even locked. Why bother? They never believed they'd return. As expected, the house was empty of belongings, just a few empty hangers in wardrobes not worth saving, several dented pots and pans, cracked plates, even a mangy sofa in the living room. I rummaged in a small pantry, waded through mountains of newspapers, old containers and what have you, and then, bonus, a tin of baked beans. Buoyed by my bounty, I delved deeper. In no time I was cooking up a storm. Baked beans, spam, and a pack of rice out of date four years ago—I was sure it would be fine.

Meal prepped, I settled on the sofa and ate my food. Tyr's chest rose and fell as he dreamed, unworried. After eating, I washed up, stacked the crockery and cutlery neatly in case somebody came after me, then curled up beside Tyr and slept like a warrior.

No mind. No fear. No life. No death. Just battle.

Morning was action stations. No messing. Exercise routine done, smug glow because I'd not skipped it. Washed, teeth cleaned, other business taken care of, then a quick bite and on our way.

By nine, I'd ditched the bike and hiked through a sulking forest until I came to the edge and saw the house I sought up a rise in land. No neighbors, no busy road, just a nice drive leading to a smart Georgian farmhouse for a rich landowner who was long dead. The guy who owned it now certainly had cash. It looked well-maintained and the drive alone would have cost a fortune to put in, but there was nothing ostentatious about it.

I watched for a while through binoculars. Nothing stirred. It was kinda pointless to hide though—the dude knew I was coming. Either he was up there with a rifle, waiting to shoot me in the head if he was a crack shot, or he was cowering inside, hoping I'd leave him be. The alternative was he was on the lam, done a runner, and I would have to spend days tracking him down. I hated it when that happened.

I instructed Tyr to stay put, out of sight, then readied myself for action. With my knife in its sheath, everything else left behind, I shook out my arms and legs then morphed. In the blink of an eye, I was at the front door, winded, sick and hurting, but it had been so fast I recovered quickly and wasted no time. Doing the obvious first, I tried the door handle.

Result.

Weird Elevator

I opened the front door and found not a lavish hall-way but an elevator, no other means of entry. Stupid, but I walked straight into it. Once the blood was upon me I acted irrationally, but it wasn't as daft as it seemed. If there was gas, I'd morph, same for hidden blades, all that nonsense.

But more importantly than any of that, I'd seen similar things many times. Smart men, cocky men, thinking they could overpower me with their words, their minds, their ideals, did crap like this. Without a doubt, this guy wanted to talk. He also had a helluva lot to hide.

He could talk, for as long as it took me to kill him.

Cool blue lights illuminated the interior, right out of a spy movie back when real people starred in movies. I turned and looked in the mirror behind me as the lift descended. Damn, even I looked impressive. Deep shadows under my eyes, cheekbones highlighted, my chest defined. I needed me some of this lighting at home in the bedroom. Phage would be overwhelmed with my hotness.

The elevator shuddered then binged as the door slid open to reveal a very cool open-plan interior. It was full of timeless furniture. Somewhat brutal for my tastes, but the owner had style, I'd give him that. Tech was everywhere. Curved monitors, stuff with little lights that blinked, even a bank of servers along a wall if I wasn't mistaken, which I may well have been as me and technology had a hate hate relationship.

Directly in front of me was a large desk. A man stood beside it. Behind him a huge oil painting, abstract of course, hung smugly, aligned perfectly with the desk, just asking for me to question its meaning.

"You should have run," I told him. "Half of them run."

"Does everyone know you're coming?" he asked, in an accent so devoid of accent it made me nervous.

"No, most don't have a clue. But there are always a few like you. One's who know, who find out. You're a Necro."

"No, not as such."

"Never had a note? Ever killed?"

"No note, yes to the other."

"What about the bird?" I asked, as I moved closer without giving the impression of moving.

"Ah, the bird. My talent, to communicate with them. Just birds. Nothing more." He spread his hands apart as if to confirm he was harmless.

"Then you're a Necro, and you have had notes. Why the games?"

"I am not a Necro," he spat. "I refuse to be labeled. I refuse to take part in this sick game. I refuse to kill."

"Bullshit," I growled, moving closer. "You have and you would again given the chance."

"It was worth a shot," he smiled weakly. "Now, shall we get down to business?"

"You know what's coming, don't you?' I asked, not unkindly. "I'm sorry, but there is no other way. No choice."

"There is always a choice, my friend. And I am here to tell—"

"You are not my friend." I was close to him now, close enough to smell his fear.

"Maybe not," he said, smiling, confident despite his fear. "But I have a deal for you."

"No deal."

"Not even if it meant I could tell you who is behind all of this. The Necronotes, how they discover us, how they decide who lives and who dies? All of it?"

"So, let me get this straight, you know all of this? You know it and you will swap the information for your life?"

He grinned, shoulders relaxing. "That's exactly right. Haha. I can tell you, whoever you are. I can tell you and maybe you can act. You will be free."

"Like you, you mean?" I sneered. "If you have this information, if there is something to be done, then why the fuck haven't you done something?"

His smile wavered, but he tried his best. "You can know it all. I have found the answers. Searched and searched until I uncovered the truth."

"What is the truth?"

"First you make the deal. You let me live, I will tell you all I know."

"And what would I do with this information?"

He frowned in confusion. "You will know the truth! You will know who pulls your strings. All our strings. The truth."

"What's to stop me torturing you to get the answers, then kill you anyway?"

He backed up, suddenly aware how close I was. "You wouldn't. You're like me. We're the same."

"We are nothing alike. Why have you done this?" I was genuinely intrigued.

"So I'd know. I'm sick of being manipulated. I had to know. Even with the risks."

"Don't you think everyone in the world wants the truth about how the world works? You think people don't wonder why there's no water, why they can't drive a car, why they can't go on holiday? Why there's not enough food for some and too much for others? What the government is really up to? What they're hiding?"

"Of course! But that's different. This is us being made to murder each other."

"You think everyone else isn't in a similar boat? All the wars, soldiers dying, not being told the truth about why they're invading, what the real reason is? People sunk into poverty then locked up when they steal to feed their families? Crime? The never-ending murders. Prisons overflowing. Everyone's made to kill, one way or another. You don't think it's all a fucking conspiracy, all messed-up, that there's something going on, a big dark secret?"

"No, not really. The powerful play games, it's always been the way. As to one single big worldwide conspiracy? No, I don't think so."

"Haha, me neither, not really." I smiled. I liked him.

He relaxed a little. "So, you won't torture me?"

"No, I won't," I admitted. "I'm not that guy."

"So we have a deal?" he asked brightly.

"No, we don't."

The words sank in slowly, then he understood. I would kill him if I could, or die trying.

He didn't just accept it and roll over, which would make my job a lot harder, actually. Instead, he surprised me. I kinda liked it; kept me on my toes.

Something dark and deadly wrapped itself around his human form. Like a snake with legs. Sharp claws, loads of heads, all that jazz. The menace emanating from this summoning was almost overpowering. My energy was being sucked from me. Strength, hope, the ability to enjoy life, all being drained by his power, this thing's power. It was a dangerous symbiosis, the melding of your mind with a creature from beyond the mortal realm, and it confirmed this guy was seriously deranged.

Dark arts practitioners were the worst. They never knew what they were playing with until it was too late, which was fine if they kept it to themselves, but they always had to show off.

"I gave you a chance to know," he shouted. "You could have known about the Necrotrons."

"And what good would it do me?" I called back, locking down my emotions, refusing to allow this thing to suck me dry as a desert.

One of the many heads darted forward, but I dodged aside. The head snapped at empty air. I sliced down with my knife, severing the shroud head, but it did nothing. This wasn't manifest, it was a concept, an energy source, the mind of something far removed from this plane, never to become flesh.

"Then you will die," he screamed, as he locked himself to the creature.

"Not today." I readied for the hurt, then with a mental flick of a switch I became dust. One moment I was there, the next I was circling the spirit and man combo at a dizzying rate. I spun faster and faster. Heads snapped at me but I was like it—energy transmuted, not solid. More the thought of Soph than the man.

As fast as I was one thing so I became the other. Entrenched in pain and hunger, with an ache for sleep so deep it flayed my mind, I stabbed the man in the kidneys from behind, then stepped aside and slid over his desk to give myself some distance.

He spun, he shrieked, his control lost, and with it the creature he had conjoined with.

I lunged forward, but he pulled a gun from a drawer and fired without taking proper aim, too keen to act fast. A bullet grazed my side but there was no permanent damage. My arm slammed down on his wrist and the gun slid across the table. I grabbed his collar, dragged him across the desk, and smashed his head backward until his skull cracked. He snatched at my face, trying to gouge my eyes, but already he was losing his will to fight, like they all did when it got nasty.

With a grunt, I yanked his head forward and slit his throat without hesitation. Blood flowed freely, his eyes rolled up. His body was limp. He died.

Panting, and still on high-alert, I calmed my nerves as I scoured the room, just in case there were any nasty surprises.

Nothing stirred. Just the hum of the servers.

It was over.

I had fulfilled my duty. My job was done.

Relief washed over me.

I had another year. Another year to watch my daughter grow, marvel at Phage's desire to be with me, and get annoyed with idiot unicorns and uppity cats.

I smiled. May I rot in hell.

Truth Dawns

I jabbed at the elevator button, impatient to leave this freaky-ass place. I wanted fresh air, even if it was hot and stale. Anything beat the hum of tech, the weird static charging the air, doing who-knew-what kind of damage to my brain.

But mostly I wanted to escape my own foulness. To put as much distance between me and what I'd done as possible. Of course, there was no escaping the fact I'd just murdered a man. It would always be there, gnawing away just like the others, but I had to get out of here.

"Come on, come on," I hissed, as the elevator door refused to open. I prodded the button again and the doors finally opened. The cold blue light cast its deep shadows over me as I walked in facing the mirror. I didn't look so cool now. I looked haunted. The blood at my side had stained my shirt, making it look like a chunk of me was missing, so dark was it in the subdued glow. My cheeks had hollows, no longer defined, and my eye sockets were black pits of cruelty, like a skull with long-dead eyes.

I turned to press the button, glanced back into the room where the man lay dead in front of his desk. How long had he been at this, uncovering the truth about Necronotes? What had he called them? Necrotrons. Sounded like some stupid superhero name, but they were far from superheroes. Guess he thought it sounded cool. It didn't.

He'd wanted to tell me, to share the knowledge he had, and I don't think it was just to save his own skin. He must have known it was coming eventually. Any-one who delved too deeply was eradicated, we all knew that. You did your job, didn't ask questions, and you lived to fight another day.

He must have taken more precautions than most, as he'd certainly been at this for years. They'd found out what he was doing, like they always did, and now I'd solved the problem for my invisible overlords.

The doors closed, the elevator rose, and suddenly the truth hit me like a smack in the face.

I was next. I was fucking next.

They wouldn't risk it. They'd sent me to slaughter him and then they'd send someone to kill me. All nice and neatly wrapped up, no loose ends. They never left loose ends. Never.

"Bollocks!" I slammed my fist into the glass. Cracks spread.

Blood trickled from torn knuckles as I pulled my fist back.

Staring back at me was a man in the cross hairs of a circular target made of fractured glass.

"I don't know a thing," I shouted, wondering if they could hear me. Maybe they'd been watching the whole thing. It wasn't beyond their capabilities, but this dude had been so careful, would have all manner of protection in place for his secretive research. So no, chances were high they weren't watching and had no idea that I'd refused the offer of knowledge because of this very reason. Knowledge meant death.

Now I was dumb and dead, which was a far worse state to be in.

As the doors opened, and I stepped onto the porch, the clear light of day chased away some of the demons.

Maybe I was being utterly irrational. Maybe I was just paranoid. I'd dealt with others who wanted to bargain for their lives, who promised they knew the truth, said this was why they were chosen. I'd never believed any of them like I'd believed this man, though. He was the real deal. I felt it in my bones. He'd known, or at least thought he did.

Where did this leave me?

It was fine. I was fine.

They'd be watching. They were always watching. I scanned the sky; there were several drones overhead. Could they listen in? Could they see through walls? Couldn't they have just bombed the fucker and left me out of it? Of course they could have. They could have sent daemons, they could have done countless things, destroyed this man in any number of cruel fashions, but what was cruelest of all? Make us do the dirty work. Watch and laugh. Amused by the way we tore each other apart. And for what?

It was all too easy to have fanciful ideas about a strange race controlling us, but it was much more likely to be some faction of the government. A super-secret police department ensuring any Necros who got troublesome were eradicated. And what better way to ensure the job was done than to send somebody with powers just that bit better than the one you wanted eliminated?

I settled with these thoughts, knowing it was probably the truth. We killed each other because lots of us were unhinged, couldn't handle the gifts we'd inherited. This was their way of keeping Necros underground, not upsetting the general populace. Leaving them to go about their business of ruining the world, then making us pay for their mistakes as they gradually sank us deeper and deeper into a net of dependence we could never escape from.

The world was sliding back into the past. Was it all part of some master plan to ensure the rich got richer, the powerful become almost godlike, and everyone else just shut up and tried to stay alive?

"I've got to stop doing this to myself every bloody year," I grumbled. "Stop thinking about it, Soph, just do your job, enjoy your life, and stop trying to understand things you never will."

Suitably chastised, I actually felt better, then I nearly crapped my pants when my phone rang.

"Phage, you okay?"

"There's a man here, Soph." She sounded worried. "A Constable."

"I don't suppose you mean a policeman, do you?" I asked, knowing it wasn't.

"No, the other kind. He told me to ring you. Said he knew you'd finished, and wanted to see you. Make sure you understood what happened next."

"Okay," I said, trying to sound calm. "Make him a cuppa, love, and don't worry, I'll get there as quick as I can. I'm fine, so don't worry."

"Okay. Love you."

"Love you too." I hung up.

"FUCK!"

I almost lost the plot. A Constable? I was in this deep now, but they had better not touch my family.

Dazed, I walked away. At the tree line, a buzzing overhead from the drones filtered into my consciousness, then there was a loud whoosh. I watched a missile leave contrails as it sped to the house then hit. Then another hit. The place blew to bits, the main house gone. More missiles launched, obliterating the underground structure.

"Could have done that before I arrived, you bastards," I whispered. But then, they wouldn't have been able to test me, truly discover what he'd known, so at least I knew one thing for certain. They had seen and heard every last detail.

A Little Help

"Pam, it's Soph. Yes, no. Sorry, there's no time for a chat. Listen carefully, and I'll answer your questions another day. Can you message me your dad's phone number? Like, right this instant. It's important, Pam. Very."

She agreed and we hung up.

A moment later the message arrived. I called Dover and it rang and rang as I tapped my foot manically and prayed he'd answer.

"Hello? Now's not a good time."

"Dover, it's me, Soph. We met at Pam's."

"I remember. Listen, Soph, I'm, ugh, about to do it. Just getting my nerve up. I'm leaving this pain behind once and for all."

"Wait! You do what you want, but before you do, how about being the good guy for once? Going out with a smile on your face, knowing you've helped someone?"

"Rather than spilled their guts, you mean?" He sounded depressed as hell, although, to be fair, he was about to top himself.

"Yeah, something like that. I need your help, and I mean now. I have to get home, and all I've got is a bloody bike. Can you come get me, take me there? I need this, man, I really do. It's life or death for innocents I'm talking about."

"There are no innocents," he whispered. "Not any more. Not in this world."

"There are, and you know it." I was losing him. "Look, Dover, it's the most important thing you will have ever done in your life. You can die anytime, right? Come get me. There's a Constable at my house. My wife and kid are there."

Dover was silent so long I wondered if he'd just finished the job, but then he sighed and said, "Give me your exact location." I read him the coordinates from my phone and he was obviously checking the route then said, "I'll be forty-seven minutes."

"Make it half an hour," I told him.

"See you soon. And this better be life or death, Soph. I am not happy about having my final day interrupted like this."

"It's more important than puppies," I sobbed, as I hung up.

The Constable

"You want me to come in?" Dover asked as we pulled up at the gate beside a battered brown Volvo estate.

"No, thanks, you've done more than enough."

"You sure?"

"Sure." I nodded. I held out my hand and we shook. "It's been nice meeting you, Dover. You take care of yourself, you hear?"

"I will. Haha, I mean I really will."

"Wish you'd change your mind. But look, sorry, I gotta go."

"I understand. Good luck, Soph. Be calm, answer his questions, you should be fine. I've had a few visits over the years, always worked out. Just remember, Constables are lackeys. Don't take out your frustrations on the guy. He's as in the dark as the rest of us. It's not like they get to choose their own career path. They're stuck, same as all Necros."

"Okay. Thanks."

I hurried from the car, retrieved my pack and bike, and ran into the house, my heart beating so fast I feared a heart attack would finish me off.

There was nobody inside, just some dirty cups in the kitchen. I headed out the back, but it was quiet there too. Where were they? Was I too late? Had Phage paid the price for my sins?

"Woofer," I called silently. "Where are you, boy? Missed you."

"You're home. Woofer missed Soph," came the mental reply. I got an image of his tail wagging, ears pricked up, then I saw him bounding towards me.

"Hey, buddy. Missed you."

"Woofer so sad when Soph not here. I can come next time? You promise?"

"We'll have to see. I told you, you're still young. Maybe soon, okay?"

Woofer's ears flattened. "Woofer sad now."

"Sorry." I ruffled his head and he perked right up. "Listen, I need to go see Phage and that man. Can you leave us alone for a while? It's important."

Woofer sloped off to the house, as forlorn as a dog could be.

I ran down the garden, out into the various enclosures, then on into the paddock at the far end of our property once I spied Phage and the Constable. They were just standing there, seemingly chatting. Where was Jen? What time was it? What bloody day was it? Ah, she was in school. No need to panic.

"Hi," I called, as I slowed to a casual walk. Nothing wrong here. I'm chilled. All under control.

Phage waved and held a forced smile as I approached. I nodded to the Constable; he nodded back solemnly. He looked like so many of them I'd encountered over the years. World-weary, as though constantly about to sigh. He was surprisingly tall and very thin, with a lined face. Frown lines. He didn't smile much, that was obvious. He kept one hand in the pocket of plain black trousers that matched his dark shoes and shirt. The cuffs were frayed, his shoes well worn. He held a mug tight in his other hand.

"You okay?" I asked her.

"Fine. You?"

"Been better, been worse." Phage nodded. She understood now wasn't the time for a conversation about my trip.

I turned to the Constable who'd remained silent so far, just watching, observing. They were good at observing, it was their job.

"Constable." I nodded a greeting.

"Necrosoph." He nodded in return.

I balked at the use of my full given name. "So, what's up?"

"Just a few questions, if I may?" he asked, like I had a choice.

"Sure, but you already know what happened. Then you blew the bloody guy and his house to smithereens." Phage raised an eyebrow but said nothing.

"Hmm, yes, well, I'm sure that's all for the best. Your mission was accomplished, but I have questions." I understood the tone, the unspoken words. He didn't care, would happily leave me alone. But his masters had questions. His job meant he had to ask, to uncover the truth. He'd rather be at home putting his feet up, same as we all would.

"I'll answer them. First, can I get a drink? I'm parched. Shattered too."

"Of course, how rude of me."

"I'll make it. Constable, would you like another tea?" asked Phage.

"That would be wonderful." He handed her his mug.

With a backward glance, Phage headed up to the house.

"So, what now?" I asked the Constable. He didn't offer a name; they never did.

"Now you have to satisfy me that you went by the book."

"Ha, the book? What book? I killed the guy, then he got blown up. Overkill, but I did my part."

"Look, Necrosoph, don't make this any more diffi-cult than it needs to be." He sighed as he removed his fedora and ran a hand through soaked hair. "Damn, it's hot. Let's move into the shade." We crossed the paddock and stood under the relative cool of the hawthorn.

"I'm just tired, okay. It was a helluva trip. The guy ended up being more difficult than I'd anticipated, and I need to rest. Sleep. I need sleep and food."

"That's the magic for you."

"Magic? Ha! More like a bloody menace."

"Yes, well, we each have our burdens to carry. Now, what did he tell you?"

The Constable stared hard at me, inscrutable, reading every tic, every movement, working his way into my mind like he could see my thoughts. He couldn't, not exactly, but they were trained within an inch of their lives to read people like books. I relaxed. I had nothing to hide.

"He told me he knew the secrets of the ones in charge. Necrotons he called them, but I think that's just a word he made up."

The Constable rubbed his large nose. "Indeed, sounds like something from a Clive Barker novel. Continue."

"He said he'd tell me everything if I spared him. He told me he knew who they were, the secrets behind it all, that kind of thing. A lot of talk, if you ask me. Half-baked ideas. Speculation. But hell, even if he knew, I told him the same thing I've always told them. And then what? What difference would it make? And we aren't meant to know, are we? Look, Constable, I don't want to die, I want to live a happy life with my family and my animals, so I said no, and then I killed him. Are you happy with that?"

"I'm never happy. It's not my job to be happy. My job is the truth. To be sure. Be a hundred-percent certain that you are doing as asked."

"Asked?" I couldn't help myself. Nobody ever bloody asked.

"There is always a choice." His lips twitched, a hint of a smile.

He was screwing with me, doing what was needed to read me better. Ugh. These guys were difficult to deal with. You never knew how much they were manipulating you, what they were finding out. What they would do with that information.

"Maybe. But it's not much of a choice, is it?"

"No, it isn't. So, he gave you no information? Told you nothing of the Necronotes. Of who sends them, or why? Anything else he said?"

I tried to think back, but there wasn't anything to tell. He'd pleaded for his life, tried to bargain, but I knew better than to ever think I could get out of this. Nobody ever had. I was in the system. This was the way it was, the way it had always been. For as long as gifted had told stories, passed down knowledge, there had always been notes. Always.

"Indeed," said the Constable, replying to my thoughts. So creepy. "The notes endure. Through the ages, the notes have been a constant. Keeping the Necros pure, strong, to pass down their gifts, to ensure the survival of our kind." He frowned, as if wondering why he had shared so much with me. It was surprising. Guess he was in a good mood.

"So, are we good? Do you believe me?"

"I believe you. I believe you don't think he told you anything of merit. But a few more questions before I am totally satisfied."

Phage returned with the tea, which I took gratefully. The Constable nodded his thanks and Phage sensibly left us to it.

We drank in silence. I didn't break the peace, or try to push him. He was assimilating, letting his observations process. He had to be sure, I got that, and I wanted him to be. A man needs to know where he stands, know he isn't going to wake up dead.

When he finished his tea, he placed his mug on the grass and put his hands in his pockets. "Tell me something. Do you ever wonder?"

"Wonder?"

"About the notes? Your role? Your duty?"

"Of course I wonder. Doesn't everyone?"

"You'd be surprised."

"I doubt it. But it's human nature to think about it. Even though I've lived my whole life with the Necronotes, and my parents before me, and back and back and back, they all wondered, same as I do. But no, I know the rules. I've never tried to find out as what would be the point?"

He nodded. "There is no point, and yet we still think of these things. Why do you think that is?" He cocked his head to the side, genuinely interested. He watched me like a hawk and it made me feel so uncomfortable I had to resist the urge to run away. "Don't worry, many people get the same urge."

Ugh, he was reading me so well. It was utterly unnerving. "We can't help it, can we? It's just the way we're wired. We are curious. Even though we know we can't know, we still speculate. Just the way it is," I shrugged.

"Just the way it is," he repeated, as though my words held hidden meaning. Did they? Was I digging my own grave here?

Just like that, he snapped upright, straightened his back, adjusted his hat, retrieved his mug, and said, "Thank you, Necrosoph. That will be all. Shall we?" He swept a hand towards the house. He was leaving.

"Um, yeah, sure. So, did I pass?"

"You know the answer to that. I am merely here to understand what you know. I am not in the habit of telling people what they know."

I nodded. That was all I'd get from this guy.

We walked in silence. He stood at his car, lost in thought for a moment, then handed me the empty mug. "Be well."

"You too."

He got in, started the engine, buckled up, then drove away, carefully. He even indicated. This dude played by the rules.

My shoulders sagged. I felt heavy, leaden, and clomped back to the house. Phage waited at the porch, surrounded by perfumed pink roses.

She was such a beautiful sight. Why, then, did I feel so low?

I shivered despite the heat.

Absolutely Not

I followed Phage into the kitchen and almost walked into the back of her as she stopped dead.

"Hey, careful," I laughed. "Not that I mind backing into such a lovely behind." I snuggled up to her but she was stiff, trembling. I caught sight of it on the table and my head hung. My guts gnawed me a new ulcer. I squeezed Phage tightly then released her. "It's okay, honey. Don't worry. I'll sort this."

I stared at the simple folded piece of paper on the scrubbed pine table. Necrosoph was scribbled in inky calligraphy, handwriting I hated with a vengeance.

Woofer was growling from the far end of the room. He hated the notes; wouldn't go near them.

"It's not fair," whispered Phage, a lifetime of hurt behind her words.

"Goddamn," I sighed, slumping into a chair, too tired to even shout.

Phage sat beside me then reached for and grabbed my hand.

"Five times in my life I've had two in a year. But never a second one before I've even had my dinner. Bugger. God, I'm so tired."

"It isn't unheard of," said Phage on auto-pilot. "But it's rare," she agreed. "They never come this soon." She was trying to hold it together for me, be calm and composed, but she was shaking like a leaf. She understood only too well what was involved, and we hadn't even spoken about the job I'd just accomplished.

I reached for the note; my fingers trembled.

The damn thing leapt up as though sensing the heat and slashed across my palm, cutting deep. Blood trickled onto the table as the note sliced up my arm then across my face, tearing my lip and cheek. Tangy iron dripped down my throat as I licked my lips.

Woofer went mental, barking so loud it felt like my head would split open. Sometimes animals talk, other times it's just the noise everyone else can hear.

Phage yelped as the paper flapped at her face too, drawing blood in multiple places. As she reached for her eyes to protect them, the note carved across her throat then slapped down onto the table. The pooled blood spread away from the note as if scared.

"Open it, quick," shouted Phage, as she tried to stem the tide of crimson.

"You're bleeding," I protested. "Are you okay? Woofer, quiet!"

"I'm fine. It isn't deep." She grabbed a tea towel and wrapped it around her neck, but not before I saw the wound. Shallow, but deep enough to hurt some. She wasn't about to die though.

"These fuckers! I can't stand this any more. What the fuck are they playing at?"

"They're teaching you a lesson, Soph. Both of us. A reminder. Do not ask questions."

"But I told the Constable I knew nothing." Then it hit me. "Um, he asked me if I ever thought about the notes, about the ones behind it. I couldn't lie, had to say I did. Everyone does, right?"

"Course they do. You think he reported differently?"

"I don't know. They know everyone wonders, why wouldn't they? It's our lives they're playing with. God-damn."

The note squirmed, so I grabbed it with my blood-ied hand and unfolded it.

"Mace. Daisy."

"I hate this new way," complained Phage.

"Me too. Where's my damn phone?"

"Probably in your pocket," Phage told me, without a hint of sardonic wit.

"Yeah, right. Ugh." I wiped my hands then input the words into the app. I stared at the screen, my heart sinking. Numb, I placed my phone on the table and rubbed at my temples. Could this birthday get any worse? Yes, it was just about to.

"I think I just got a promotion."

"What? Let me see." Phage moved to look at the note, but I snatched it then closed my phone. "Sorry."

"Come on, honey, you really want to risk looking? You know you can't."

"It was just automatic. Sorry."

We both glanced around nervously, knowing we might be observed. How could we tell?

"I hate all this spy crap," I told her.

"Me too. It's the worst thing about it all. Not knowing what we went through, never being able to tell each other. Why does it have to be like that?"

"Because they want us to work without help or interference, to act alone, never tell anyone because it might compromise things."

"But it wouldn't," Phage protested.

"It's how secret organizations work. Nobody gets the full picture, everyone works at their part, and you keep it to yourself. If a mission fails, nobody is going to complicate things by seeking revenge. Crap like that."

"So stupid."

"I know, but let's be honest here, do you really want to know what I did? I know for damn sure I don't want to know what you do. All the death, Phage, the things we do. It's better this way."

I had no idea if it really was, but I did know I absolutely did not want to picture my wife killing some poor person in all its gory detail. Did I want her to be able to unburden herself, share the load for her mental health? Absolutely. Did I want to tell her the things I did? Yes, but also no. I didn't want my family knowing the depths I sank to, the things I did to stay with them.

Maybe for once our masters were right. Wrong about so much, but maybe not this.

With the new job already gnawing away at me, I took a deep breath then said, "Okay, and may I rot in hell for saying this. We need to go visit your m... Your mo... Ugh, we need to go visit your mother."

Phage stared at me in shock. Her mouth opened and closed, but no words escaped.

I couldn't help myself. I laughed. I laughed at her face, at the fact I had another note, and because I really did just offer to go visit the maddest, baddest, most disgusting old witch-bitch I ever had the misfortune to meet, let alone call family.

Phage nodded, knowing it meant this was dangerous for our family and I absolutely had no other choice. Then the spark returned to her eyes and she grabbed me, laughing hysterically, as she too succumbed to the utterly, unfathomably ridiculous nature of the world we inhabited.

Sometimes you just have to laugh at life. It is nothing but a game. A game you know you'll never win. Doesn't mean you have to be a sore loser though.

"Hey, what time is it?" asked Phage, suddenly all business.

I checked the wall clock. So did she.

"Damn," we both exclaimed.

"We'll be late getting Jen. Bloody notes, bloody Constables. Come on, let's go. Woofer, stay. Be back soon, buddy." We cleaned ourselves up, Phage put a scarf around her neck, then we raced out of the front door and grabbed the bikes and were down the road in seconds flat.

Tyr cried from above, then swooped and landed on the handlebars of my bike as I pedaled furiously. "Tyr can meet Jen now?" he asked, eyes full of hope.

"Not now, Tyr, you know you can't go to her school. People will see. You have to remain hidden, re-member?"

"Tyr know, but I need to see her," he whined.

"When we get home, okay?"

"Woo-hoo." The wyrmling launched and soared high then was lost to sight. Hopefully, he had the sense to return home.

"What did he say?" asked Phage, as we both ped-aled for our lives.

"He wants to meet Jen. It's time, honey. No avoid-ing it now they've seen each other up close in that call. She knows there's a dragon and I'm guessing she's been giving you hell, right?"

"You wouldn't believe it. She hasn't stopped talk-ing about Tyr since she saw him. All I've had is when are you coming home. Oh, and she wants to know if Tyr can sleep in her bedroom."

"He absolutely cannot," I said in a panic.

"I know that! I told her they would meet soon enough, but no dragons in the house. It's strictly forbid-den."

"Phew. Good. So, they can meet today?"

131

"I don't think we have any choice. This is all happening too fast though. We haven't had a chance to discuss it. Is everything okay? Did it go okay? How are you?"

"We'll... talk later, when I'm not knackered. But I'm here now, and in one piece, just about. So nothing to worry about. Apart from our daughter and her growing up."

"She takes after us. I began to understand things very young, and so did you. It was inevitable. But I do wish she hadn't seen Tyr."

"Sorry, I kind of messed up."

"It's not you fault. Not much." Phage smiled. I got off lightly, as it undoubtedly was my fault.

We pedaled hard and focused on the road until we hit the village and all the other parents, red-faced, sweating and panting as everyone converged on the small school to pick up antsy kids from impatient teachers who couldn't wait to get home and have a drink.

It was at times like these that I really missed having a car.

"Daddy!" Jen came running through the school gates and flung herself at me. Phage looked put out by the lack of attention so I shrugged and mouthed, "Love you." She smiled and let my daughter and I have a moment.

"Missed you, honey. How was school?"

Jen gave me a quick cuddle then stood back, frowned, and began to list a litany of complaints ranging from not enough pudding, to a boy who called her funny face, to having too much work to do and not enough play time, and on and on it went as we collected her bike and headed home at a very sedate pace.

I smiled the whole way.

It was awesome to feel normal, if just for a while.

Besties

"Where is he? Where is he?" shouted Jen as she skipped through the garden in search of Tyr.

"Ssh, quiet," I warned. I ran up to her. "You have to be quiet. We don't want the neighbors to know, remember? And poor Woofer's locked in the house, so don't let him hear how excited you are or he'll mope around all day. Now listen, you must promise never to tell a soul about Tyr. Dragons do not exist, right?"

Jen frowned at me and Phage as she came to join us. "But they do."

"Yes, I know they do, but there is no such thing as dragons, okay?"

"Daddy, but you just said there are." Jen turned to her mother, confused. "Are there dragons?"

"Yes," said Phage. "But there is no such thing as dragons. Do you understand?"

"No," wailed Jen. "What are you talking about? You said there's dragons, now you say there aren't."

"What we mean," I tried again, "is you mustn't tell. Got it?"

"Got it." Jen saluted and grinned, then hopped about like she wanted to go pee.

"Okay, let's get down to the zoo and then you can meet Tyr." I watched her run ahead, so excited she'd forgot that I hadn't been around for a while. She'd even foregone her after-school snack.

"Blimey, what a day. I'm beat."

"You sure you're okay?" asked Phage. "Anything you can tell me?" I looked to the sky out of habit, then held her hands and said, "All good. Just tired. Freaked by the damn Constable, and now this new note. But we'll get through it like we always do."

"Daddy!" yelled Jen.

"Come on, let's go let our young, innocent daughter meet a dragon," said Phage, smiling. But we both knew this wasn't good, that it signified the end of one chapter and the beginning of a much harder one.

We beckoned Jen over to us and led her to a nondescript small barn at the rear of the zoo, a building of zero interest to a young girl. Until now.

"Now, there is plenty I have to tell you about Tyr, but we can do that later. All you have to know at the moment is that he's what's known as a wyrmling, which means he's still young. Like you. He's small, but you already saw that. He will grow and—"

"Jen!" Tyr shot out of the small gap at the top of the barn and practically slammed into Jen's stomach, sending her careening backwards. She landed on her bum then was flat on her back, with Tyr on her tummy, licking her face then her arms and legs while she laughed and called out, "Tyr, Tyr," repeatedly.

"You were supposed to stay inside and wait for us," I scolded Tyr. "Come on, get off her and let's go inside."

I checked we weren't being watched by Mrs. O'Donnell, then unlocked the barn and led Jen inside. Tyr shot in and flew around while Phage closed the door behind us.

The small stone barn was devoid of straw as that hadn't ended well, and the walls were still black in places as a result, but Tyr had a high perch of a metal pole, the roof was constructed with steel purlins and corrugated tin, and the only flammable thing was a pile of blankets in a corner.

"Tyr, come and say hello nicely, please," I called up to him

Tyr's strange eyes glinted in the gloom. His tail swished, then he spread his thick leather wings and sailed down to land on my shoulder as we'd discussed.

"Jen, meet Tyr. Tyr, meet Jen."

"Hello, Jen. We're best friends," Tyr told her. "We'll grow up together and have awesome adventures, and I will save you from anything bad and kill the monsters for you. We'll fly in the sky and you can ride me and we'll be best friends forever."

Jen nodded in agreement. "We'll be besties for ever and ever. We're going to have so much fun. We can play and you can make fires and when we're older we can go on trips together and I can come and live with you in this tiny barn if I can have a bed and my tablet and my books and the teddies and can I have my desk in here? Hey, where do you sleep and how long do you sleep? How old are you and what does Tyr mean? Daddy, can we have a drink please? I'm really hot. It's very hot in here, isn't it?"

"Whoa there you two, calm down a little," said Phage, laughing. "You have plenty of time to get to know each other. All evening and the rest of your lives. It's hot because dragons like it to be hot. The metal roof makes it warm and the thick walls stop the heat escaping. Jen, dragons don't drink. You must never give Tyr water. It will put out the fire that is growing inside him. Understand? It's very important."

"You have a fire inside you?" asked Jen as Tyr left my shoulder and landed on Jen's like it was the most natural thing in the world. She didn't even flinch.

"I do. I can even make a small flame already. And I'm seven."

"I'm seven too," Jen told him, looking serious.

"Gosh," said Tyr, as it was clearly the most amazing thing anyone had ever told him.

"I already told you that, Tyr. Remember, you were both born on the same day. You are exactly the same age. Although, Jen is maybe a minute or two older."

"Wanna see Tyr make a flame?"

"No! No flame, Tyr. Remember what I said? No flames near Jen. You could burn her. This is important, guys, so listen up. You must not be seen together, by anyone. Ever. Understand?" They both nodded solemnly. "There are to be no flames or fires anywhere near Jen. If I find out there has been, then you will not be allowed to be together. Fire is dangerous, Tyr, it can burn Jen's skin so easily. Think of her like paper. You know how easy it is to burn paper? Yes, that's what Jen's skin is like."

"Can we go play now?" asked Jen.

I threw up my hands, exasperated. I turned to Phage for support.

"You can't play outside as people might see. Someone might come. You can play in here, and if you both promise to behave, then later on we can go into the far field where nobody can see and have a little play. But only once Mrs. O'Donnell has gone to bingo. But listen, you are not to go outside without an adult. You are not to play unless you ask first. Understand?"

They both nodded again, itching to have fun.

"Okay, now, do you guys want to be left alone for a little while?" I asked.

"Yes!"

"Tyr show Jen his wings."

"Behave," I warned.

Uncertain of the greatness of this idea, we both reluctantly left and stood outside for half an hour while they basically told each other their life stories. Jen recounted every single event of note she could recall of her life, including what'd happened in school that day.

Tyr found it fascinating and then proceeded to tell Jen how great he was at killing monsters and that he would grow to be larger than a bus, whatever a bus was, and they would be together for always.

It went silent eventually so we hurried back in, panicked.

"So sweet. Look at them both." Jen smiled at the sight of our daughter curled up on Tyr's blankets with the tiny dragon cuddled tight like her favorite teddy bear.

"Can you imagine when they're teenagers?" I asked, smiling despite the worry I felt.

"Bloody nightmare," agreed Phage. "And we'll need a bigger barn. Somewhere hidden, and much, much larger."

"Time to plant some trees to cover the sight of a monstrous dragon flying about the neighborhood.

"Make them big ones, and fast growing," said Phage. "In a few years he's gonna be bloody massive."

"He will. But maybe we won't need the trees, not to hide him, anyway."

"The camouflage thing?"

"Yes, but I'm not certain. It's always very sketchy, the information I can find. But I think once he's old enough, he can hide himself. He's about as magical as they come, right? So my guess is once his size becomes a problem he'll just poof, vanish."

"Let's hope so. I guess Bernard can hide his horn."

"There are lots of stories, but let's be honest, who the fuck ever has a dragon?"

"Nobody."

I scooped Jen up, ready to carry her up to the house. Tyr opened an eye and winked at me, then went back to sleep. Sometimes I got the distinct impression he was playing at being young, and was a lot wiser than he was letting on.

"Good night, Tyrant of the Sky."

Phage locked the door and we went up to the house to sort out dinner and have a meal before I had to leave once again.

I had to keep telling myself that once this was done I would have a whole year of peace, time to be with my family.

It felt like a lifetime away.

Kill Me Now

"Seriously, kill me now. Do some nasty witch stuff to me. Turn me into a goat. No, wait, not a goat, pesky buggers. A bat. Anything. Tie me up, singe my toes with a cauldron, tickle my armpits with a feather, but do we have to go?" I knew I was whining, but it was entirely justified.

"Ssh. What if Jen hears you?"

I turned and checked on her. She was snuggled down in the back of the cart, covered in blankets. She looked like a dormouse hibernating. "She's snoring like a trooper. Don't sweat it. Unlike me. Do we really have to go?"

"Yes," snapped Phage. "We haven't seen her for ages." She gripped the reins until her knuckles turned white. "And let me remind you, this was your idea." Phage stuck her tongue out to lighten the mood. Deep down, we both knew this was no laughing matter, that there was no choice in this decision, but it wasn't helping much. A visit to her mother was fraught with danger, both mental and physical, but it beat my two precious women being left alone in the house while I was off doing who knew what. They'd be protected with her mother, but it wouldn't be easy.

"Should I take over the reins?"

"No, you know you can't do it properly."

"She's right," said a miserable Bernard, turning his head to scowl at me. "You always end up steering into a tree."

"Hey, you're the bloody one at the front. You should know better than to walk into a bloody tree. It can't be that difficult."

"I go where you direct. Isn't that what us poor slaves do? This is so demeaning. Not my fault I got my horn stuck."

"Took ages to get him out," I muttered.

"You used an axe!" scolded Phage, now an expert at following these one-sided conversations.

"Could have had my horn off," agreed Bernard.

"I was tempted," I mumbled. "Anyway, I can too control a stupid unicorn and a cart. It's just all these bloody others, they get in the way. I remember when—"

"Blah, blah, blah. When it was all mud tracks and a lone horse and carriage, and then roads with just three cars on and whatever. Well, this isn't then, this is now, and you need to get up-to-speed on how it's done. I don't know why you aren't. You've lived through it all, it should be easy."

"Well, it isn't." And it wasn't. It was hard to adjust, the longer you lived. You remembered such different times that things became overwhelming. I mean, you couldn't even hear a bloody car when there was one. I wasn't even sure if they had proper engines. I liked my cars to be nice and rattly, to feel the bumps, but now it was like sitting at home and having a cuppa. I mean, there was even a little TV screen, and a woman that told you directions, and a fucking cup holder. What the fuck was that all about? I sure did miss driving though. Such comfort, so easy. No moaning unicorns.

"Where was I?" I asked.

"Complaining."

"Oh yeah, right. So, do we have to go? Okay, I know we have to. But... But, ugh."

"She hasn't seen Jen since she was five. It will be good for them to get to know each other. I think this is the right thing to do. Don't you?"

"I guess," I said, deeply regretting my spur-of-the-moment decision. Why didn't I just ask the neighbors to keep an eye out? Or just go do the damn job and hurry back? Everything would have been fine. Probably.

"Please, Soph. Be nice. We really haven't seen her for the longest time."

"And whose fault is that?" I asked rhetorically.

"Hers." Jen gritted her teeth.

"It was rhetorical."

"What was?"

"The question."

"What question?"

"About... Ah, forget it. You know this will be a bloody nightmare, don't you? You sure you want to go? We can make other arrangements. Think about poor Woofer, all alone there. He'll pine something rotten."

"Mrs. O'Donnell is going to pop in, look after things, so don't try that on me. Anyway, I think it needs to be done. My bloody mother would wait years before visiting, you know what these damn witches are like. Always got something 'super important' to do. No, we're going, we're staying, and you will come get us in a few days and then we'll go home and everything will be fine. At least until my birthday... Damn, Soph, I'm so sorry I forgot. What is wrong with me?" Phage's eyes welled and she slowed then directed Bernard to the side of the road and pulled back on the reins for him to stop.

"Could have just said stop," Bernard muttered.

"Shut up, Bernard. You're the one who wanted to come out. I told you it wouldn't be all frolicking in fields and licking rainbows."

"I licked one rainbow and you never let me forget it."

Ignoring the idiot unicorn, I turned to Phage. "I told you, it's fine. You've had a lot on your plate. You're worried about Jen, we both are. You just got caught up in our crap, got stressed. Don't worry."

It wasn't long before Phage collected her thoughts and we were back on the road, heading into the lair of my mother-in-law. The steady rhythm of the road, of the wheels and Bernard's hooves on the hard surface, lulled me into a waking reverie.

Phage was absolutely not herself.

Once this was over, we'd have a long chat and figure out a plan of action. What neither of us wanted was to have to put Jen in a secret school for Necro children. They existed, but I had never been comfortable with them. More like indoctrination gulags if you asked me. Who knew what the teachers put into their heads about the Necros in such places? The kids came out weird. I should know, I grew up in one. But that was a different time, a different place. Although, from what I'd heard, things hadn't changed enough for me to consider sending my kid somewhere they encouraged their abilities at such a young age, and taught them about their future and what they would have to do.

Jen was an innocent, I couldn't take that from her. The selfish part of me also didn't want to lose that purity of soul. She was my little girl. I hoped she'd remain that way for ever. I knew she wouldn't, couldn't, but I'd hold onto it for as long as I bloody well could.

"Giddy-up," I called to Bernard, just to piss him off.

Happy Unicorn

Bernard may have been as thick as two short planks, but he was a good guy. And we'd been together longer than most people lived. He understood the seriousness of the situation, and although he grumbled and complained a lot, he was on our team, part of the family. So he made good time. He was fast, and I mean seriously fast. Like, hold on to your hat, we're almost flying, fast. Sometimes we were.

When it was possible, which was a lot of the time, Bernard came alive in a most fanciful way, much to Jen's utter delight.

"He's a rainbow," she clapped with glee, her cheeks red with excitement. "Bernard is flying. He really is a unicorn. I knew he was."

"Sure am," said Bernard, as he turned and winked, then galloped harder and we sped along open roads faster than any road vehicle possibly could. We were a blur of colors, speeding up until we were invisible. Fast as the speed of light, traversing miles in a second. Bernard the dumb unicorn was a true creature of the Necroverse. Gifted with all the magical ability you'd expect from such a rare and important creature.

As we sped through the land, leaving nothing but a gentle breeze to signify our passing, I reminded myself that I had a very special collection to make when this was all over. Bernard was too special, too wondrous an animal, to ever let his kind die out. There weren't many like him, so I had to make good on my promise as it would surely bring a smile to his long face.

Jen enjoyed every moment of our speedy travel. So did Phage and I. Much as I hated traveling with Bernard when he wasn't fired up and doing his magical unicorn thing. It was like he had no spacial awareness for the bloody massive protrusion from his forehead.

But when cloaked in magic? Oh boy, it was the best. The world turned sweet. You got this sugary taste on your tongue. Colors were all pastels and somehow felt soft. Words melted in the air, and you thought nice thoughts about puppies and having a naked sauna, although that last bit might have just been me.

It was the one time I enjoyed magic. Usually, it was associated with pain, or death. Mine, or someone else's. But Bernard was different. He was a pure being. Not a malicious thought had ever crossed his mind. Sure, he'd killed plenty, mostly by accident, and mostly Mr. Wonderful, but never out of malice. For survival. For friendship.

We moved fast as a plane, and felt like we were flying as high too. Engulfed in fluffy clouds. It was awesome, and each time was like the first. It seriously cut down on travel time. What would have taken several days by bike with Jen along, was going to be cut to a single day, and not a long one at that.

When Bernard finally slowed and we came out of the magic bubble, we were already three-quarters of the way there. We were now deep in the heart of Mid-Wales, where roads were narrow and potholed, and the hedges loomed like daemons ready to swallow you whole. Not that I mentioned that analogy to my daughter. Jen complained about it being so slow now, and she wanted to taste the sugar again, but Phage explained that Bernard needed to rest up a little, and it was very bendy on the lanes, so we were going to have a picnic.

When the daft horn-head came to a farm gate and an absolutely massive group of willows, he stopped when I called, "Whoa there, boy."

Bernard turned and hissed, "I hate you." I winked at him.

Phage slapped my arm playfully and said, laughing, "I'm in charge, not you. I have the reins, so stop giving commands. And anyway, you know he doesn't like it."

"I know. That's why I said it. Come on, you two, let me help you down." I held out my hands, all chivalry, and my two favorite ladies in the whole world hopped down onto the green grass.

Phage sorted the tack out and freed Bernard. He moved deep into the shade and began to complain. "It's too hot. I don't know why humans let it get to this. What is wrong with you all?"

"Don't blame us. Um, blame someone else." But everyone had their part to play. Nobody was free of blame.

"What was it like, Daddy?" asked Jen.

"Huh?"

"Before. What was it like when you were young and we had cars and trains and you could go on holiday on a plane whenever you wanted? Did Mummy see it too? Did you, Mummy?"

"I did. Everything changed so fast. It's still hard to believe it was only a few years ago when we had a car and went a hundred miles without even thinking about it. We used to go on holiday to Spain, go to Cornwall all the time. Lots of things were different. But we have to think of the planet now, honey. We can't ruin the world, can we?"

"No, Mummy. Did you like it, Daddy? When you were young? You're older than Mummy, right?"

"Yes, a little. Just a few years, you know that. I liked the ease of travel, but it always bothered me a bit. I preferred it when it was just horses, you know, more like now."

"Haha, you're so funny, Daddy. Horses was ages ago."

"I know, little one, Daddy's just messing around." To avoid any further talk about just how old Daddy was, I poked out my tongue, whisked her off her feet, and swung her around as she yelped for joy while Phage sorted out lunch and Bernard enjoyed being miserable in the cool. Poor guy wasn't made for the heat. Unicorns liked it somewhat on the fresh side, which is why his head was always up in the clouds, or away with the fairies. And that may well be literal.

We had a lovely picnic lunch, then a short doze under the trees just because it was so cool and refreshing. Poor Bernard was knackered, so it was a good job we'd brought a ton of food for him because he needed it. Such speed, even for a unicorn, takes its toll. I can't imagine how many calories traveling that way requires. The laws of energy still apply, as far as I'm aware. So he ate until his tummy looked fit to burst, which Jen found hilarious. She repeatedly poked it, which made Bernard fart, which was even funnier, although Bernard wasn't too impressed.

Soon enough, it was time to be on our way. We loaded up, I helped Jen into the back, where she snuggled down again, and Phage took the reins once more. We had a short stretch on a busy road to navigate, then onto a quiet route for the remainder.

We moved at a leisurely pace, no need to rush now as we had plenty of time to arrive before the evening, so enjoyed the road, the sights, the company of each other. I refused to think about the note, about what I might encounter, just tried to focus on the present. I'd learned over the years that it made no difference whether I worried myself sick or didn't give it a second thought, the outcome would be the same regardless. So why worry?

Damn it, I did worry, couldn't shake it, but I did my best to put it to the back of my mind. It remained there, nagging at me, gnawing away like it always did. I was amazed I hadn't died of a stroke centuries ago. And yet, as the day wore on, I found a place of calm in my mind and I forgot about the job for a while. Phage and I held hands and stared at Bernard's rear; I wondered how he could possibly walk with such a fat tummy.

With only a few miles before our turn, an ungodly sound began to overwhelm all else. Jen sat up and leaned out the side to get a better look.

"Hey, be careful," I warned. "You might fall out."

"What is it? Is it a plane?" cooed Jen, peering up, super-excited as you saw them so seldom.

"No, I don't think so." I looked behind us down the long stretch of road. Heat haze shimmered off the surface, wobbling the air.

Within seconds colors crept up, a blob of something or other encompassing the whole width of the road and moving fast.

"Phage, pull over. Bernard, get off the road," I called.

He turned, questioning, but Phage had already pulled on the reins to direct him and he moved out of instinct.

"It's another group, I assume?" she asked, much calmer than me.

"I guess so. Jen, it's nothing to worry about, but I want you to stay in your seat and absolutely no getting out onto the road. Understand?"

"Okay. What is it?"

"It's cars. Lots and lots of cars."

Bernard bumped the carriage onto the verge and we stood as the noise became almost overwhelming.

A convoy of cars maybe fifty strong roared past, blaring horns. People waved, standing up on the seats of convertibles. Cars of all description. Old gas-guzzlers, electric vehicles, sports cars, and bangers. You name it, it was there.

"There's so many. It must be a million. No, a thousand. Maybe a hundred?" Jen shouted, clapping her hands.

"Maybe," I shouted, smiling at her excitement.

"Where are they all going?" she asked, the vehicles already receding in the distance, just the smell of fumes remaining.

"No need to shout now, honey," said Phage.

"Oops. Sorry. Wow, so many cars. I thought they weren't allowed." Jen frowned. "Naughty drivers. Are they allowed? Can we drive too? Will they get into trouble?"

"Calm down." I told her. "Come here a minute, let us explain." Jen came to the front and sat between us on the bench. I looked to Phage and she nodded. She'd tell Jen what the deal was.

"So, you know people get a little allowance for fuel if they want it, right?" Jen nodded. "But some people have figured out how to make their own, or they scavenge it."

"What's scavenge?"

"They search for it. Old cars, find it in barns, that kind of thing," I told her.

"And others can charge their vehicles if they're electric, which most are now," Phage continued.

"But we aren't allowed to drive, not unless we're important," protested Jen.

"That's right. But up until very recently all those cars you saw, well, it would have been normal. Not all in a line like that, but this road, it would have had hundreds of cars passing us by every minute, and we certainly wouldn't be parked here. It would be too dangerous."

"We'd get squished," clapped Jen with delight.

"Sure would. But it used to be normal. Just recently. And then we had the new rules, and for a while everyone obeyed. Most people, anyway. The police would tell you off if you drove without a permit. You got into lots of trouble. But now people are fed up, and the police, well they can't stop everyone who breaks the rules. So people get together. They go for rides in big groups and the police mostly just let them."

"Cool. So, can we do it too?"

"No, Jen, we can't," I told her. "If we got stopped, and it would be just our luck, then the police can lock you up, fine you, and they will definitely take the car. So no, not unless we get a permit."

"Aww."

"Sorry, kiddo," I said, ruffling her soft locks and laughing. "And besides, isn't it better to go places with a flying unicorn rather than by car?"

"Yes! Bernard, you are amazing," she yelled.

Bernard shook his head and whinnied. He also got his horn stuck in a tree.

"You fu—You fool," I grumbled.

"Daddy was about to say a swear," said Jen, face serious.

"He was. Naughty Daddy," agreed Phage.

"Sorry. Dock my pocket money."

"What's pocket money?" asked Jen, suddenly all ears.

"Oh, nothing for you to worry about just yet," I told her, then jumped down to make fun of Bernard for being such a dick.

Once his horn was out of the tree, and Jen had rubbed it clean for him, we set off on the final leg of our trip to Bitch Witchville.

The fun and games were over. Only misery lay ahead. Especially for me. Witches, at least this lot, weren't too keen on men. One in particular.

Mother-in-Law Blues

"But why can't I come?" whined Tyr as he sat on Jen's lap, staring at her full of adoration. Jen stroked his head, smiling as only a young girl who has a dragon can.

"I already told you. They don't want dragons there. You aren't on the list, so you can't come."

"Daddy, don't be so mean."

"Be nice," warned Phage.

"Okay, I'll be nice. Tyr, Pethach refuses to allow creatures as powerful and awesome as you into the compound, or to fly anywhere close. She is secretive, and believes it will put her and her, ah, friends, in danger. I'm sorry, but you'll see us soon enough. Jen and Phage will stay for a while, but tomorrow you can catch me up as agreed, and we'll be together then. Sound good?"

"But I'll miss Jen," he whined.

"You only just met!"

"But we love each other, Daddy," said Jen, stroking his head.

"We do," agreed Tyr.

"Gosh, you two are going to be inseparable, aren't you?" Phage laughed. "Imagine all the fun you'll have once we're back home. But you have to wait a few days and then you can be together. Besides, Tyr, you need to help Soph with his work, remember? It's important work and only you can do it."

Tyr puffed out his chest and roared. A small flame erupted, then he farted a much better flame and singed the bench cushion.

Jen clapped with delight. "Haha, you're so funny, Tyr. I love you." Without warning, she grabbed him and squeezed him. Tyr let out an involuntary belch and almost burned Jen's face. He flapped away and landed on Bernard's ample backside, which made him jump and lunge forward, jolting us all.

"Careful, Jen. You mustn't just grab Tyr. He's a dragon, don't forget. You must ask first."

"Sorry."

"It's okay, just be very careful. Tyr is a dangerous creature and you could easily get hurt. He could burn you."

"Is that how you got your scars?" she asked me.

"No, nothing as exciting as a fight with a dragon."

"Okay," said Phage, all business. "Tyr, say goodbye. Jen, say goodbye gently to Tyr. We have to go."

"Good riddance," muttered Bernard.

"I heard that," Tyr shouted down.

"I know."

"Tyr, come down," I told him.

He did as he was told, apologized for the accident, then the two best friends said goodbye. He flew off with the hump, but he'd get over it.

"Okay, let's get this show on the road," I said brightly. "Bernard, lead the way."

"Don't I always?" he grumbled. Nevertheless, he got us back onto the road and the final leg of the journey began.

Pethach, "affectionately" known as Peth to those who loved and loathed her in equal measure, was Phage's mother and clan ruler of a bunch of utterly dark witches. This woman, this "doorway", was super-skilled, super-powerful, and super-scary. You did not mess with her. How Phage had come out of her care relatively unscathed by the experience until I "kidnapped" her is still beyond me—even now, sixteen years later, Peth hadn't forgiven me. She made it clear every time we met. The woman and her gang of witch bitches were so far down the rabbit hole of dark magic that I would have preferred we had absolutely nothing to do with any of them.

But that's family, right?

What's the saying? You get to choose your friends, but your family should be avoided at all costs if they enjoy raising the dead for kicks?

Something like that anyway.

They took Necro to the extreme. They were true Necromancers. Many could morph, if not all of them, and they dabbled in things that would turn your hair white with fright if you even got a glimpse. They played on the edge of sanity, and many, including Peth, had paid the price. They were obsessed, enraptured, and half-insane because of the things they did, the powers they played with, and the sights they'd seen.

And they loved it.

Magic, this thing, this energy, pervades the Necroverse, the multitude of worlds that includes the human realm and those associated with it, but the Necroverse also includes much deeper, darker realms never meant to be accessed by the human mind or soul. Where corrupt eldritch horrors lurk, right out of Lovecraft's imagination. He must have caught glimpses of these places, these colossal creatures born of stars, riding out eternity in unfathomable places. Taking on horrific, unimaginable forms that made no sense to the human mind. With brains the size of moons, thoughts so alien, so all-encompassing, vast, and unlike our thought processes, that to encounter such a being would turn your mind to mush in an instant.

And this is what they sought, what they encountered. They felt it their mission to discover as much about the Necroverse as was possible, seeking out encounters with the colossi of the universe, the hidden realms where the beasts slept away the millennia in the gaps between realities.

To be blunt, they were a bunch of fucking lunatics. But they did have nice hair.

I dwelled on Peth and her mad bunch of witches as we moved off the roads and into what I guess you'd have to call an enchanted forest. Hidden by the witches' magic, the dirt track to their compound was impossible to traverse unless you knew the access points and were given safe passage. The track knew who was and wasn't allowed, and if you weren't on the list you would never find them, never even get close.

They were a closed community, special invite only. Which meant they lived how they wanted, did as they pleased, and answered to no-one.

Almost no-one.

They still got their notes.

The forest was pleasant. Nice trees, nice flat track, shaded and cool, but there was an edge. Bernard kept his head down, Phage gripped the reins a little too tight, stressing over seeing her mother after such a long break, and Jen went from super-excited to needing a cuddle the further into the woods we got.

"Why is this place different?" Jen asked.

"It's Grandma's road, and she and the others keep it secret," I told her.

"They don't tell anyone?"

"Nope. Nobody. Apart from us. You will always be welcome at Grandma's," I told her.

"I don't like it. It feels... Hmm, don't know, just... wrong. That's it! It feels wrong."

"It's just because it's the woods. Sometimes it can make you feel a bit funny inside."

Phage focused her attention on us, but it was a struggle as her mind was elsewhere. "It's okay, honey, nothing bad will ever happen to you here. I promise."

"You too, Daddy?"

"Yes, I promise too. Hey, won't it be great to see Grandma again? Are you looking forward to it?"

"Yes! I like Grandma. She's so funny. Always does those amazing tricks. But, um, I can't really remember much. What does she look like?"

Phage and I exchanged a glance, and I saw the hurt she felt. It was tough for her. On one hand she wanted Jen to know her Grandma, it would be important as she got older and her skills were revealed for Peth to guide her in some matters, but on the other hand, Peth was nuts and it would be better if we had nothing at all to do with her. That would never happen, though. Peth loved Jen and Phage, but she was reluctant to make the trip to visit, hated the outside world with its rules. And she abhorred regular folk, seeing them as mindless fools, which she was happy to relate to any person she encountered. Let's just say, when she did visit, we didn't have many dinner parties or barbecues with the locals.

"Daddy?"

"Oh, sorry, I was miles away. So, what does Grandma look like? Well, she has very long black hair, and it's very shiny. Like in a shampoo commercial. She is pale, looks very young to be a Grandma, and loves to wear black clothes. All the other women do too. Some of them are very old, even older than me, and others are young girls, just learning."

"Learning what?" asked Jen.

"Oh, you know, how to live like they do. Out in the woods, away from the rest of us. To search for plants and herbs, make medicines, that sort of thing."

Jen laughed. "You're so funny, Daddy. I know she's a witch. Haha, so silly." Jen gave me a hug, then went to sit beside Phage like it was the most natural thing in the world.

When Phage turned to me, I mouthed silently that we needed to have words with our daughter. She nodded.

And now we were bringing her here? Into the heart of darkness? I had to keep telling myself it was for her protection. Peth would protect her with her life. So would the other witches. She would be safe. I just hoped she wouldn't also be corrupted.

"We're here, we're here," cried Jen as we moved from the path into a wide clearing several acres in size. There was no gate. They didn't need one.

"I forgot how beautiful it is," said Phage sadly.

"You okay?" I asked, knowing her old home always brought back a lot of memories, some not so nice.

Phage squeezed my hand. "I'm fine. We'll be fine. Don't worry. Let's just have a nice evening, then get back as soon as you can, Soph. We'll miss you."

"We will," agreed Jen.

"And I will miss you both too. So very much."

Jen smiled then hopped down and ran ahead.

"I don't like it here," said Bernard.

"I know, but it's for Jen, so please be nice."

"Nice? I'm a unicorn, I have to be nice."

"You killed Mr. Wonderful the other day," I reminded him again.

"Some would call that nice," he snorted.

"True. Anyway, let's get this over with. Phage, you sure you're okay?"

"I'm fine. Come on, let's catch Jen up."

Bernard trotted forward into the witch compound. Surrounded by large trees, the enclave was not what you'd expect. It was a botanical paradise—lawned areas, patches of fabulous wild flowers, orchards, vegetable gardens, numerous large herb gardens, beautifully tended herbaceous borders, a lot of fire pits, places to sit, huge wood sheds, a substantial central open-air communal meeting hut, and dotted randomly about the place were neat, compact houses of all description. The main theme was wooden lodges, but there were several tin shacks, a large stone cottage, and even a modernist glass and steel home.

The witches were free to build as they chose as long as it got the okay from the others, but as in all things here, when you got right down to it, Pethach made the final decision. It was a democracy of sorts, but Peth was the matriarch, and what she said was final. Pethach—the name meant many things. A doorway, opening of the mouth, even of the earth itself. Peth could do all of these things, and much more. She was well-named, for she opened doorways that ought never to be opened, and she helped her witch sisters unlock the power within themselves, opening them up to the true terror of pure magic in its rawest form.

But she really did have lovely hair.

Bernard stopped beside the stable block where other animals greeted him with respect, and his mood immediately lifted. Phage went to catch Jen while I sorted out the cart and harness then got Bernard some food and water. By the time I'd finished, the coven was out in full force to greet their visitors.

The cooing and adoration of Jen had already begun, and I smiled despite myself, because if there was one thing witches loved, even dark ones, was a young, innocent girl. They couldn't help themselves. They would spoil her rotten and vie with each other for her attention. They were all kids at heart, they just usually hid it well.

Bitch Witches

I left Bernard with his fan club and headed into the heart of darkness. Scores of women of all ages were gathered around Jen and Phage, chattering excitedly, vying for their attention, exclaiming how much Jen had grown, how pretty she was, and how well Phage looked.

I wandered over, feeling like a true outsider. A lone male amongst the most powerful women in the country. There were dozens of clans, but none with the clout or strength of this one. It was all down to Pethach. She'd been the matriarch for as long as anyone could recall, was old in a way the word lost meaning, had scores of children, grandchildren, and so on, but there was never a permanent man, and her descendants were strictly forbidden from living here full-time once they came of age. At least, all but one. Phage had been an exception. It was normally her strict policy that they were welcome to visit, and she would sometimes deign to visit them, moreso in the past when travel was easier, but they had to go their own way, find themselves in the big, bad world.

"Hi," I said, but they were so occupied with Jen nobody even noticed me. I moved forward next to Phage and finally I was acknowledged. Immediately, there was an atmosphere. Not of hate, nothing that strong, but of distrust. They were on their guard. The mood settled once I acted respectfully and greeted everyone, but it was obvious they'd rather I wasn't here.

"Don't worry, I'm only staying until the early morning."

They laughed and joked, said not to be silly, and I was welcome, but it was clear they were relieved.

And then here she came. Queen Bitch herself. Pethach. Necro-extraordinaire. Necromorph, Necromancer, Necro bloody everything. Necromum, maybe not so much. Necrogran too. I smiled at the thought of calling her that. Not that I ever would.

The women quieted as Peth waked lightly across the clearing. A vision in black wispy clothing. Long shining hair hung down to her backside. She remained slender, unshakably confident as always, with chiseled cheekbones and a defined jawline. A collection of trinkets hung from leather thongs around her perfect neck; they tinkled as she swayed. Peth fizzed with magic.

But it was the eyes that got you. They sparkled with mirth, as though she knew a joke she would never share. Even this wasn't what stopped me in my tracks every time. She had the eyes of a goat. The palest of blue, the horizontal slit pupils were arresting, and quite unnerving. Apparently, it helped her see to the sides better, but I think that's bull. She did it to look freaky. End of.

She held out her arms as she approached; the women cleared a passage for her.

"My beautiful daughter," she said, smiling, revealing perfect teeth and her forked tongue, which made her lisp somewhat.

"Hello, Mother," said Phage, almost shyly.

They grasped each other's elbows and kissed, then hugged each other. Peth took her daughter's hands and stepped back. "Let me look at you. So pretty, so grown-up. It's great to see you. It's been so long."

"Several years," agreed Phage. "You look great too."

Peth nodded, as if it was a given. "And Soph, good to see you too," she said perfunctorily, losing some of her spirit.

"And you, Pethach. Keeping well?"

"Always. And who is this? I thought you were bringing my granddaughter, not this beautiful, sweet teenager. Who are you?" Peth laughed and bent to Jen who was almost beside herself with excitement but was acting shy. She hid behind my legs, then peeked out, grinning.

"It's me, Grandma. Jen. I'm all grown up!"

"So you are. Come here, child, let me hug you."

Jen grabbed my leg, but I nodded to her that it was okay and then she lost her shyness instantly and lunged at Peth, who scooped her up and swung her about in a deep embrace.

"Missed you, Grandma. You should visit us more. Ooh, your hair smells lovely. Is it peaches? Have you got any pets? What's for dinner? Can I sleep in your room tonight? Can I? What's this for?" Jen lifted a crystal from Peth's neck and studied it.

"Oh, haha, so many questions. Let's get you inside and fed and watered and then we'll see about answering some of those questions, shall we?" Peth turned to the other women and told them, "Tonight we shall feast in celebration of my beautiful daughter and grandchild." And then she turned and carried Jen up to her house. A simple barn structure that belied her status.

Everyone ignored me as they went about their business. Phage stifled a giggle.

"What?" I asked her.

"Feeling all left out, are we?"

"Couldn't care less," I shrugged. "But a hug would have been nice."

"Come here." Phage wrapped her arms around me and we hugged before we followed Peth and Jen into the house.

Inside was as I remembered from the few times I'd visited over the years. Minimally furnished and tasteful. Like so much here, the exact opposite of how you'd imagine. There were no skulls, no ravens on perches, no weird liquids bubbling in cauldrons. No arcane books, not even bunches of dried herbs. Nothing to signify she was anything but a woman living an alternative life-style.

Nice furnishings, expensive rugs, plush sofas, a big TV, quality speakers, modern kitchen, and an envy-inducing multi-fuel stove with stacks of wood arranged neatly to one side.

Oh, and a lion curled up on the rug. He opened one eye as we entered, then closed it again.

"Hey, Oz," I called brightly.

"I'll eat your face if you talk to me again while I'm trying to sleep."

"Nice to see you too," I called back brightly.

"That isn't a big cat," said Jen, standing in the middle of the room, hands on hips, utterly affronted.

"Well, technically it is," said Peth, as she busied herself making drinks. She turned on her expensive kettle and poured a soft drink for Jen.

"It's a lion," she said, resolute. "You all told me he was a big cat. You said it was glands... Gladnul... Glandular. Whatever that means."

"We didn't want you to be scared," said Phage. "But you're learning a lot these last few days, so yes, Jen, Oz is a lion. But leave him be, he's sleeping."

Oz opened an eye, stared hard at Jen, then with a sigh he got to his feet, yawned extravagantly, just to show off his teeth, stretched, then padded slowly over to my little girl.

He bowed his head and stared into my daughter's eyes. Then he sniffed the top of her head, making Jen laugh and say, "It tickles."

168

"She is powerful," said Oz.

Peth, suddenly interested, came over and stood beside them both. "Aren't you afraid of the big lion?" asked Peth.

"No. Should I be?"

"Yes."

"He's nice, aren't you, Oz?"

"Not really. You can understand me? My thoughts? My words that are not words?"

"Yes, I just learned. I can talk to lots of animals now, even Tyr."

"You still have that dragon?" asked Peth, voice tinged with disgust.

"Yes, and he's learning fast, same as Jen," I told her.

"We're best friends," Jen told her with all the sincerity of a seven-year-old.

"I expect you are." Peth nodded to Oz who returned to his spot by the fire.

"My, my, you are growing fast," said Peth. "So, what else have you learned?"

"Mother, there will be time enough for that tomorrow. Can we just enjoy the evening, please? It's been a long time."

Phage was nervous; the less Peth knew for now the better, but we both understood she'd uncover Jen's abilities. It was time, and deep down I knew that was part of why I'd suggested we come here. She needed guidance, and there were some things only one such as Peth could teach our daughter. If she was to survive, then we needed her help, her knowledge, her power. Jen would have whatever it took to ensure she survived and flourished.

"Yes, of course," said Peth. She went back to the kitchen to make the drinks.

I put an arm around Phage; she looked like she needed it.

"Do you still have that idiot unicorn as well? Bernard, isn't it?" shouted Peth.

There was a crash of smashing glass and the idiot himself poked his head through the window and asked, "Did somebody call?"

"Bernard, how many times have I got to tell you? They aren't holes, they're windows!"

"Oops."

"Silly Bernard," laughed Jen.

"I'll get a brush," said Phage, giving Bernard the daggers.

Peth scowled at the dumb unicorn; Bernard had the sense to beat a hasty retreat.

I wished I could do the same, but I had to remind myself tomorrow I'd be out of this hellhole and back facing unknown dangers. I couldn't wait.

Adoring Grannies

I was grateful for the disturbance, as it took me a while to fix the window. In the meantime, the girls got settled in the guest room, then helped prepare a large dinner with the other witches out at one of the fire pits. We would all eat at the communal hut, as was usual.

After several glass cuts, a lot of swearing about idiot unicorns, and more putty than a professional might use, I was finally done. I cleaned up in the bathroom, stared hard at my reflection in the mirror, and told myself that I just had to hold out for one night and then I'd be gone. I hated this place. The women, the magic, the vibe, the grumpy lion. Everything. I even hated the towels. Who had towels this soft? How was that even possible? Even the water felt cleaner, and I knew for a fact that wasn't even a thing.

Reluctantly, I wandered outside and offered my assistance, but it seemed that nobody here agreed with the worldwide fact that men did barbecue. Their loss, but I guess some of the old-timers had even more experience than me. It was tough to remember that many of the most beautiful women here were almost primeval. The more immersed they became, the more youthful their appearance, and I dreaded to think exactly how that came to be. Once again, I was humbled by Phage's strength of character that she diverged from the path most in her situation inevitably followed. And she was still a damn sight prettier than the rest of them put together.

The women chattered. Jen had a whale of a time being pampered and coddled. Phage was uneasy but did her best to be sociable. I kept to myself mostly and was happy for it.

Dinner was plentiful but simple fare, and it was delicious. The meat was succulent, the potatoes crispy, the vegetables fresh as fresh could be. There was even strawberry wine. A little sweet for my taste, but it took the edge off. Jen couldn't sit still if her life depended on it, and was far too excited to eat much. She had a billion questions and a score of witches only too happy to blather on for fucking ages about their nonsense. But the longer dinner went on, the more they drank, so the darker the mood became. Finally, they began saying things they should have known better than to discuss with a young, impressionable child present.

"I think someone's looking sleepy," said Phage lightly.

"Am not. I'm wide awake," said Jen. She opened her eyes as wide as she could, but it was clear she was flagging and would be asleep soon enough.

"I think it's time to kiss everyone goodnight and then how about I read you a story?" I said.

"I want to stay up late. Can I? Can I stay up super late, just for tonight?"

"And what time is super late?" I asked, feeling superior as I knew I had her in my cunning trap.

"Maybe half eight?" she ventured. "Nine?"

"Okay, you can stay up until nine," I told her.

"Yes!"

"So, say goodnight."

"But... You just said I could—"

"Stay up until nine. I did. And it's quarter past. Haha. Gotcha."

"Aw, no fair." But good girl that she was, she did the rounds, gave everyone a kiss goodnight, then had a special hug from Grandma before coming to sit on Phage's lap for a late night cuddle.

"Come on, hold my hand." I took my little girl's hand and led her away from the pissed witches.

Once she was settled, I read to her for longer than I normally would. Partly because I knew I wouldn't see her for a while, but also for the selfish reason that I didn't want to return to the madhouse.

Jen fell asleep after twenty minutes, so I tucked her in tight, turned out the light, and pulled the door to. I headed back to the others. No need for lights in this place; you could hear their caterwauling a bloody mile off.

I smiled at Phage as I sat beside her and told her Jen was asleep and happy. She took my hand and held it tight. Words weren't necessary; I understood how she felt. Torn, concerned, happy, sad, you name it. This was a strange place full of strange women, but it had been Phage's home for many years. She had grown up here, been taught so much, knew the women very well. Yet she hated them, what they stood for, and in some ways she hated her mother too. But there was love also, and isn't that what it all comes down to? What was she to do?

We joined in the conversation and drank more wine. When in Rome and all that.

The tales were tall, even outlandish, but I knew much of what they boasted of was the truth. Nobody talked directly about their notes, but they trod a fine line. Even here, well away from anyone, they never, ever, discussed their jobs directly with another witch. At least, not as far as I knew.

"I got my note this morning," said one woman.

"Happy birthday," the others chorused, and clinked their glasses.

"Thanks, everyone, and thank you again for the gifts. So generous. I'll set off in an hour or so, get a good start on the job."

"Is it far?" asked a young girl who couldn't have been long into her teens.

The air was instantly heavy with palpable menace.

"What have you been told repeatedly?" snapped Peth. "You do not ask about other's notes. Nothing. You understand? If you are to become like us, then you must try harder. Listen, learn, and remember your lessons."

"Yes, Mother. Sorry." The girl, mortified, stood and addressed the table. "I apologize." She ran off, tears streaming.

"Silly child," hissed Peth.

"She's still young," said one.

"Don't be too harsh," said another.

"I may have been a little brusque," conceded Peth. "I'll speak to her in the morning. For now, let's continue the celebration."

Everyone drank guardedly; the mood remained dark.

Over the next half hour, three quarters of the women made their excuses and left. We remained because of Peth, but also because I wanted to have a word with her and other senior witches without the young ones present. Now was as good a time as any, I supposed.

I gulped a glass of sweet wine, wiped my mouth, and had at it.

Risky Questions

"How far back does the history of notes go?"

The mood darkened even further as the witches exchanged glances. Not so much worried, as questioning if they should deign to tell this lowly Necro, and a man to boot, anything.

"This stays between us," said Peth. "You will not utter a word spoken on these premises to another living soul. You swear?"

"I swear."

"You know what will happen if you break that oath?"

"I do." I swallowed nervously; they always made me feel like this. The scariest thing was I knew they would follow through on their threats, their promises, regardless of family ties.

"They go back to the beginning," said Peth. "We know this world, and many others. The realms of the fae, of goblins and sprites, even angels. Even daemons. Our kind have been there, traveled to all places. Our sisters know. You understand? We know."

"I understand."

"You have never asked before. Why?"

"Because we aren't supposed to ask, I guess. At least, it isn't encouraged. But, ah, something happened, and now I just want to know. So...?"

"Our history is long. The roots are deep, our branches sturdy. The oracles, the history keepers, our oldest and most beloved of sisters, they have the memory of their lineage in its entirety. You know what that means?"

I was about to make a quip, but this was not the place, certainly not the time. "That they have all the knowledge back as far as it's possible to go?"

"Exactly. Right back to when magic was in its infancy. When humanity was barely new. When we dwelled in caves and had no written language, hardly any words even, and yet, there was always a note in one form or another. A scrawling on a cave, a scratch on a rock, then millennia later came paper, and the true age of the Necroverse dawned. It is as much a part of our magical existence as any other. The notes endure."

"The notes endure," echoed the sisterhood.

"And nobody has ever discovered how they are sent? Who sends them? Why they send them?"

"The why is clear. To keep us alive. To ensure only those of us who are worthy may pass on our DNA. Survival of the fittest. Only the strongest endure. As to how, or who, then no, it has never been discovered. Many have searched, many have made false claims, all have perished. The Necronotes are sacred, part of what makes Necros the blessed, but it is like asking who made God. Some things simply are."

"But somebody, or something, sends the notes," I protested. "They have to."

"Of course," snapped Peth.

"He's a fool. Tell him no more," protested another.

"No, he might learn something. He's not like the others, this one. My daughter chose well. For a man."

Blimey! Praise indeed.

"It's obvious," began Peth, "that the notes are sent by numerous entities. There are too many for it to be otherwise. Messengers, nothing more. But even their identity has never been discovered, and trust me when I tell you there have been those amongst us who have kept vigil over our sisters for decades, waiting to catch the note being delivered. To follow it back to its source. It is impossible. They come through magical channels, traverse the void, are nothing then something. You cannot find the answers you seek, and you should cease your search."

"I don't want the answers. I merely wanted to know how far back their history went. When this all began. If it will ever end. Damn, I know the rules. I want to protect my family, but there is a part of me, after this latest fiasco, that just wondered."

"I understand." Peth put her hand on top of mine, almost kindly. "But let this be the end of it. Some things in life are taken on trust, on faith. We are Necro, we endure. When the world destroys itself, we shall remain. Magic endures. The Necroverse in all its myriad facets endures."

"The Necroverse endures," echoed the witches.

Peth nodded down at me as she stood, her freaky eyes boring into my mind. A beautiful, terrible creature. I pitied her, but damn she scared me.

"Leave us now, we must work."

I rose and nodded my thanks to the table. Phage took my hand and we scarpered.

Neither of us breathed until the cloying night air hit us like a reminder.

These women were dangerous.

On the Road Again

I hummed the Willie Nelson classic as I pedaled away from my family, strangely chipper about the whole thing. What was wrong with me? A calmness, a confidence that all was well with the world, enveloped me as though I had no cares at all.

They were safe, that was why. I hated leaving them alone when I had a note to fulfill, but here, with these mental antiquarian bints, my family were safe. Nobody was deranged enough to come anywhere near them.

"On the road again," I sang, as Tyr swooped above me, his heart full of the joy of youth, reveling in his freedom, the taste of the air on his highly sensitive tongue.

The early morning was fresh and cool, a pure delight, so I made the most of it and got in a good workout as I wended my way through the dirt tracks of the forest, following the route the wonky witches had given me to get north-west without being able to offer my destination.

It would be nice to stay mostly off the roads. I might even get some privacy for a while. Harder to be watched when you have the cover of the trees. At least, I could pretend it was so, even though it was probably just as monitored.

Mid-morning saw me sipping happily at a bottle of water and enjoying the comfort of a rotten tree stump. I liked the woods. I belonged here. Sunlight streamed through the canopy like lasers—pew, pew—picking out individual flowers that poked their heads timidly through shy patches of luscious, emerald-green moss. Birds sang, tiny woodland creatures rustled in the thick carpet of fallen leaves, and the trees sank their roots ever deeper into the loam in search of moisture.

It was still like the old days here—damp, rot, lush growth—but there were telltale signs all was not as it once was. Trees were patchy, more were dead than was right, and there were fewer saplings able to get a foothold in the drying earth and the thinner air.

But right here, right now, I could imagine I was still a boy playing in the woods, not a care in the world.

Such a long time ago, but the memories were clearer now if anything, as though all those intervening years had been nothing but a dream.

I lay down on the earth and put my ear to the ground. Far below me, echoed the dull thuds of the dwarves tunneling. Grinning, I pictured them arguing, fighting, frantic to protect their hoards. There were other sounds too. The hum of electricity, the slight background cackle in the air as a billion conversations flew by, invisible, leaving trailers of broken nature in their wake.

Microwaves, radio waves, zeros and ones dashing this way and that, signals filling the world, the universe, with messages. I wondered how much more it could take before it all imploded.

I shook my head at the wonder of it all. Technology was so impressive, had given so much to so many, but at what cost? Almost everything. But with new tech came a glimpse of a future where maybe we could have clean air, do minimal damage, and still have the information age. It was getting closer, the ability to generate clean fuels, but was it all too little, too late? We would find out.

Rested, I pushed on for a few more hours until the heat and humidity in the forest became almost unbearable. I dismounted, found the deepest, darkest shade I could, and stripped down to my underwear. Not a pretty sight, but there was nobody here to see apart from this scruffy badger.

Badger?

I stared at the fat striped creature; he stared right back at me.

"Hey," I said, wondering if he was just a regular woodland creature or something more.

"Hey yourself," he replied. "Nice undies."

I looked down at the plain shorts and shrugged. "It was hot. I took my clothes off." Why was I explaining myself to a tubby badger?

"Not the smartest, are you?" he grumbled, pawing at the dirt then sucking up a worm with relish.

"I can hear you, you know?"

His head snapped up like he had suddenly realized. "Yeah, I'm talking to you, aren't I? How great, and me a lowly badger. What a treat for me. Not." He returned to his grubbing. Large claws ripped through the dry earth with ease, delving deep where it was still damp to find worms.

"Wow! Got a lot of friends, do you?"

"More than you," he said with his mouth full.

"How would you know how many I have?" I asked suspiciously.

"Stands to reason. You have one. Human like you, out in the woods in your underwear, up to no good, you're a Necro. Always in trouble, you lot. Met a few of you."

"How do you know about Necros?" This was a smart creature, but I wanted to find out what he knew.

"I can read 'em, hear their thoughts a little, but mostly it's just from being around for like ever."

"Oh, you're old too," I said. "Been around a while myself."

"Yes, I see that," he said, studying me carefully with his tiny pink eyes. "Andrew Blaine, now Necrosoph. I've heard of you."

"Nothing good, I hope. You can really read my mind then?"

"Nah, just screwing with you. Heard the witches talking, and I knew you way back, back when you weren't much bigger than me. Don't you remember?"

Suddenly I was transported to being a young lad, a kid really. I couldn't have been more than nine or ten and I'd had the most awesome day playing in the woods near our house, rolling around with a young badger I called Stripe, digging for worms and feeding him.

"Andrew Blaine, you better not be getting those clean clothes dirty," called my mother into the woods. I'd stopped playing, stared down at my clothes in horror. I was filthy, stains all over me, worm juice on my tunic. I was in trouble.

"I've gotta go," I told the badger back then. I ran off, calling over my shoulder, "See you, Stripe. Nice meeting you."

And he'd replied, like he was talking directly into my mind. "See you, Andrew Blaine." It had stopped me dead in my tracks.

It was when it all began. Everything came suddenly after that. More gifts. More animals found me. The waifs, the strays, creatures unlike their siblings. Some had gifts, others just needed to belong.

So long ago. Hadn't thought about that for centuries.

"It's you," I said to Stripe. "You remember."

"Badgers never forget," he said, as though insulted.

"Um, isn't that elephants?"

"No, it's definitely badgers. So, here we are. You never did come back, but I saw you, heard you grow, felt your mind. And then one day you were gone."

"We moved, my parents were concerned, wanted more privacy while I grew up. And they sent me to a 'special' school."

"Don't we all? So, the mighty Necrosoph, the most venerable Necro this quadrant has ever known. Although in other places there are some pretty decent Necros, you know?"

"I'm nothing special," I told him.

"You are. You're one of the oldest, maybe the oldest left."

"My neighbor's got more years than me. There must be loads."

"Nope, not that get given proper jobs. Most of the old-timers are just kept on for the small stuff. Easy work, nothing taxing. You're the real deal."

I didn't know whether to feel honored or horrified. Why couldn't I take it slow, get easy jobs? How the hell had he heard of me? But their world was different to ours. Animals that belonged to the Necroverse shared intel more freely, and there were a hell of a lot of them.

"I don't feel like the real deal. I'm a fraud."

"Don't put yourself down, Soph. Everyone's a fraud. Everyone's blagging it, hoping nobody notices they have no clue what they're doing."

I studied this rotund badger carefully. There was something about him, an otherness. He was different, even in a world of so many different animals. "You're a smart one, aren't you?"

"I have my moments. Can't believe it's really you. That young, grubby kid. Bet you have some stories to tell, right?"

"I have stories, but not many I can tell."

"I get it. Sworn to secrecy. Mum's the word. Anyway, I've seen my fair share, done enough, seen more than enough. You keep your secrets."

"So, what you doing here?" I asked him.

He looked at me in surprise. "Isn't it obvious? I'm here to help."

"Oh, right. Um, help how?"

"In any way I can. I want to strike a deal."

"That I can do," I told him. "You want to help me out, and in return you want to come home with me, right?"

"You got it, Soph. See, I said you were one of the smart ones."

"Then why do I feel like I've just been duped?"

Stripe smiled at me, revealing a set of very sharp teeth. "No idea," he said, then returned to snuffling in the undergrowth.

Once he'd had another bite of worm, I asked him, "Why? Why do you want to come live with me and a whole bunch of annoying animals when you have this?"

"Because the world is different now. I'm getting older and it's getting harder. Less land, less freedom. It's hotter, and there's more competition for prime burrow sites. The bloody badgers are everywhere now, it's a nightmare. Always some young boar wanting to challenge you, take over your sett. It's exhausting."

"Ah, no cars, right?"

He nodded. "We used to curse the roads and vehicles, not that most of my kind understand the dangers, but now we're bloody everywhere. You can't get a minute's peace. But that's not the reason. It's the food. It's a problem. This forest, it's rare now. Worms are going deeper every year, trying to find moisture, and it takes it toll, Soph. So you'll feed me, right?" I nodded. "Provide shelter? A place to be warm and dry. Comfortable?" Again, I nodded. "And when you want help I'll be there for you."

"Okay, you have a deal." I didn't push it, didn't ask what on earth he thought he could do to help me once we got back home. He wanted alms and I would give it. Leave his pride intact. He was ancient, knew a thing or two, so shelter in return for information was fair enough anyway.

"Great!"

"Hey, what's your name? We haven't been properly introduced."

His ears flattened against his head and he shuffled about on stubby legs. He looked away, suddenly interested in a tree. "Promise you won't laugh?"

"Why would I laugh?"

"It's your fault, you know. I didn't know, and it sounded nice."

"What are you talking about?"

"You called me Stripe," he snapped, then stared at me, defiant.

"You kept the name I gave you? That's cool." I smiled at my new friend.

His shoulders relaxed and he angled his head. "It is? Oh, great. Thanks."

"So, it's Stripe the badger then?" I said, my smile widening.

"Actually, my full name is Stripey Shortlegs," he said solemnly.

"Oh, right, I see. Anything else?"

"Well," he said, glaring to see if I was taking the piss or not. I remained stoic. "Actually, when you were in a good mood, and you were a happy kid, you used to call me Stripey Shortlegs Tubby Tummy."

"Course I did. Makes sense," I chortled.

"I knew you'd laugh. Don't you dare."

"Just messing, old friend. My oldest friend. It's a great name. It's a true bond, isn't it? We were meant to be."

"We truly were," said Stripe.

I couldn't help it, the laughter burst from me like a broken dam.

"I bloody well knew it!" Stripe flung a worm at me. It slapped against my forehead then slid down my nose before dropping to the earth.

We both stared at it.

"You going to eat that?" he asked, after a few seconds of eyeing up the prize.

"Help yourself."

Stripe snuffled up his worm.

I reminisced about a childhood when the world was an innocent place, at least to the young.

New Friends

A small object darted from the sky before alighting on a low branch. Ochre leaves rustled.

"Shall I kill it for you?" shouted Tyr in his squeaky voice.

"Kill what? Who said that?" grunted Stripe as he looked around.

"No need, Tyr. He's an old friend. Come down and meet Stripe. He's a badger," I offered by way of explanation.

Tyr flew down and landed gracefully on the back of Stripe. "What's badger?"

"That thing you're standing on."

Tyr looked down at Stripe's back. "Oh, Tyr thought it was a rock." He flapped to my shoulder to get a better view.

"Hey, what do you think you're doing? You can't go landing on a guy without their say-so." Stripe squinted, it was clear he had poor eyesight, then asked, "Is that a dragon? A real life dragon? Bit small, isn't it?"

"I am Tyrant of the Sky." Tyr spread his wings to show his true size and belched; a tiny spark escaped this mouth.

"Are you now? And what do you tyrannize? Tiny birds? Moths? Haha."

"I will grow to become a mighty warrior. I am best friends with Jen and everyone will tremble in our wake."

"What's he going on about?" asked Stripe.

"Tyr is still a wyrmling, only seven. He's got a lot to learn and a lot of growing left to do, haven't you?" I rubbed under his chin and he leaned into it, happy as only a wyrmling can be.

"He sure has got a long way to go."

Tyr growled, trying to sound menacing.

"Okay, guys, let's start this again. Stripe, this is Tyr. I hatched him from an egg and he's been with me ever since. My daughter, Jen, is already best friends with him. In time he will be hers, her companion. I am currently training him. Tyr, this is Stripe. He is a very old friend with a lot of knowledge. He's a land animal that makes his home underground and—"

"Like a dwarf? Has short legs and big tummy."

"No, not like a dwarf. Um, although there are similarities. No, he's a badger, and I knew him when I was a young lad. He's tagging along, and coming home to live with us."

"Will he eat Tyr's food?"

"No, don't worry, he won't eat your food. Will you, Stripe?"

"No, promise. Unless it's worms? Is it worms?"

"It isn't worms."

"So, you two going to be friends?"

Stripe squinted, paws forward, head down like he was about to charge. Tyr puffed out his chest to show he wasn't scared, then stepped a little closer to my head.

"We'll work on it."

Suddenly, Tyr took off then landed on Stripe's back again. "Can I have a ride?" he asked Stripe.

"Get this bloody undersized reptile off my back," he grumbled, but Tyr didn't move. Stripe sighed then said, "Fine, you can have a ride. But you fulfill your duties. You know what that means, right?" he asked the grinning dragon.

"Sing songs?" ventured Tyr.

"No, you miniature moron. You get the ticks out of my fur, check for parasites, that kind of thing. It's called a symbiotic relationship."

"I'm too young to have relationships. Soph said he'd tell me all about that when I'm older."

"Much older." It wasn't a conversation I was looking forward to having. I mean, I hadn't even had the conversation with my daughter, how did you go explaining it to a dragon? Maybe they did things differently.

"Not like that. It means, you take care of me, I take care of you."

"Deal," said Tyr. "The Tyrant of the Sky loves ticks. They pop in your mouth, squirt blood down your throat. Tasty."

Tyr got straight to work. Stripe sighed with relief as the wyrmling yanked out several ticks and enjoyed the taste of badger blood.

"Ah, love is such a fine thing," I laughed. "A match made in heaven."

"What's heaven?" asked Tyr.

"Heaven is giving thanks for your life, for the miracle of being you."

"Then I'm in heaven," said Tyr, as he snapped off another tick and squirted blood down his chin.

Stripe laughed. "I like the kid. I can't believe I'm saying this, but I like him."

"Yeah, me too. Come on, you two, we have a long way to go and I want this over with as soon as possible."

"You better fill me in on the details," said Stripe.

"I think I better had.

While I packed up and got back onto the path, I began telling Stripe of recent events. Tyr took a keen interest too, having seemingly up until now been utterly oblivious to what was going on.

Stripe understood only too well what my concerns were. He'd been around long enough to know about notes, the underground world of Necros, the dramatic increase in the use of technology and the impact it all had on his world.

What he failed to understand was why I didn't just run away and hide.

"You can't," I told him, as I rode slowly along the path, him trotting along beside. Tyr alternated between flying, and hitching a ride.

"Why not?"

"Because there is nowhere to run, nowhere to hide. Every city, every town, most roads, they are all under surveillance. It's been like that for years and years."

"So, use paths like this, and hide somewhere."

"And when I need money? I can't use a bank card, pay for anything, buy anything. How would that work?"

"Dunno. Grow it? Hunt it? Can't be that difficult."

"There are people who live like that, but they aren't Necros. More people are returning to the land to live simpler lives, but even they need to buy some stuff. And they do it in groups, pool resources. But anyway, it's different for us. They watch us, always have, and they will find us. You can't break free, it's part of the way things are. If we did run and hide, what kind of life would that be? Always scared, always worried about being caught. About another Necro getting a note with your name on it. No, I couldn't do that to my family. It isn't possible in this day and age. Even way back when, nobody ever stayed hidden for long. Now it's impossible."

"I get it, but aren't you scared now? Don't you worry? What's the difference?"

"Of course I am scared, of course I worry. But there is no choice. I do what I have to do to survive. End of."

Stripe knew better than to push it, and I may have been a little harsh, but it wasn't like I hadn't had this conversation with myself a thousand times over. Was there a choice? No. This was the way it had always been. Every country, every culture, everyone had rules. Law and order. Crime and punishment.

Necros were dangerous, that went without saying, and the notes controlled those who would risk our very existence. Was it so different from jails and corporal punishment? In many ways no. In some ways it made it fair. Everyone was involved; you played your part.

But who was I kidding? It was barbaric. The weak, those not cut out to kill, they were obliterated by their lack of ability at an early age. It was nothing more than a cull.

This was not a fair world, but I was not in charge and never would be.

We kept going at a slow pace for several more hours, my thoughts deep and dark as usual. Soon the heat became too much once again and we made shelter in an abandoned barn. Thick stone walls and a heavy slate roof meant it was a pure delight inside.

Stripe curled up in a corner and began to snore immediately. The old guy wasn't used to such a hike, and his little legs must be aching.

I settled down and ate the food the witches had provided, wondering how Phage and Jen were doing under the care of the insane hoary hags. Safe, Soph, they were safe. That was all that mattered.

Forging Ahead

"Hold up, hold up," shouted Stripe, wheezing.

I stopped the bike and left it beside the path. The raggedy badger coughed and panted, which caused him to choke. He collapsed and pawed at the air like an upturned turtle, albeit a fat one... with stripes.

"I can't go any slower. I'm sorry. Time is limited and my nerves won't stand it. Maybe you should wait here? I'll pick you up on the return journey."

"No way. You need me now. You can't do this alone."

"Soph not alone, has Tyrant of the Sky," admonished Tyr.

"That's great for when he needs his pipe lit, but not much else. Damn, I can't get my breath back."

"Stripe is a miserable thing," said Tyr, then took off to show he had endless energy.

"Hole up somewhere," I told him. "Take it easy. I'll be back soon."

"No chance. Give me a minute, then I need to have a chat." Stripe panted heavily while I grew impatient. I really didn't have time for this. I had maybe fifty miles more to go and at this pace it would take days.

When he'd recovered sufficiently, he came over and asked, "How are you about Necromorphs I think you lot call them?

"Fine. There are probably a few things I still have to tell you, actually."

"Like you can morph? I know that. What about animals? Ever met any that can morph?"

"Well, I've got a unicorn called Bernard who can hide his horn. Does that count?"

"Bloody unicorns. Dumb as rocks, the lot of them." I didn't disagree. "Any others?"

"I've met a few in my time. Why?"

"Now, this may surprise you, but I'm not your average badger. I can do things, to my body. Change it. You okay with that?"

"Will it make you go faster?"

"I'll be like lightning. But I want you to know, it's kinda intimidating. Bit scary like."

"Nothing much scares me. Unless you're going to turn into a six foot spider," I added hurriedly. "If you're gonna do that, then count me out. Ugh."

"No, not a spider. More of a humanoid type thing."

"Animals can't turn into humans," I told him. "Can they?"

"Some can, for a while. But humans can become animals and then turn back right?"

"Yeah, course."

"But it's not that. It's something else."

"Fucking hell, Stripe, will you get to the point? You're killing me here. I am getting beyond stressed."

"Okay, okay, but don't say I didn't warn you. Turn away, I don't like anyone watching."

"Fine." I turned my back and tapped my foot impatiently. What was he going to do? Morph into a motorbike, an invisible one, so we could speed away and not get caught?

Strange cracks and loud groans scared away the birds, with a generous smattering of creative swearing thrown in.

"You can look now," he said, his voice different, like he had a mouth full of rocks.

I turned. It wasn't rocks, it was tusks. "Oh." I was genuinely surprised. "You're a... A..."

"I'm a goblin. You know what a goblin is, don't you?"

"Little hunched green men with big ears and tusks and a bit lumpy like. Stubby, bandy legs, and a bit dumb. So, you pretty much fit the bill. Except for the height. Damn, you're big. Really big. How can your legs look so short even though they're longer than mine?"

"Enough with the wisecracks," he said, sounding hurt, also sounding like he had a speech impediment. "Ugh, I forgot what the tusks feel like. So inconvenient. It's nice to be on two legs again though. Shame about the knees. They are a bit knobbly."

He stared down at his green legs, so misshapen it was hard to tell what was leg, what was buttock, what were toes. Everything seemed to have a mind of its own. He towered over me by a foot and a half, his torso oversized in comparison to his legs. Chunky arms almost dragged on the ground because of the hunch. His face wasn't really like Stripe's, and free of fur, yet I could recognize him. Same piggy pink eyes, weak chin, but on a long neck.

"This isn't a thing, is it? Animals can't become goblins, can they? Is this what a goblin is? An animal on steroids? Or are you a goblin who can turn into an animal? Ah, that makes more sense."

"Anyone ever tell you you talk a lot?"

"Only people I've met."

"I'm a goblin. Then I became a badger for a while. I liked it, made life easier. I could move about freely, didn't have to stay hidden, and... Okay, I like worms. There, I said it!"

"How long have you been a badger for?"

Stripe shrugged. "Half a millennia, maybe a little less. Who knows? Time doesn't mean much. I sleep a lot," he offered, like that explained everything.

"So, how does it feel?" I asked, noting how unsteady he was.

"Weird, like I'm missing two legs. Let's give it a go." He lifted a leg to step forward and promptly fell flat on his lumpy arse. "I'm alright, don't panic. Give me a minute and I'll get the hang of it."

He scrambled to his feet and tried again. He made it several steps, began to wobble, but grabbed a tree for support. He nearly snapped it in two.

A few more steps, a little rest, and he repeated it several times until he smiled, at least I think he did, and said, "Right, shall we be on our way then? You pedal like mad, I'll run alongside. This will be fun."

"If you're sure?"

"Positive."

"Attack, attack. Intruder." Tyr plummeted from the sky and darted at Stripe's face. Stripe knocked him aside with a shake of his head.

"Oops, sorry. It was automatic."

Tyr shook off the hit, readied to launch again, shouting, "Intruder," but I grabbed him by his tail, lifted him off the ground, and looked him in the eye as he dangled there.

"Cool it, Tyrant. It's Stripe. He's a goblin."

Tyr spun and looked at Stripe. "Oh, okay."

"Okay, just like that?"

"Yes, why? Can you put me down now? I'm getting dizzy."

I laid him on the ground gently. Tyr flew straight to Stripe, landed on his hunch, and began searching for tics.

I shook my head in wonder, then was about to say something but instead just got back on my bike and pedaled off. Sometimes it's best not to ask.

With Stripe loping along beside me easily, I picked up speed, making the most of the shelter while it lasted.

I'd met many creatures in my time, being a part of the Necroverse meant most of us were linked one way or another, but Goblins were rare. Maybe several over my lifetime. Not much was known about them. They were secretive, lived far away from humans, and as we spread around the globe so they retreated further into realms not seen by ordinary humans.

Some were good, some were bad, so the lore went, same as everyone else, but they were renowned for their strength and stamina. Legends told that they could, and often did, become other creatures for long periods of time. Sometimes because they preferred it, but often because they either got stuck in animal form, like many morphs did, or because they simply forgot they were goblins.

No matter how hard you try, once you become something else your mind is altered. You take on the traits of the animal you become. Maybe a badger was the perfect fit for Stripe, so he retained more of his sense of self than most, or maybe he was so stubborn he kept his identity that way.

One thing I knew for sure, he would have to return to badger form if he wanted to live with us. The others wouldn't stand for it, and he'd scare the kids who loved petting the animals at Uncle Soph's "Zoo." Haha, how the pesky critters hated that word.

We sped through the forest, just a regular guy on an outing with his wyrmling and goblin companions.

A Stranger

We kept going late into the evening. Stripe apparently had unbounded energy. Tyr flagged after several hours, but was content to ride on either the handlebars or Stripe's hunch.

I was knackered, a gross sweaty mess, but the exercise felt good, stopped me from thinking. Something I was prone to doing way too much of when alone. So I pedaled hard, savored the build-up of lactic acid in my legs, then coasted for a while when we hit easy spots on the track.

On we rode, hurtling through the forest towards unknown trials.

Tyr started from a bumpy sleep on the handlebars and shook himself free of dreams of being a mighty dragon, then spread his wings and launched.

He circled us several times then was lost above the canopy, the shrill cry of the little fella the only sign of him.

"Danger, danger," he called as he plummeted with less control than I would have liked. He thumped into my chest and I nearly fell off the bike; I steadied myself then stopped as he dug claws into my t-shirt, piercing cotton and flesh alike.

"What's the problem?" asked Stripe, eyes darting, looking like he could club a mountain to death with his gnarly fists.

"A woman, coming down the path. Should we kill her? Should we attack now?"

"Whoa there, little wyrmling. You guys just hide. It's probably nothing. No attacking," I warned Tyr. "You either, Stripe."

"Hey, I'm a goblin, not a homicidal maniac."

"No offense, but we only just met, this time, anyway. I don't know what your morals are."

"Hmm," he pondered. "Cloudy. Yes, cloudy."

"So go and bloody well hide," I told them.

The moment they ducked into the undergrowth they were gone. Bloody witches and their magic paths.

I pushed my bike out of the path and waited for the traveler to arrive. Chances were high it was just someone going about their business, but it always paid to be prepared these days. Plus, access here was very select. Not that the country was full of marauding pillagers and rapists, but because you just didn't see the same numbers of folks about the place away from built-up areas. Cities were still chock-a-block with shoppers, workers, more bicycles than you could throw a troll at, but there was definitely an edge in the air. A woman alone out here was either innocent as the summer days were hot, a barmy witch, or plain daft. Or maybe a pillager and rapist.

So I acted polite, remained at the side of the path, and waited for her to pass on by.

I heard her whistling before I saw her. A woman of middle age with flowing red hair, a tad padded, with bright red cheeks from pedaling a very cool looking mountain bike. I looked down at my sorry excuse for a bike, all ugly welds and patched together, and got a case of bike envy. But I wouldn't change mine. It was an old faithful, and I could never find another bike that felt so comfortable.

"I like your bike," I said as she approached, smiling warmly, gesturing for her to pass.

"Thanks," she said, returning the smile. "I, er, think yours is interesting."

"Haha, it sure is. Fits like a glove though," I called as she passed.

She broke and came to a stop, then wheeled it back still sitting on the seat and asked, "What do you mean?"

"You know, it fits like a glove. It's really comfortable. Nice and snug."

"But you aren't wearing it," she said, nonplussed.

"No, guess not. I just meant, um, if it were a glove, it would fit perfectly. It feels right, you know? Like it's a part of me. Damn, how do I explain this?"

"You like your bike?" Her eyes twinkled with amusement.

"I do," I admitted. "Well, sorry to interrupt your journey. Bet you get nutters blathering away to you all the time. Ignore me, I'm just tired."

"Haha, no, it's nice to stop and have a chat. This is, er, kind of a private track, but even so most people just look right through you, or act extremely dodgy, but you seem nice."

"Oh, I'm lovely. Haha."

"Going anywhere nice?" she asked, laughing.

"No, afraid not. Just some things I have to attend to. Nothing fun. You?"

"Same. We do what we have to do to get by, right?"

"Right. Well, enjoy the peace. It's quiet for miles up ahead. Um, unless there's anyone coming, I suppose."

"Haha, you're a funny guy."

"Yeah, even when I'm not trying to be."

"Well, nice meeting you...?"

"Soph, I'm Soph."

She paused, as though she recognized the name. Then she shook her awesome locks and said with a sweet smile, "I'm Roux. Pleased to meet you, Soph." Surprisingly, she reached out a hand. I took it and shook.

We smiled at each other and then she nodded, put her foot on the pedal, and pushed off.

"Good luck, Soph," Roux called back over her shoulder, red locks dancing behind her.

"And to you, Roux."

My smile faded as she rounded the bend and was gone. "Fuck." I pulled out a small bottle of alcohol and cleaned my hands. Second nature now.

"Hey, what's up? She was nice," said Stripe.

"Lovely hair," agreed Tyr. "So red. Like blood or fire."

"She's a Necro, same as me. She's got a note. Fuck."

"There was certainly something about her." Stripe put a fat finger to his mouth, scraped a brown fingernail up and down a yellow tusk as he pondered. "She's a witch, a powerful one. Old too. Not cruel. She didn't seem cruel like so many of them, but she was strong of spirit."

"Yeah, I got all that. But who's she going to visit? Who's her mark? Why is she on this track? Damn, what do we do?"

"I could go and splat her," offered Stripe.

"Tyrant of the Sky can rain down hellfire on her lovely hair, make her face melt," offered Tyr hopefully.

"Thanks, I appreciate the support, guys, but let's think this through. We're closer to our mark than she is to the witches and Phage and Jen, so even if she's going there we could be done with our job before she arrives. But then we have to get back to them, which means she could be gone by then. Ugh, where is she going?" Why was nothing straightforward?

"Phone them up, tell them," offered Stripe.

"Damn, yeah, haha, of course. I can't get to grips with this technology, it's so easy to forget. Hey, how come you know so much about recent stuff? And your vocabulary is excellent. What gives?"

"I've been around," he said. "I listen to people, watch, go anywhere I please. I used to sneak into a farmhouse and watch TV for a few years. I was kind of a little girl's pet. Learned loads. All about phones and internet, not that I ever used any of it, of course. And Soph, you know I don't really sound like this, don't you? I'm a bloody goblin. I speak goblin. We understand each other because of what we are. Creature of the Necroverse."

"Yeah, we all speak different languages, but yet we all speak English. Makes my head hurt, always has. Wonder what you really sound like?"

From his oversized mouth came a non-stop stream of garbled nonsense. Harsh, guttural, almost cruel sounding. His accent was different, there were a lot more grunts and lisps because of the teeth and the tusks, and it hurt my head just to listen.

"Yeah, stick to the English."

"And you too," he said, grinning.

"So, I'll just call up Phage, tell her what I saw, and the witches will go deal with Roux. But what if she isn't after any of them? What if she's going somewhere else? I don't want to kill an innocent."

"Nobody is innocent. She's a Necro with a note. She's on her way to kill someone."

"I know that! But so am I. So are we."

"That's different," said Stripe.

"How?"

"Because it's us. Are you going to take the chance? Risk her attacking your family and killing your wife? Your daughter?"

"They don't kill kids," I reminded him. "Ever."

"No, not on purpose."

He was right. I couldn't risk it.

Mind made up, I called Phage and checked they were all okay. She was fine, hanging with her mom and her cronies while Jen played. All was well. I told her about the woman I'd met, about my concerns, and she said she would tell her mother and they would send people out to investigate.

"Don't let them just kill her," I said. "She's just doing her job."

"I know, but she's going to kill someone, Soph. I can't guarantee anything. You know what these lot are like," she whispered.

"Yeah, I know. But tell them, if it isn't one of you, leave her be. Sometimes our job is important, Phage, you know that."

"I know. And other times it doesn't seem that way, does it?"

"No, it doesn't. Damn, I don't know what to do. What do you think is right?"

"I think we'll do the best we can," said Phage. "But you have to admit, if you were stopped, asked who you were going to see, would you tell a bunch of strangers?"

"Not bloody likely. You know the rules. Never divulge that information, not even if it means your life. Because it doesn't just mean your life, does it?"

"No. So I'll try, Soph, but once they go to intercept her, you know the likely outcome. Shall I tell them?"

"Yes, tell them. We can't risk her coming to you without you being prepared. Get her checked out, or watched. Yeah, just have her watched. If she heads for you guys then intercept. If she passes on by then that's the end of it. Let me know, okay? She'll be there tomorrow unless she travels all night. Call me anytime, but make sure you call me as soon as you know anything. Okay, honey?"

"Okay. And be careful. Love you."

"Love you too. Give Jen a huge cuddle from me."

"Will do."

We hung up.

"See, all sorted," said Stripe, looking hopeful.

"Yeah, maybe. Okay, it's getting late. Let's make camp and get an early start in the morning.

We moved off the path, gathered firewood, and sat around the fire, talking late into the night after Tyr crashed out. Stripe and I had a lot to learn about each other, and I knew I wouldn't sleep well as the red witch headed towards my family. I had to keep reminding myself my wife was formidable, her mother even more so, and they were surrounded by a cacophony of utterly rabid antediluvian crones who would protect their matriarch and her offspring with their lives. No way would anything happen to them.

More Revelations

Morning brought a call from Phage. All was well. The witch had slept through the night some miles from the enclave, then skirted around them and continued on her way. Seemed like she had business elsewhere, so everyone could relax. They'd keep an eye on her, but it was a false alarm as far as anyone could tell.

Mind and guts eased, we packed up then forged ahead. The path petered out eventually, so we left the peace of the forest for the relative bustle of the main roads, heading for North Wales.

I could already smell the tang of the ocean, and it lifted my spirits. I hadn't been to the coast for years, and there was always something refreshing, freeing about the emptiness. The call of the gulls, the ionized air, the vastness of it all.

Going was slow because you can't very well have a goblin trundling along beside you, especially a hairless, naked one, so we had to travel right next to the verge so Stripe could remain hidden in the undergrowth, but countless times there wasn't enough cover and he had to make a circuitous route and I had to wait for him to catch up.

The road was busy with travelers. Some on horse-back, others riding donkeys or walking beside them. A surprising number of cars passed us by, unable to get up much speed, but it sure beat walking.

There was also a very heavy police presence. The moment I got a bit of speed going, there was a road-block where I had to hand over documents that gave me a pass without too many questions by bored police who checked my papers with little more than a superficial glance.

The further north we went the more checkpoints we encountered, until it became ridiculous. It was happening every mile or so now and seriously hindering progress. Never mind that the roads were in a terrible state, that the young recruits didn't really care, and would rather just wave everyone through, they were still an annoyance.

Ostensibly, they were to ensure nobody was break-ing the rules of travel, of going places without good enough reason, but it was obvious half the folks on the road were doing little more than visiting friends or fam-ily. People were sick of quarantines, the lack of trans-port, and being so isolated. The police clearly felt like-wise.

Eventually, I'd had enough. I waited for the road to clear, then called for Stripe who bounded over the rise and down the bank to the road.

"You're gonna have to revert to badger form," I told him. "This is taking for ever. You'll have to hide under a blanket on my lap and if anyone asks I'll say I found you beside the road and and I'm going to try to heal you."

"I am not doing that," he said, crossing his arms.

"You got a better idea?" I asked him.

"Yeah." He snapped his fingers and as I watched, bones crunched, sinew snapped, and lumpy bits smoothed out. His tusks retreated, his jaw narrowed, hair sprouted on his head, and within a minute there stood before me a very ugly man with way too much body hair and genitals that made me urge.

"Um, yeah, that's better. Just," I told him. "You okay like that?"

"No, it hurts. It's not really my thing. I'm more of an animorph. I can hold this, but not for long."

"Let me ask Tyr about the checkpoints. You don't have papers so this might not work." I called out silently to Tyr who dutifully noted the blocked roads. I thanked him then turned back to Stripe.

"Okay, we only have a few more miles until we can ease up, pick the smaller roads, maybe even go cross-country. Hang in there." I fumbled in my pack for some suitable clothes and gave him the best I could find. He dressed quickly, looked utterly ridiculous with the tight fit, but it was better than the naked alternative.

I pushed off and pedaled hard while Stripe ran alongside, puffing and panting almost immediately. Guess the strain was a lot in an unnatural form for him, same as all Necromorphs, but if it gained us some time he would have to put up with it.

Several people gave us funny looks, but nobody bothered us, and soon we took a turn off the main road before we'd have to show ID, and onto a small lane where we'd hopefully be alone.

We slipped into a field and with inadequate shade and dried blades sticking into my legs, we waited out the worst of the heat, ate and relaxed while Stripe recovered from his morph and rubbed his tusks happily. It was a very annoying habit, but I let him be. We all had our vices, and his was tamer than mine as I puffed away on my pipe and tried not to think of the day ahead.

How was Phage doing? Fine, no need to keep pestering her. She'd call if there was a problem, but it had only been a few hours ago and the woman was heading away. I pulled my phone out anyway, checked the charge. It was getting low, so I plugged it into the power bank then stuffed it back into my pack. Last thing I needed was to be out of juice; my nerves wouldn't take it.

We made good progress for the next few hours as we joined a quieter road that led to the main coastal route. We were heading downhill now, and the lower we descended the more breeze we got. Cool air rushed in from the Irish Sea, low pressure bringing a taster of how things used to be. Salty tang on the tongue, the cry of gulls, the clean air, the scrub climbing high on the cliffs, it was like the world used to be. Untouched, as though humanity hadn't arrived.

Down, down we sailed, freewheeling. Stripe kept pace easily even with his bandy goblin legs, and Tyr reveled in the eddies, swooping this way and that, gliding on thermals, catching bugs on the wing. Improving his skills, slowly learning to become what he would one day be.

And then there it was. The ocean. Blue and dazzling, dotted with white surf. Vast, purer than it had been for centuries, the tiny plastic particles slowly fading, a return to its former glory. We had a long way to go, but every year it got cleaner, less of a threat to the wildlife. Fish returned, including new varieties, and we become more self-sufficient in all manner of ocean goodies than we had for over a century.

Far out at sea, small independent boats bobbed about. Scores of them, each allowed to catch their quota of sea life. It was all monitored, recorded, keeping everything in check and balance, but bountiful for our country.

It all came at a price of course. Limited freedom, limited travel, less variety in the diet. Minimal exports meant less in the coffers, but we weren't unique. It was the same everywhere now. Many countries were suffering terribly from the new laws, but here with our fields, our animals, our waters, we were doing okay. For now.

I rode on, hugging the coast. Gulls screeched, Stripe panted, Tyr called with joy, and I emptied my mind, let the day unfold as though a mere observer, not a man on his way to kill another human being for the second time that week.

My stomach rumbled. It must have been kismet because out of the heat-haze came a patch of pristine road, newly surfaced, leading to one of the ever-increasing number of ubermarkets. Well, I was peckish, and we were almost out of food now there were more mouths to feed. Time for a detour. It might be the last chance I got to stock up. A nice dinner could be had, and then tomorrow was crunch time.

First World Problems

The ubermarkets had become otherworldly places. Vast, sprawling museums testament of the ability to produce all manner of food on an epic scale. No matter that the worldwide shipping on most items was at an all-time low, no matter that there were no longer mile-long container ships traveling the world's oceans, bringing endless supplies, our country and our European partners were doing pretty well on their own. If anything, there was more choice than ever.

For many, it still seemed strange if not damn annoying that the fruit and vegetable selections were less varied. But it felt like a blink of an eye ago for me when nobody had heard of oranges or bananas, and you never saw a pineapple. Kiwi, avocado, we never had that stuff so we never missed it. Well, after a brief hiatus, they were back on the shelves in limited numbers.

The prices for such homegrown exotics were astronomical, but it didn't stop people wanting to buy to recapture times gone by.

What we did have in abundance was seasonal veg. Although the seasons were different, we were still temperate enough here to have potatoes of all shapes and sizes, more carrots than anyone could possibly think was healthy, and apple varieties in the hundreds.

Meat was still relatively plentiful, but red meat not so much—had to watch the methane. We had cheese and milk and yogurts in every imaginable combination, rows and rows of the stuff almost as far as the eye could see. But prices were high and most people had nothing left over at the end of each month.

Consumerism was alive and well, however, and you can tell the state of a country by its snack aisle. In this case, half the store. All manner of confectionery. Cakes, biscuits, and crisps labeled under thousands of different brands, probably all coming from the same factory, left you bewildered and spoiled for choice. I grabbed sausages, steak, a loaf of bread, and a few cheeky bottles of wine, although the wine nowadays was so poor I longed for some of my homemade brews. Oh, how sweet it would be to get home and sit in the Necropub and enjoy a tipple with Phage.

The overhead lights were so muted, the racks of produce loomed like multi-colored monsters. Goods wrapped in colored cardboard that you were required to recycle on penalty of imprisonment.

Blaring speed metal hammered at my head as I hurriedly stocked up. Gone were the days of leisurely shopping trips. Now they wanted you in and out quicksmart, as the opening hours grew shorter every day in order to keep running costs and electric use to a minimum.

At checkout, my food and the packaging were weighed on the self-serve scale, and after I paid with my card, out popped a receipt for my records. It was all logged and come recycling day the numbers had to pretty much match up—you recycled the glass, card, paper, and tins, and you'd better not be short. Once loaded into my bag for life, I got the hell out of freaksville. I'd only just got used to bloody supermarkets and now they'd changed again. I longed for the days of small corner shops and doing a daily shop. Guess it wouldn't be long until that happened—once the choice was no longer viable and running fridges and freezers became a luxury for most.

That, or as I suspected, there'd be a "miraculous" breakthrough and energy would suddenly become plentiful. I mean, we had the oceans, the sun certainly shone nowadays, and there was plenty of wind. What was the problem?

I almost crashed into the rows of bicycles as I mused, so got my act together, loaded my backpack, then headed off to meet up with the others. Time for a refeed, a rest, then get close to our destination and figure out how to play this.

I was so tired of this shit. So utterly drained mentally and physically by it all. How much longer could I deal with this without breaking? Without just falling apart? Either giving up or making a mistake and ruining everything?

Stay strong, Soph, you have no choice.

Suitably chastised, I nodded to my fellow glum shoppers, hopped on my bike, and coasted along shiny black roads. Seemed the only ones that were maintained these days were the ones that led to you parting with your hard-earned. Not that I worked these days—a long life and a few judicious investments centuries ago meant we would never starve but were never flush either.

We weaved through the coastal hills, the sea coming in and out of view as we took sharp bends only for the vista to open out, lightening my mood, letting my spirits soar like Tyr as he called down to us. The little guy was enraptured by the emptiness, the sense of freedom, the sheer infinite vastness of it all.

Stripe wasn't as impressed. He moaned about it being too empty and grumbled about the lack of trees and dirt, but mostly he was concerned by the scarcity of worms.

Stunted trees clawed at us from steep banks as I freewheeled down a long strip of open road, not another soul in sight. We were on a road to nowhere here, well away from the sprawling masses of humanity. Hardly anyone came to such places now as the effort was too great. There were much easier beaches and places of interest to visit without it taking all day or wearing you out so much.

I liked it.

On a whim, even though now wasn't the time for sightseeing, I missed the turn that would take us down to the river Conwy and remained on the coast road and continued on past deserted seaside towns until we hit Llandudno. We sailed through the sleepy town, past the pier and beach, until we hit the Great Orme. The cable cars no longer ran, the tramway was a rusting relic, but the surroundings were as picturesque as ever.

I shouldn't have come here, shouldn't have let old memories surface, but I might never get the chance again. And besides, it was past dinner time anyway, so now was as good a time as any to set up for the night and gear myself up for the final push tomorrow. How commonplace this all was now. Was I so indoctrinated that I would call it a final push when the truth was I had come to kill a person I didn't know and without reason? I was, and I accepted it. I had become beyond jaded; I had become what they wanted.

I hid the bike in the trees, then climbed the limestone headland with Stripe back in badger form. I didn't blame him; it was one helluva climb. I clung to roots and tufts of tough grasses, dragging myself up until we emerged victorious onto a bluff overlooking the sea. A huge herd of Kashmir goats scattered as we arrived. Their numbers were vast now they were no longer culled to stop them terrorizing the tourists. Around the headland a beautiful beach stretched for miles; clean sand hugged the coast like a scarf.

Beat, I slumped to the dry grass and sat there, staring out to sea, watching the boats bobbing in the distance. Wind buffeted my hair, the salty tang almost overwhelming. Gulls screeched as they bickered over fish. A peregrine falcon hovered, motionless, high above. People like ants walked their dogs on the beach far below, a few holiday-makers played in the water, kids screaming with delight to be on such a rare treat of a vacation. The famous pier was all but deserted. The rides and amusements were gone, what remained was slowly rotting.

Off to the south, a community of green static homes shone in the evening light. There were still such places, people still came. Maybe not in the numbers they used to, but they came and they stayed for months at a time now to make the trip worthwhile. That would be nice, to while away the hours staring out to sea, go for a morning dip. No worries. No cares. Just isolation and freedom.

Several horses galloped across the sand, riderless. It wasn't unusual to see these semi-wild creatures now. The horse population had exploded out of necessity, which meant, inevitably, some were discarded, left in remote areas, or plain escaped. It was nice to see, a naturalness to it all, as if it was right.

Too hungry and tired to think about why I'd chosen this spot, I moved back into the shelter of the hillocky land and set about making a small fire away from prying eyes. With plenty of dry wood gathered on the way up, I lit an almost smoke-free fire and began cooking a veritable feast for myself and Tyr, then sat staring at the roasting meat and vegetables while Stripe went off to hunt for his own supper. Tyr continued to explore the sky.

When the meat was cooked, I whistled for Tyr and he appeared almost instantly, if less than gracefully. With a flutter of wings and a snapping of twigs, the daft sod landed in the middle of the fire and looked at me expectantly.

"Let's have another little lesson," I told him.

"Aw, do we have to?"

"Yes, we do. It's probably not the best for you to land in fires and just stand there," I told him. "You can cause other fires by sending the burning wood all over the place."

"But you made the fire."

"Yes, but only here. Just this little area. You ruined the fire, now it's smoking. We don't want smoke as then others can see it. Hop out, let me sort it."

Tyr shrugged, then jumped from the fire and I assembled it again, adding plenty of fuel to get it roaring and crackling fast to disperse the smoke.

"Tyr like fire. Nice and warm."

"I know you do, but you must remember that it's dangerous to others. Only dragons can withstand the heat. Everyone else burns. Tyr, the lessons on fire are the most important ones. You cannot risk hurting Jen. Remember, her skin will burn just like the meat you like. You must be careful. Always."

"I understand. I would never hurt Jen."

"I know you wouldn't. But accidents happen and one day you will be able to breathe huge geysers of flame. But even jumping into a little fire like this one is dangerous. You mustn't do it. Not unless it's absolutely necessary. Understand?"

"Tyr understand."

I nodded, then ripped off some of the juicy steak and threw a scrap for him.

He missed.

I said nothing, just let him swallow it then tried again. He got maybe three out of five which was an improvement, then I tore him off a big chunk and placed it beside him. Famished, I got to work filling my boots with probably more food than I should have eaten.

By the time I was finished, and I even ate some vegetables, I was stuffed. Nothing beats the feeling of cooking on an open fire, even if you hunted for your meat in a rather different way than our ancestors.

Stripe returned eventually, muttering about tiny worms and skinny slugs, then promptly curled up by the fire and began snoring fitfully. I was somewhat disgruntled, because he knew what the morning meant, but I had to remind myself he was a different kind of creature. His mind was not a human's. Life, death, killing, it wasn't the same for him. Whether a badger or a goblin, there was little sentiment involved. He didn't know the stress a human brain was capable of. Stripe had fewer worries and much fewer qualms. He would do what it took and not dwell on it.

For my own sake, I prayed I never felt nothing as I took the life of another. Would I even be human anymore?

Tyr joined his new buddy and curled up next to Stripe's belly for the warmth and the comfort and then it was just me. Buffeted by the wind, far from home. The sun was low, astonishing in its intensity. I enjoyed this strange time between day and night when the world takes on a peculiar pinkish glow and the sea suddenly seems ablaze with the dying embers of sol.

The looming eye watched us all, then winked out. All was drab and gray, the life sucked from the world until tomorrow. I watched the fire to find some comfort, not warmth, and added more sticks to lift my spirits.

Zoned out, empty of thought, a snap of a twig forced me into the present. I listened, I waited, then there it was again. Someone was coming. A sneak. A thief maybe? Something else? Slowly, silently, I drew my knife and crawled away from the fire and my sleeping friends. I slid behind a bank on my belly, then turned to peer back at the campsite. My breath was loud in my ears, my heart beat fast, but I wasn't scared. I knew my abilities, had faith in my corruption.

A crouched figure stalked around the fire. He was cautious, stopped often to check for anyone. What the fuck was this chancer doing? If he was here to rob me then he got his timing seriously wrong. You do that in the middle of the night when people are asleep, not just as the sun goes down. Maybe he was desperate, maybe he didn't care. Maybe he was dumb.

Definitely dumb, I told myself as he bent to my pack but was distracted by the food I'd left.

"Take the food if you want. Leave the pack," I said as I stood and walked towards the crouched form.

"Stay back!" he hissed. "I'm warning you."

I kept moving forward, knife hidden by my side. The stranger stood and I got a glimpse of him. The fire reflected off pale skin, his chin and neck in shadow from a thick beard. He had a hoodie and tatty jeans, but he wasn't malnourished or an obvious addict.

"Like I said, you can take the food, but leave the pack. You've got some balls, buddy, but you picked the wrong guy on the wrong day to try this shit."

"Fuck. Fuck. Look, just stay there. I'm taking the food, the pack too, all of it. Where's your phone?"

"There is zero chance of you getting my pack or my phone. I have to call the wife later to check on her and my daughter. There's a problem, so I need to know they're okay. Understand? You are not getting it." I glanced quickly at Tyr and Stripe who were awake and itching for a fight. They bored holes into the guy's head but remained hidden by the sleeping bag. This dude was lacking in observational skills; they weren't that hard to see. It was a fucking badger and a tiny dragon, for Christ's sake.

"I said, give me your phone." The jittery intruder pulled a wicked knife from a nice leather sheath and waved it about. "Haha, not so smart now, are you, old man? Hand it over."

I moved forward into the light of the fire so he could see me and I could get a proper look at him. "You're no spring chicken yourself." He must have been early thirties, pretty fit, well-fed, a bit soft around the middle. Nothing to write home about.

"Drop the sass, grandpa."

"Sass? Haha. What is this, the old wild west? Yeeha. Giddy up, cowboy."

"Shut up, this isn't funny."

I stepped up so he could see my face, my eyes, and I told him, "No, it isn't. What are you doing here? Why are you doing this?"

"Easy, that's why. You tourists, campers, whatever the fuck you are, think you can do what you want. I show 'em. I take what I want, teach 'em a lesson."

"What lesson? That people need a break from the everyday shit? Come here to relax after an arduous journey, and you ruin it for them? Leave them stranded without a phone? Nice job, buddy. Not today."

"I said hand it over." He lunged for me with the knife pointed straight at my middle like a complete amateur. I stepped aside and shoved his back. He sprawled into the bank and grunted.

"Stay low," I hissed to the others as they shifted. Tyr was puffing out his chest, dying to get in on the action. I shook my head no. This kid still had a chance to walk away alive. I didn't want any complications because of bloody dragons.

"Haha, that all you got? I'm gonna kill you slow, old man." The boy, although he was definitely a man, just acted young, jumped to his feet and sneered. He rubbed at his head, his hoodie pulling back as he did so. I locked my eyes on his and read him like an open book.

"You're like me," I told him, relaxing slightly, but still ready for action.

"I'm nothing like you. Look at you, all alone with your little cozy fire and your meat. You're mine now."

"You don't get it, do you? Shit, man, how old are you? You should know better than this by now. We don't do this to our own. Not like this, anyway. You go about your business, I need to get about mine. Do you understand?" I asked slowly. "I have business to attend to. Business."

He scowled hard but kept eye contact, and suddenly realization dawned. "You're a Necro too?"

"Duh. Why the fuck do you think I'm up here hiding out? Look, what's the deal? What's with the spiel about tourists and crap?"

"It's the truth," he mumbled. "I gotta get my practice in. Gotta hone the mad skills."

"Mad skills? You're a beginner. And what, you go around threatening innocents, killing people so you can practice for when your note arrives? Come on, that's not good."

"What difference does it make? They make us kill. And how the fuck do I know if they deserve it or not? Nobody's innocent, or maybe everyone is? I don't know."

"You have a point," I admitted. "But still, these campers, hikers, whatever, that you attack, they are definitely innocent. They aren't involved in this. You can't practice murder on normal folk."

"I don't care. It's them or me. So, like I said, hand over your shit."

"No. Look, kid, I'm trying really hard here not to just tear you apart. Leave me alone. Final warning."

His eyes shifted, nerves building, the cockiness waning, but I knew he wouldn't back down. I tried one more time.

"It's okay to walk away sometimes. Learn something from this. Don't attack innocents, it isn't right. You have to hold on to your humanity."

"They made me a monster," he hissed. As his anger built so his gift was unleashed. He morphed from a well-fed human man into a rather mangy dog in less than a heartbeat. He pounced from the pile of clothes with incredible speed and knocked me backwards. I stumbled around the fire, arms waving, as he landed to my right, hackles up, teeth bared.

"Don't do this," I warned, but I knew it was fruitless. He'd made his decision.

Time slowed as I became the moment, followed every twitch, every tensing of a muscle, and as he launched again I was relaxed, poised, and ready.

The scrappy mutt attacked, ready to rip out my windpipe. I shifted my torso to the right and as his teeth snapped down on air, a fraction from my neck, I sliced up through his belly. Warm innards coated my hand.

The body, still with a little momentum, sailed past then hit the ground hard.

He changed back to human form instantly, a naked man covered in various wounds from previous fights, his stomach in tatters. He panted heavily as he put a hand to his spilled guts and scooped them up then tried to put them back inside. Shock had set in and he didn't have much time, but it was long enough for him to know what had happened, that these were his last few moments.

He began to shiver and shake. His skin paled. Sweat formed on his brow.

"Tyr, finish him," I ordered, my voice cold.

Tyr looked from me to the lad and hung his head a little, the reality clear.

"Now!" I barked.

Tyr flapped over to the young Necro and with a glance at me he snapped down hard on the dying man's carotid artery. Tyr groaned as he bit deeper, sucking the remaining life from this poor, broken soul. His eyes closed. The body slumped. He was dead.

"Tyr, he's dead. You can stop now," I told the wyrmling.

Tyr continued to hold tight; his throat expanded and contracted as he swallowed blood. Was this right? Was this how dragons acted? Was it instinct?

"He's sure enjoying that," said Stripe, eyes glued to Tyr. I scowled at him. "Just saying." Stripe shrugged, but didn't move.

"Tyr! Stop!"

The wyrmling convulsed, his body spasmed, his hold released. Tyr shrank away from the corpse then shook out from tip to toe like a wet dog. He stood, more energized than I'd ever seen him, and then the weirdest thing happened. His body flickered, like a TV screen with a bad reception, and for a moment he wasn't a dragon, he was the mangy dog. Then he was the man, then he was Tyr again.

But not the Tyr I knew.

He turned and stared at me, eyes full of a deeper knowledge than he'd had moments ago. It was as though he'd aged a lifetime with his kill, with what he took by feeding. Blood red orbs bored into me; I shivered inside at what confronted me.

Then it was gone. Tyr remained, a small wyrmling. Blood dripped from his mouth, his entire head stained red. Nostrils flared as he breathed deeply. In. Out. In. Out.

Scales enlarged, his tail stretched out and fattened. His head expanded and elongated, tiny ears became more pointed, his teeth grew longer and sharp as needles. A ridge appeared along his back. Small horns, little more than nubs, poked through the skin on his bony head then grew and swept back. He changed through every conceivable shade and for a moment vanished entirely.

The wyrmling lifted its head to the sky and roared.

A Geyser of flame shot up seven feet in the air, lighting the world blood red, then died. The dragon convulsed once more then stood there, panting, eyes gleaming, and Tyr said, "What happened?"

"I don't know. Something. How are you feeling?"

He shook out his legs, his tail, opened and closed his jaw, arched his back, then locked his eyes, now back to purple and orange, on mine. "I feel amazing. I feel... Bigger. Stronger. Did Tyr breathe real flame? Oh no. Tyr killed a man. A human being."

"You killed out of mercy, Tyr. He was dying. In pain. You helped him. And I told you to."

"Tyr never kill a human before. Never killed anything but baby birds and grubs."

"I know. I thought this was what you wanted. What you needed to help you become the ferocious dragon you want to be. To help Jen, to be powerful and mighty. Tyrant of the Sky, remember?"

"I remember." Tyr hung his head, then his body twitched once more and the little wyrmling, now twice the size, vomited over the corpse's face. The man's skin hissed as noxious fumes contaminated the air. Flesh and meat spat and bubbled as it melted off the guy's head, revealing bone and gristle.

The corpse stared at me accusingly as lips melted away, revealing all his teeth in a death snarl.

The eyes popped, making me jump.

"I think I did a bad thing," I said, looking away.

"What happened?" hissed Tyr in a panic.

"My best guess," said Stripe as he joined us, "is that the blood of a large animal, in this case that man, a human, fired up the furnace inside and activated some of your abilities. Your stomach acid, your ugh, not sure, fire production center, got kick-started, so now you can produce flame, and the byproduct is all that acid. Damn, your insides must be like lead."

"Hell, I didn't know that could happen. Not like this. And the acid, that's a new one on me. You shifted too. You changed into him, into the dog he became."

"Everyone knows that happens," said Stripe.

"Did you?" I asked Tyr.

"Tyr takes on the gifts of his prey," nodded the wyrmling.

"So, what, you're an animorph now? You can become a mangy dog?"

Tyr clamped his eye shut and concentrated. He flickered, became the dog, then back to Tyr. "For a moment. Ugh, don't feel well."

Tyr stumbled over to the blankets, curled up, and fell fast asleep.

"He's gonna be a handful," said Stripe.

"Yeah, I think you might be right. I just thought it would help him develop, make his first kill. Get the feel for it."

"He needs to learn," agreed Stripe. "But dragons aren't like other Necros, other magical beings. They have abilities we can never obtain."

"Like puking acid?"

"Exactly. And they take the powers of their prey. Watch him, Soph, if he kills the wrong creature, the wrong person, his abilities may become impossible to control. He needs to take it slow, not develop too fast, or he'll be a babe in an adult's body, with an adult's gifts. I don't even want to think about the problems that could cause."

"No, me neither."

"Well, goodnight." Stripe yawned then padded over to Tyr, moved warily around the sleeping dragon, then curled up next to him and began to snore.

I was left alone. With the corpse of a stupid young man who should have known better. The now-cooled skull stared back at me with accusing orbs. The death snarl made me shiver. I threw a blanket over his head and hugged my knees as I sat staring at the fire, trying to process what had just happened.

Dead Dudes

In days gone by, not that this happened on a regular basis, I would leave the corpse and be done with it. I'd be long gone by the time it was found and it could never be traced back to me. But times were different now. Cameras everywhere, tracked by your phone, your credit cards, your damn recycling quotas. Drones and satellites and other stuff I'd taken no notice of, or forgotten about as who could keep tabs on it all?

But now? Now I had to do something about this guy. Like what? Chuck him off the cliff? Nope. Check his pockets and take him home? Ugh, no way was I delving into the pockets. What if I found out he had a family? Kids? I did not want to know that stuff.

Why did he have to attack? Sure, this life was hard, but killing innocents? The truly innocent. Stupid. Cruel. He did it for kicks. I'd met others like him, people jaded by the Necronotes, ruined. Others were born for it, loved the excuse to kill with permission. But they never lasted, as soon enough they were unstable, too much to handle, and along would come another Necro to put them out of their misery.

Marks, those identified by notes, were never a concern. The corpses were dealt with. At least, I assumed they were. There had never been any comeback from a killing for me or anyone else as far as I knew. Covered up, sanctioned, accepted, but you never had to worry. But sanctioned kills aside, this was the real world and you didn't go killing twats, melting their faces off, then leaving them for hikers to find. You'd get into trouble. Haha. Trouble! You'd be locked up for life and never see your kid grow up.

There was only one thing to do.

I smashed his teeth in and collected them in a ziplock bag. I cut off his fingers and toes and cooked them on the fire until they were just bones. Then I bagged them too. I didn't have to worry about the eyes, they were long gone. Reluctantly, I searched his pockets thoroughly, bagged a phone after I'd removed the battery and destroyed the chip, and threw his wallet on the fire. I did not open it. There was a set of keys so I bagged them too. I searched the area and found his pack, lightweight with just a sleeping bag, some meager rations, and a bottle of water. Guess he lived close, and I hoped he was on foot. Although, if he had a bike it wouldn't mean much to anyone who found it.

Then I cut up the body into manageable pieces, manhandled the torso and all the bits and bobs down into a deep ditch, and got digging with my fold-out spade. Yes, I came well-equipped for such eventualities. A Necro has to be on the ball to survive in this game.

After an hour's digging, I figured I'd gone deep enough, so I dragged in the torso, then the limbs, then the wrapped-up head. I buried it all, patted down the ground, swept it over with snapped off bushes until it looked like nobody had ever been here. I'd throw the teeth and small burnt bones into the sea, although once I'd finished burying the guy, I realized I didn't need to as any prints were gone—that was all that mattered. Ah well, better safe than sorry.

Exhausted, and sickened, I shuffled back to the campsite, got into my sleeping bag, and slept away the early morning. I sweated with nightmares until I awoke, groggy, thirsty, and hungry in the early dawn. All I could see when I awoke were the empty orbs of the skull and the melted lips revealing his crooked teeth. It's impossible to describe the feeling inside when you have dismembered the corpse of someone you helped to kill. It's beyond sickening once it becomes the norm. You feel ruined. Abhorrent. Disgusted with yourself for not breaking under such a strain, aware of what you are capable of, amazed you can still function. Still cuddle a sweet, innocent child, hold a regular conversation, as what kind of perverted person does these things?

Necros. That's who.

We survive for a reason. Because we are the toughest, most capable, scariest people on the planet.

And we are broken.

Onward

There was no water to wash with, no beautiful waterfall to slake away the dirt and grime. Nothing to cleanse me of my sins. All I managed was a rub of the face with a handful of water from a bottle and to brush my teeth. Bits of meat from supper remained stubbornly stuck, even though I had awesome pearly whites after all these years.

Breakfast was dismissed. I had no appetite. My body ached, and I needed more sleep, but I had business to attend to. Stripe was worn out as he wasn't used to being his old self and preferred badger form. Didn't blame him; he looked much better that way. Tyr was the complete opposite, which was a worry. I sat and puffed on my pipe to calm my nerves as he babbled on about now being a mighty Tyrant and was he an adult now? Could he come live in the house, and when could he eat another human? A bad one, he added, but that was absolutely a problem. He danced about, he jabbered constantly, he practically glowed with energy from his meal, and his new size brought all manner of issues. He had little body awareness now he was twice as big, so was ten times as clumsy.

When he launched and landed on my shoulder, I got smacked in the face by a leathery wing, he sank his claws deep into my flesh, and nearly burst an eardrum when he tried to peck lovingly at my earlobe. He was heavy, roughly the size of an eagle now, plus a long meaty tail, so I told him there would absolutely be no more human flesh or blood for many years as he needed to grow naturally, not take massive jumps in growth like this.

Once the nicotine did its job, I knocked my pipe against a rock to dislodge the embers, then covered the fire with dirt and checked there was nothing left behind. I absolutely did not want anyone snooping in this area. Then I packed up, and sat on the bluff watching the early morning activity down below. North Wales was always a popular tourist spot, and Llandudno had been one of the main attractions along with places like Rhyl. Now it was eerily quiet. Not so long ago, the place would have been brimming with early risers out for breakfast and to nab a choice spot on the beach.

Several fisherman were leaving, others returning, and there were a few people getting in some sightseeing before the day became too hot, but mostly it was how it used to be before cars. Nothing like in Victorian times though, when the craze for fresh coastal air hit hard and there was a flurry of building all along the British coast as large houses overlooking the sea were constructed at an astonishing pace.

From my hidden spot high up on the Great Orme, I looked down on the empty pier and the shore, then moved up higher to take in the panoramic view. What a place. What a view. What a country. If I had to be somewhere, then this wasn't half bad.

Wistful memories surfaced as I knew they would, and my mood darkened. Memories of another time, the pier thronged with people in their Sunday best, laughing and joking, me walking hand in hand with two young children, a woman turning, her auburn hair blowing into her face from the strong sea breeze, laughing and running ahead down the pier, us chasing after her. Ugh, not now, Soph. Not now. They are long gone. That was then. Focus on the now.

I held back the memories and tears and stared out at the fathomless water, lost to the emptiness for a while, grounding myself.

Then I was all business. Thoughts of the past, of family, banished. I had a job to do and the sooner I got it done the sooner I'd be home. I returned to camp, where Tyr was blathering away to Stripe, who was doing his best to ignore him.

"Right, time to get this over with. Stripe, best if you hold back with Tyr. Okay?"

"I'll come with you for a while, just in case. Could do with stretching my legs."

"Tyr needs to fly. Needs to breathe fire."

"Okay, Stripe. Sounds good. Tyr, no bloody fires. Wait until later, when this is done, then you can light a fire to cook on. Deal?"

"Tyr want to burn."

"Told you he's gonna be trouble," said Stripe.

"Yeah. A real headache."

My motley gang of fools descended the Great Orme past the now defunct tram line and I pushed memories of riding it down and locked them away. What use would they serve now? We had several hours to go and I needed to get a move on. Why had I come here? This wasn't where I needed to be. Stupid. I smiled as we passed the hundreds of names written with large lumps of white rocks. A tradition that dated back to my time. Wonder when the last one was made?

We bypassed the high street and cut across to West Shore Beach. I threw the remains of the man far out into the sea. Then it was onto a good clear road for the twelve-mile trip down to Conwy. Even with my tired legs it could be done in less than two hours.

With nothing eventful to note, we made good time and crossed the suspension bridge with the stunning thirteenth century Conwy Castle directly in front of us while the sun was still low. Damn hot already though. We left Tyr near the castle, under strict instructions not to show himself, and he was happy to oblige. He slept so much anyway, and after yesterday it was obvious he was done for, so he curled up behind a dense hedge and promised to remain there until I called him or he needed to stretch his wings.

Stripe, currently human, said it was a bit of a strain, so decided to hide out as well. It suited me. I needed to be alone, get this done solo. So I headed into town, just another dude on a bike, although mine was better than theirs and my thighs were stronger.

People came and went, just going about their day, but they were mostly locals, stopping and chatting to each other like it used to be in the old days. Nobody gave me a second glance. There was no reason to. I chained my bike at one of the numerous new bike racks and wandered about, just getting familiar with the place, checking out side streets, lamenting the closing of so many stores, surprised how many others had opened to take their place. Commerce had changed, but it still thrived. Just different.

Eventually, I found myself at the marina. It was beautiful. Just a few tourists, a handful of fisherman, plenty of boats, and a looming vessel out at the end of what looked like a new stone harbor wall, moored like someone wanted to be able to get away quick. More likely, it was simply because of its size. Nobody paid it any heed, and for all I knew it was a familiar sight. Could have been here for years, or might have arrived recently. I wasn't about to ask anyone as I didn't care and wanted to stay in the zone.

The murder zone.

I cracked a smile as a dum, dum, dum sounded in my head at the ominous thought. Murder zone? What was I, a cool spy on an important secret government mission? No, I bloody well wasn't. There was no glory to be had here. No thanks for my services. I needed to get a grip.

Like the few other tourists, I milled about, marveled at the view, took a few snapshots, and sat on the walls and admired my surroundings. But I saw things they didn't see. Things they couldn't see.

For Necro eyes only.

"Damn, there I go again. I am not James Bond. I am not James bond." I shook my head in wonder at my utter idiocy even after so many years, and focused on the task at hand.

"Oh, hello, what do we have here?" I asked myself as I watched the boat. "Damn, gotta stop doing this." I slapped my head and laughed quietly to myself, then got up and walked away as I was acting stupid. Brazen. It's how you got killed.

I moved back to somewhere more discreet, hidden by a sign for boat trips, now defunct. I sat on a bench, and watched. There was movement, fleeting, there but not there. Ripples of the air, a slow fading in and out.

There are people, and then there are special people. Like me. Oh-so-fucking special. Gifted, or cursed, depending on your mood, the time of day, and how much you've had to drink.

And then there are the others. Lots of other things.

This was an other. One of the increasing number of feral. No home, no permanent base, no possessions. A roamer. A damaged, wild thing from another place. Things like this, they had a name. Doesn't everything?

They were wraiths. Necrowraiths if you want the full, cooler sounding name.

Trapped beings. Spectral. With form yet without form. Fleeting glimpses of corporeal intensity only for it to be ripped away again and left in limbo, neither wholly dead nor wholly alive. Imprisoned by those with the ability to do so, the pitiful wraiths were under control by one more powerful than they. Used and abused for the jailer's own nefarious wants and needs.

They made damn good bodyguards.

You couldn't kill them as they were already dead, kind of, and you couldn't reason with them either. So what was a poor Necro to do when he wanted them gone?

He panicked.

First one, then two, then a half dozen of the enslaved creatures moved around the boat like the wind. They slithered over the hull, around the wall, in and out of nearby boats. Up, down, bloody sideways, they flew with just a hint of form. But the more I watched, the more I saw, until I was attuned to their wavelength, and followed these ancient humans, now something else, as they patrolled the boat in their own psychotic way.

If you had the strength and the inclination, you could ensnare a wraith, keep it in limbo, have it do your bidding. But this was powerful witch territory, not for most Necros. Wraiths were part of the other side, of death itself. They'd been there, done that, got the spectral t-shirt, but became trapped for one reason or another. Lost in purgatory, roaming the realms. Some were lucky enough to return to our reality only to find themselves untethered, insane, with little mind of their own.

Easy pickings for those with the fortitude, but they were unstable. Wraiths could turn, devour your mind, leave you little but a husk, locked in a nightmare that would last for all eternity. Or, you know, until some numnuts came and fucked you up because you were in their way.

Mind made up, annoyed this was not looking in any way easy, I took a break for a cup of tea at a cafe and ignored the writhing mass of ungodly non-flesh while I watched the fishermen load up their boats and head out for the day.

Something caught my attention as I sipped the dregs of my meh cup of tea.

I slowly turned my attention back to the boat, a stupid grin on my face like I was having a whale of a time. I scanned past the figure, turning my head to the left, smile still there, and focused on a group of tourists with a young child, all covered in protective clothes—hats, sunscreen, umbrella, the lot. They were gonna have a good time at the beach, weather be damned.

My heart raced, and I was usually as cool as a rapper with a name made from an ingenious play on words. All I could think was, I didn't know what to do.

After all, who the fuck kills an elf?

Birds

They say beauty is in the eye of the beholder. And that's true. To some extent. But there are some people who are simply gorgeous, right? Handsome men, beautiful women, just people with something about them that everyone would agree makes them different. They stand out whether they are in rags or designer clothes. They have a presence, an aura.

Now, times that by ten, a hundred, a thousand even.

Then give that person that information. Not just tell them, but imbue the certainty that they are perfect into every atom of their being. They are unshakably confident in their superiority. Look better. Are brighter, smarter, more knowledgeable than everyone. Are lovers that would make you weep, long for their touch with every ounce of your being. Perfect in every way apart from one.

They treat you like you are nothing, like an ant under their toes, and they are cruel beyond measure. There is no humanity, no moral compass. They are dead inside when it comes to empathy. Utter sociopaths. Psychotic. No thought for others. Unable to care about the suffering of another being.

That's about as close as you can get to describing an elf. Plus the pointy ears; that goes without saying.

And they are not allowed to walk amongst us. It is forbidden. They must not be seen, they must not be heard, they cannot take part in human affairs.

Doesn't mean they don't.

Elves scorned the Necro culture, refused to submit to the whims of our hidden masters. And they paid the price.

There was a zero tolerance policy for their presence. They entered our world at their peril. They were not to be abided. Our world, our rules. Necros got notes. But not the elves.

I knew of nobody that had ever spoken to an elf apart from very powerful witches. Those at the absolute pinnacle of their game. Scary witches. Although most of them were. Excluding the lovely Phage, of course.

"How the fuck am I going to kill him? Damn, he's so handsome."

"Sky Tyrant will rain down hellfire on elf."

I turned at Tyr's voice as I hissed, "What are you doing here?"

"He's a bit of a dick, isn't he?" said Stripe.

"Hell, you too? C'mon guys, what gives?" At least Stripe was in human guise, and somehow Tyr was holding the form of the mangy dog, although it was clear he was struggling. He kept writhing, and I saw the dragon beneath. I glanced around nervously but nobody paid us any heed.

"I will burn your head. Make eyes pop. Singe the fur on your fat behind," promised Tyr, with a hiss and a puffing out of his chest. He didn't budge, though.

Stripe rolled his eyes and ignored the mangy mutt.

"Tyr, you need to stay well away from this guy."

"Only because Soph wishes it," he said proudly.

"Good boy. Your time will come, don't you worry, but for now let me deal with this one."

"Okay."

"Now, what are you doing here? No, don't answer. Just follow me. And try to act normal." I led them away from the cafe and the view to the boat and down a narrow side alley. Nothing but large green bins for recycling. Ducts belched out greasy air from the cafe.

"We wanted to help. And Tyr hungry." His stomach rumbled.

"I offered him some worms," said Stripe helpfully. He fiddled with a pair of oversized shorts that kept slipping down. He wore a pink vest that was way too tight. I didn't even ask where he got them.

"Bleh." The dog poked out a pink tongue.

"You saw that? The elf, the wraiths?"

"We saw," confirmed Stripe. "Bloody elves. Horrible creatures. Shouldn't be allowed."

"It isn't allowed. I mean, strictly, you aren't meant to be here, but it's different for elves. Like, they really, really aren't allowed. Have you ever met one?"

"A few times," shrugged Stripe. "Don't see what the fuss is about. All those stupid ears, smooth skin. Skinny bastards the lot of them. All airs and graces, like they're better than us. I kicked ass."

"What do you mean? Where? Here?"

"No, not here. You know, other places." Stripe scratched at his face, evasive.

"It's okay, I know you can't say. Can't explain about the other places. Your worlds."

"Phew, good, because it hurts even thinking about it here. The words don't come, you know that, right?" I nodded. "Yeah, once I tried to think about home properly, about what it was like, even to describe it out loud. I was sick as a dog for a week. Awful business."

"Anyway. Moving on. Come on, be quick. You guys have got to leave."

"So, yeah, I kicked elf ass. Didn't kill the bastard, you can't really do that. But I gave him a whooping. Only thing that kills them is true magic. You know, like unicorns and shit."

"What about dragons?" I asked, about as reluctant as a man draped in animal flesh is when going into the lion's den.

"Yes, Tyr will destroy elf. Burn to crisp with mighty fire." The dog looked at me, pining to be let loose. His form was faltering; we had to leave.

"No chance. He'd have to be bloody massive, and what, you gonna let a dragon loose at the seaside?" Stripe scowled and picked his nose.

"Okay, fair point. I'll just have to go have a chat with him, then. See what the deal is. Wing it. Usually works."

"Suit yourself." Stripe rummaged deep in his nose, then inspected the prize before sucking on his finger.

"Okay, definitely time to go. Come on."

I guided them away from the marina, through alleys and across roads when needed until we got to the beach and up into the dunes. I stayed with them for a while, enjoying the sea breeze, hating the heat. I popped to the shops later in the day and we ate limp sandwiches and warm fruit for a meager supper. Once evening came and the beach was all but deserted and the marina should be dead as my insides, I left them there under strict instructions not to stray. I headed back to the boat with nothing but my wits and a cruel knife. Plus a dose of dread.

Lights were on at the boat, dotted around the deck and the cabin at the front, but there was no sign of life, just death. Wraiths circled, protectors of the man I had come to kill. Or had I? There was always that doubt. The note never specified, just gave the location. Maybe it was a test? Maybe I wasn't meant to kill him. Maybe I just had to check he was going to leave. Sometimes I didn't kill, when it felt right, and it always worked out. You never knew until you met them face-to-face.

Mind made up, and with no other choice, I settled on the bench and let myself still. Before I could even begin, the wraiths had to go.

I sank into deep silence, letting my consciousness connect with the creatures around me. More specifically, the gulls. They were everywhere. Pecking at the ground in search of meager crumbs, perching on the railings, flying about, and further out to sea they congregated in vast numbers. They were harder to connect with, but I could do it, so I let their inane chatter crowd my mind until it became almost overwhelming. Just nonsense about fish and the wind. Bickering like gulls so often did.

But they stilled at my presence as I sent out a call, more an order really. Nothing too intrusive, nothing to harm them. I gathered my focus, sent mental images of what I wanted from them, and although reluctant, they followed my lead as their small minds weren't capable of much in the way of decision-making. I pressed them until they turned from their insults and name-calling, and did my bidding.

Hundreds of birds came in low over the water, and once I had them ensnared I opened my eyes. The instructions were clear—swarm the boat, attack the wraiths.

Pointless to hide now, I stood, knees creaking, and walked slowly but surely towards the boat. The gulls swooped, diving right at the wraiths. The near-silence was eerie. The only sound the beating of wings. No screeching, no calling, no bickering, just wings.

The wraiths panicked, as I knew they would. They might be able to terrify humans and stop your heart with their frightful images as they passed through you, turning you cold and full of dread, but birds? Nah. The gulls amassed in groups, each attacking a wraith, and flew straight through the poor creatures. With silent cries into the other side, they vanished, unable to re-main tethered with such a disruption, no matter what hold the elf inside the boat had over them.

All the while I continued walking. Steady, calm as the sea in the marina, full of intent. I thanked the gulls silently and they returned to their business, leaving one hell of a mess behind them.

Avoiding the guano as best I could, I marched down the stone jetty, hot as Tyr's belly, sweating like a frog in a sauna, and straight up the gangplank and onto the boat. Then I stopped. Queasiness washed over me instantly. I was not made for boats and boats were not made for me. I swayed, even though I don't think the boat was moving at all, and had to fight the urge to vomit. Not a good time. Stay strong, show no fear.

I took a moment, then moved deeper into the boat, keeping close to the rails as the rest was piled high with crates and all manner of easy places to jump out on a poor Necro and say, "Boo!"

What a Lovely Chap

Modern boats were a genuine mystery to me. I hadn't been on one since it was all wood and sails and barrels of rum. I was as sick as a dog and vowed never to do it again. So I was at a loss where to go, apart from up to the front, fore I believe, and check in the cabin. Obviously, there was nobody there.

I wandered back behind the cabin to find a trap-door that opened when I pulled on a dull metal ring sat flush with the deck. Steps led down into light so I took a breath, readied, then tore apart for a fraction of a second of intense displeasure as I morphed into the air and came back to myself standing on a carpet so plush I felt like I was sinking.

The lights were dim, the atmosphere inviting, the furnishings impressive.

252

"You've got a nice setup here," I noted as the elf put down a paperback and stared at me with amusement from a bench seat against the wall. His legs were crossed casually, smart slacks and loafers with no socks. A pink shirt and light blond hair made him look like a true nautical type. You know, a posh one who got everyone else to do all the boat stuff.

"Thank you. Comfort is important for extended stays. May I help you? Was that you with the birds? Very clever. Haha."

"Damn, but you're handsome," I told him.

"Thanks. And you. You're... a human."

"That I am, and a tired one at that. You mind?" I gestured to a small table and chairs built into the hull. So it didn't move about, I assumed.

"Be my guest. Although, I must say, this is rather an imposition. What brings you here...?"

"Soph. I'm Soph. And you?"

"My, you are a forward one, aren't you?" He chuckled, clearly amused. This elf was the epitome of good manners and so relaxed he was almost comatose.

"Just making conversation. So, your name? Not that it matters."

"No, I don't suppose it does. But there is power in names, Necrosoph. You should know that."

"That depends on what you've got to hide. What you fear."

"Haha, so wise. You truly are a Necro, aren't you? I don't meet many. Hardly any, in fact. That's the problem with staying at home, so boring. Nothing new, just others like me. But you, a true human Necro, all smelly and sweaty and grim and determined. How wonderful." He clapped his hands with glee. Made me want to smack the smile right off his face.

"Glad I could be of service. What are you doing here? How long have you been here? And how did you get here?"

"My, so many questions. Oh, how wonderful this is." He clapped his hands again and laughed. The elf reached for a glass of wine and drank deeply then replaced it on the side table. "Shame the wine isn't better though."

"My heart bleeds. So?"

"Oh, I'm sorry, am I here to answer any question you deem worthy? I didn't realize that was how it worked here. But let me summarize. I'm here because I want to be. At least for a while. I have been here for some time, and I got here because I am an elf, your superior, and I will do as I please. Does that answer your question?"

"Kinda."

"I'm assuming you have a note?" I nodded. "May I see it?" I shook my head.

"I could make you. You do know that?"

"No chance. You can't make me because I don't have it."

"Haha, oh, you humans, so funny. I can read you, Soph, like you read the animals. In fact, there are many similarities between you and I. I can understand you humans, you understand the animals beneath you."

"I don't see it that way." This guy was getting on my nerves in a big way.

"I doubt you do. So, you have your little note, and now you are here to kill me?"

"That's one option. Down to me to decide." I knew which way I was leaning, that was for sure. He was slicker than an oil spill and slimier than Mr. Wonderful's scat after he'd stolen half a pack of butter.

"Before you do, before you decide to fulfill the request of my rulers, I... I want to ask you one thing."

Why did he pause? What did he mean? The request of his rulers? Did he mean elves sent the notes? "What?"

"Do you enjoy it? Being told what to do? Made to kill? Is it fun?" He took another sip of wine, uncrossed his legs, then re-crossed them the other way as he stared with soul-searching eyes and smiled through full, ripe lips.

"The answer is no. To all of it."

"I always assumed so. What a waste. It seems like such fun. Still, keeps you all in check. Weeds out the trash, isn't that what you say?"

"I say rubbish, I'm British. But yeah, trash is a word too. You seem to know a lot about it," I said, pushing for information, knowing I shouldn't and the time had come.

"Not really. Just picked up a few things back home. Now, I respectfully request that you leave. I have no quarrel with you, and it's a shame you have your note thingy, but you best run along. Go, hide if you can, little human. I'm sure you will get your reward soon enough."

He rose slowly, casually, like an animal poised to strike. Relaxed, but aware of his surroundings.

From nowhere, a shortsword hurtled towards my head. I morphed instantly, and felt it pass through right where my heart would have been. Pain burst through the disparate parts of my being, something deep and cruel, cold and callous.

I converged behind him and grabbed him by his throat, pulled him backward off balance, and dragged him down. He vanished as I had just done and reappeared where I'd been a moment ago. He pulled the gleaming sword, intricately carved with elven runes, from the paneled wall and smiled as he turned to face me.

"My, that was fun. Haha, you're quick. But not quick enough." He was gone, and I spun, pulled out my knife, crouched low to strike when I got the chance. He tapped me on the shoulder and I turned then jabbed, but he was across the room, laughing. "Too slow. Come and get me."

I morphed, but this time I emerged on the floor, knife easing slowly up until I thrust hard and caught him deep in the inner thigh. He let out a piteous cry then laughed and bent to stare into my eyes as the wound closed.

"I'm an elf, you incompetent. You think a little knife can harm me? Fool," he spat, the nice guy act gone.

It meant I'd got to him, that he was rankled, and that was good, right? "Where there's a will," I began, then stabbed him again. He laughed.

I morphed, came back down right on his head, stabbing manically, trying to pierce his skull. But the blade wouldn't sink in, and it was then I recalled elves had bone hard as steel. Flesh not so much, but bone, yeah.

He shucked me off as blood stained his beautiful hair, and I landed hard on the table edge right across my chest. Wheezing, I slumped to the floor and he swung at me, slicing deep right across the bruise line. Flesh opened to bone, but I rolled and was gone before he could finish me.

"Where are you, little human?" he sang, as he swished the sword about, having a whale of a time.

"Here I am," I said, emerging from pain into light. My arms spread wide and I focused as every little creature, every insect, bug, fly, mosquito, spider, and tiny thing in the vicinity scuttled, flew, crawled, or ran at the grinning form of the elf. His laugh became a choke as hundreds of spiders and flies swarmed over his face, into his mouth, up his nostrils, and into his ears. Tiny things burrowed into his eyes.

"Not fucking laughing now, are you?" I spat. I kept my focus and summoned the small creatures to form hard lumps in his airways. He coughed and spluttered, his perfect face contorted in pain and fear as he slipped to the floor, clutching his throat. The elf thrashed about, then with a mighty effort of will he purged the insects and roared with rage as he ran hard at me. The confined space meant he slammed into me and shoved me hard against the edge of the small table where his wine still sat. The corner caught my lower back, almost snapping my spine, and my focus was lost.

He shook his head with rage and fear, trying to dislodge the insects, but some were still in there, burrowing, gnawing, taking tiny bites from his flesh, getting closer to his brain. I willed them on, called for more, and as spiders emerged from every crevice and flies buzzed, the air a black cloud, I stabbed out into his eyes, over and over. Warm aqueous humor ran down my hands, made the knife slick, but I was lost to the bloodlust now, unable to control myself.

Still the insects came, swarming over me to get to him, feeding on the blood and the raw, exposed flesh of the elf. The air was dizzying with elf power. Cloying, thick, and sweet as he healed from wounds generated on the human mortal plane. Wounds insufficient to destroy such a being, but certainly an annoyance, haha.

Tiny bugs invisible to the eye formed in masses. Millions of them that live all around us, in cracks and crevices, in cushions and beds, in wood and manmade fabrics. The unseen things that live amongst us. They came at my call and sucked and gnawed and excreted and vomited and dissolved the open wounds and holes of the elf as he screamed and lost his mind.

I stabbed over and over, anywhere, everywhere I could, all focus lost, all restraint broken, and yet I kept calling the bugs, until the room was alive. A chittering, crawling, writhing mass of annihilation.

"What's your fucking name?" I hissed as I punctured his chest between ribs and twisted the knife.

But he couldn't speak, his throat was blocked, his time near. Maybe because of my heightened state, or his weaker one, I caught it through the connection I had with the bugs. A single word reverberated through their tiny bodies, like Chinese whispers, and I knew it.

"Eleron! Well, Eleron, I will destroy you. Do you understand me? You aren't good, you aren't kind, you smug bastard. You're marked, and now I'm going to erase you." Always wanted to use that line.

Eleron sank to his knees, the fight gone. But even now, as he suffocated in the human realm, as his eyes hung from his skull, as multiple puncture wounds obliterated his beautiful face and he was devoured from both inside and out, he wasn't finished.

He laughed, he actually laughed, and with a smash of a fist into my face, I was catapulted across the small room and into a brass lamp on the wall that tore my side apart.

The elf grabbed the sword and heaved himself up then stood there, regal and composed as his face dripped gore and his body was gnawed. He spread his arms and energy surrounded him, magic some would call it. The call of home, the immortality gene at work. The wounds began to close and the insects scattered. Millions dropped down dead at his feet, a pile of black crunchy invertebrate. He stomped on them viciously, over and over, and coughed and spat until he cleared his throat.

The eyes pulled taught on damaged optic nerves and sucked back into his head, but his face was still a bloody mess, criss-crossed with scars. Strips of skin hung in tatters.

He laughed a deep, bellowing, joyous cacophony that reverberated around the room and spiraled into my mind, worse than any pain he'd inflicted.

"Touche! I wasn't expecting that! Well fought, Necrosoph. Well fought."

"Yeah, thanks. It's been memorable. Now, will you please die?"

"Die? Oh, you humans. Come, you must know enough about my kind to know we cannot die. Not here. Our lives are measured in millennia, and even then it is rare for our kind to pass. We become less, but we may live for thousands and thousands of years. We choose, Soph, we choose when we would like to pass to the next level. You think you can kill me? I am so far above you it is comical. You are like these bugs you summoned, although, again, well played. And now. Now I must leave. I cannot heal here, not fully, and with my name on your note it is only a matter of time before another comes. I have outstayed my welcome, but the visit has been, shall we say, interesting? Yes, very interesting."

"Glad you had fun," I croaked. My chest felt like it was about to split open and my heart pop out. My side was bleeding profusely, and everything else just hurt like hell.

"Oh, I did. The best time in centuries. I never expected it. You got me. Haha. I do love a good fight. Now, farewell, Necrosoph. Our paths will cross again one day, I am sure. For now, continue with your life, do your duty like the good dog you are, and don't forget."

"Forget what?"

"You know. If not, then I chose poorly."

I sank to my knees as the room filled with the scent of a thousand roses in full bloom as a rift opened. Intoxicating, heavenly. I caught a fleeting glimpse of a wondrous land with a perfect sky and rolling green hills. Emerald palaces dotted the landscape, with waterfalls and trees larger than skyscrapers. All the usual elven stuff you'd imagine. But this was real, was a world, an entire world, with its own rules, its own science, laws, and legends, that was forever out of reach to someone like me.

With a final look back, Eleron nodded and stepped through the fractured air.

And I was alone in a wrecked room on a rocking boat.

Wait. What? A rocking boat?

I grabbed for purchase and managed to get upright, then stumbled from the room and up the stairs. Out on deck, I found to my horror we were out at sea. The boat's moorings were gone. We rocked side to side; I heaved over port or starboard, wondering which it was. The pain in my chest was unbearable as I puked, but I knew it was now or never.

With a sigh, and acid burning my throat, I sucked in air then jumped into the freezing dark water.

A Soggy Scene

The numbness was welcome as I clumsily swam for shore. It was short-lived. Salt bit deeply into open wounds, every stroke wrenched my mangled chest further open, and my clothes and boots dragged me down. The effort to remain afloat took all I had. Guess Eleron had the last laugh, his parting gift.

I cursed and choked, laughed and screamed, as I scrambled for purchase in silty ground in the marina. A rope caught my leg, adding to my injuries, but I shook free and clawed my way through the mud until I got to the harbor wall close to the cafe. With monumental effort, I put hand over hand on the rusty ladder set into the wall and dug broken nails into the beautiful cold cobbles. Finally on solid ground, I rolled onto my back and laughed as I stared up at the twinkling stars.

"Haha, that the best you got? It'll take more than that to get rid of me, you bastards." I shook a fist at the sky, venting into the void. I must have lain there, giggling, groaning, hissing, and generally having an awesome time for several minutes, then I heaved over onto all fours, got to my feet shakily, and rubbed the water from my eyes.

"Oh, hello," I said pleasantly, to a young couple with two small kids peeking from behind their legs. "Are the fish and chips nice?" I asked, as I spied the piping hot food in sheets of paper clutched in shaking hands.

"Um, yes," said the man warily. "Are you okay? What happened?"

"Oh, you know. Fell in, haha. My own fault. Well, enjoy the chips. Ooh, smells so good." I eyed the grub greedily as dirty water sluiced down my body.

"Here, have mine," the woman said, as she reached for the steaming food and held it out for me.

"No, I couldn't," I said, wincing as my chest spasmed.

"You look like you need it. Here." She handed it to me and I took it numbly. They gathered the kids and hurried off.

"Could have been worse," I mumbled, as I forced molten chunks of fish covered in crispy batter into my gob between split lips. "Bit salty though," I added, then wandered off and tried to recall where my bike was and where I'd left Tyr and Stripe.

I staggered up the dunes, shouting at the sand, calling it all manner of unkind names, until I found my companions. I slumped beside them and stuffed the food numbly into my mouth as I recounted what happened. While I spat crumbs of spittle and food, Stripe helped me out of my clothes and lit a large fire to warm me through. He helped bandage my wounds, although it was rough work, and once I dressed in dry clothes I felt if not ready to dance the night away, then at least like I'd live until morning.

"See, I told you I'd be some help," said Stripe.

"Yeah," I grumbled, "it's been worth all the extra hassle." He looked crestfallen. "Ignore me, I'm just beat. Sorry."

"Plenty of years for me to be of assistance." Stripe added some wood to the fire.

My mind was slow, clouded with the remnants of Eleron's presence, his elfishness. What had he said? What was he telling me? Were the elves behind the notes? And at the end, before he left, what was it? Don't forget? Something like that. Had he pretended to let information slip, or was that why he'd come here? Had he singled me out? No, surely not? But nothing rang true with elves; they were always playing their games. You couldn't trust them.

And now what? I hadn't killed him, hadn't fulfilled my note. Maybe I had. After all, you can't kill elves. Was he playing with me? Just a game? Twisting my mind to get the advantage? But why was he even in our world? Could have been anything, I told myself. Anything at all. On the run. Fancied a break. Liked boats. A castle fanboy. Adored the Welsh accent. Wanted fish and chips.

Shivering, but with the shock receding somewhat, I put my hands close to the fire. Tyr and Stripe watched me carefully, silent. Did I look that wild, that damaged? Probably. I sure felt it.

My phone rang.

Utter Panic

"Soph, it's Peth. Where are you?"

"Peth, why are you on Phage's phone?" My heart sank. This was not good.

"Where are you?" she snapped.

"I can't tell you that. Miles away. A day away, I guess. What's wrong? What happened?"

"That bloody woman, that redhead, she came back. She tricked us, skirted around. It got nasty. Leona is dead. That bitch was good. She killed her right under our noses."

"Peth, I swear if you don't tell me how Phage is I'll come and kill the fucking lot of you. What happened to my wife? Is Jen okay?"

"Jen's fine. Don't worry about her. But Phage, well, you need to be here. Now. And Soph, don't ever threaten me again. I will destroy you, you hear? Never again," she warned.

"Sorry, I'm stressed. And how am I meant to do that? Come quick? What happened to her?"

"She got hurt. She's not well, although we're working on it, but she wants you here. She needs you. You have to be part of the healing. She's asking for you and we can't complete our whispers until you arrive. It's important. You must come. There is no time."

"I can't. Even if I had a car, it would take half a day at least. Maybe more."

"Then use your gift. You can morph, become the essence. Do that and you will be here in minutes, not hours."

"You know I can't do that! I can manage a few seconds at most. I can hold the form but I can't travel far. I'm not like you. I'm no witch."

"You can, and you must. Have faith and hurry." Pethach, that bitch, hung up.

"I bloody knew it!" I shouted. "I should never have left them there. FUCK!" I rubbed at my face, tugged my hair, tied the bandage tight around my chest. Ugh, I couldn't think straight, couldn't calm down. What if Phage died? I couldn't bear it. Jen without a mother, me without the love of my life. No. No. No.

"Stripe, Tyr, I have to go. Now. I have to get to the witches. Phage is in trouble. I'm going to try to morph there. If I don't succeed, it's been great knowing you guys. Tyr, do not kill anything bigger than a bird for the next ten years or so. Look after Jen for me. Stripe, wonderful meeting you again."

"Be careful," said Stripe. "Been a blast catching up with you. You'll be fine. I'll run on ahead and be there in a few hours."

"Tyr will fly fast with his new power. Obliterate anyone who hurts Phage. Go, go now." Tyr, rather overexcited by the commotion, shot straight up and disappeared.

"He's feisty," noted Stripe.

"Sure is. Go on, go ahead. If I'm not there, explain who you are. They'll treat you well."

Stripe nodded then morphed into goblin form and ran off.

Freaking out, I called Peth back. "Look after her, Peth. Do what you can. Don't let her die."

"Hurry," was all she said before she hung up again.

"Bollocks!" I raged, my usual composure when confronted with dire situations unraveling completely.

Panicked, beyond stressed, with wounds seeping pus and blood, my chest on the verge of splitting open through the bandages, my temples pounding, throat dry, I grabbed my pack, gritted my teeth, let the power envelop me, and dissolved into motes of pain. Utter, incomprehensible pain. My very soul ached for what I might lose. It overwhelmed the hurt of my fragmented body, threatened to send me insane, never to return to my family, my life.

Speed was impossible to comprehend as I raced through the sky like a psychotic bird hitching a ride on a supersonic jet. My consciousness remained, became heightened, but I felt no connection to a body, just the usual raging spasms of terror and hurt. Within milliseconds, the suffering intensified to levels I'd hitherto never experienced or believed possible. I was miles away from my starting point, further than I'd ever gone before. This wasn't me, not what I was made for or capable of. But I had to have faith, had to do this. There was no alternative. Witches traveled like this all the time, but they spent untold years training, pushing their bodies a little further daily, until it became second nature. The hurt endured, but they learned to channel it, to feed it back into themselves on a loop, powering them further afield and giving them strength somehow, rather than it taking anything from them.

Me, I had tried to master my morphing abilities, to travel long distances, but I'd never been able to endure the pain, the fear as my body dissolved yet somehow could become whole again. Magic isn't easy for any human, and each person has their inherent abilities. To try to force something not meant for you is fraught with risk. If I failed, I would crash to the earth and die.

I would not fail. Not this time. Not now.

Only an unconscious sense of direction kept me going. I was drawn to the place I focused on, unable to steer or think about where to go. Like a bird who travels the globe by instinct, I headed straight for the witch compound without deviation. The fear of losing Phage was all that kept me together. Even as my mind and body faltered, I grasped for her, reached out for my true love, and forced myself to forge ahead through the power of will alone. Downright stubbornness is what it was, pushing beyond my capabilities, knowing I was close to losing myself, losing everything.

And then I was Soph again. Whole, back to being a damaged human being. I felt the ground beneath my feet, the wind in my hair, tasted the bile at the back of my throat, and reveled in the warmth on my skin. I teetered, but grunted and downright refused to collapse in a heap. My chest was bleeding badly, the bandages unraveled. My arms ached, my head pulsed strangely, my throat raw—I suspected from screaming—and a hunger like I'd never felt before took me over. I ignored it all and concentrated on getting my eyes to work.

The first thing I heard were gasps.

My eyes snapped into focus and I found myself right where I wanted to be. Next to Phage.

Peth stared at me in confusion and wonder, her phone clutched tight as though she'd just hung up after talking to me.

"That's not possible," she whispered.

The other witches spoke in hushed tones, about me arriving so fast, with words like impossible, first man, no witch travels at such speed, and other mutterings I ignored.

"How is she?" I asked, staring down at Phage, prone on the ground beside a small fire, with a pile of blankets underneath her.

"We are preparing to heal her, but there is a risk. How did you fly so fast? No man, no witch, has ever accomplished such a feat." She studied me, took in the damage I'd received, the state of my soul. Her slit eyes saw everything, knew what I had done. Maybe not the details, but she got the gist of it. Witches can read the energy signals people emanate. It tells them more than you would assume. More than you would ever want them to know.

"I panicked. I thought I'd fall, die. Never see my girls again. I pushed as hard as possible to get here pronto. I knew I couldn't last long."

"But it took you a mere second. I just hung up." Peth held up her phone, like I needed an explanation.

"Can we talk about this later?" I snapped. "What happened here? Where's Jen? Is she safe?"

"The child is safe and unharmed. She is with Oz."

"You left my daughter with a lion?"

"Soph, don't be childish. You know he would never hurt her. He is incapable of such a thing."

"Unless you give the order, right?"

Peth nodded. She held my gaze. "You are being foolish. She is safe. A little scared, but safe. A sister is with her also. They are playing games. We told her Phage needs to rest after the nasty woman came. Your daughter is unharmed."

"Okay. Yeah, ugh, sorry, not feeling my best. I know you wouldn't hurt her." I knelt, ignoring the tearing of my flesh, and grunted as I reach out for my wife. I took her hand, so delicate and familiar. "She's freezing." Phage was like ice. Like a corpse.

"The Necro that came, she was truly powerful. We let our guard down, I admit it, and now one of our own is gone. It's outrageous! How dare they? They chose us to attack? Leona had done nothing wrong. She should not have been selected."

"And she's dead?"

"Yes. A sneak in the night. She was killed while she slept. There was no fight, no warning. The red witch somehow broke through our protection and entered Leona's home and pierced her heart with a dagger. So base, so pathetic. That is no way for a witch to die. So, so..."

"Human?"

"Yes!" spat Peth, disgusted that a strong witch could meet with such a mundane, uninspiring end.

"It's not all wild magic and epic battles. You know that. Mostly it's grim, fast, and just plain pointless. Anyway, what happened to Phage?" I checked her over best I could, but she just looked asleep. Pale, certainly not well, but there was no obvious injury, nothing to tell me what happened here.

"Because of our protection, only us and certain guests can use magic to enter or leave here, you know this. So the damn woman had to leave how she'd arrived. By foot. I can only assume Phage was restless, unable to sleep, pining over you no doubt, so encountered the sneak in the compound."

"And they fought?"

"Of course they fought! My daughter is a fearless warrior, one of the best. You know what she can do, how formidable an opponent she is."

"I sure do."

"Then you know she fought well. But this other woman, may she rot in hell, was a match for her. When the alarm was raised they were locked tight. Phage had disorientated her with her ability, and when I came out her multiples were vanishing as Phage snuck up behind the woman and grabbed her. She whispered her words into the red woman's ear, but even as I ran towards them, the woman laughed and threw Phage to the ground."

"Her words had no effect?" That was hard to believe. These women worked by their words, by the power they put into them, the years of work and effort behind seemingly simple mutterings.

"They had an effect, of course, but Phage is still a simple child in some regards. Rather than kill her outright, my foolish, kindhearted daughter did nothing but lock her in place. Presumably to question her, not knowing of the murder committed."

"She isn't foolish. Just hates killing. She likes to give others the benefit of the doubt. My wife believes in people."

"And look where it got her. The red devil was rooted to the spot, but she'd still thrown Phage down and refused to be beaten. She saw us approach, the end was nigh, and she spoke her own words to Phage as she bent. They were cut short when Phage ran her through with a knife, but not before damage was done."

"Will she be okay? You called me, said to come now, so what is happening?"

"We know this effect, we have our own words for this state, and it would have resulted in death if she had finished. Phage is locked in the cold, her body has slowed, and it will get worse, until she dies, unless we reverse this curse."

"And you can do that, right?"

"I hope so." Peth smiled weakly, watched Phage with sorrow, but there was a hardness too. A "been there, seen that before" behind her eyes.

This strange woman, mother to my wife, had lived much longer than I, and I had been the witness to many deaths of those I loved. It never got anything but harder, but even so, I knew how she felt. The struggle. You experienced the loss as deeply as the first time, but there was a difference, because you knew deep down inside that you would learn to live with it. That you had done before and you would again. The pain endured, but it faded. It was a hard truth to acknowledge. That your love, your utter devotion, would fade when the manifestation of everything that made you whole was no more. That you could go on, love again, experience such emotion once more.

"What happens now?"

"It's why I called. We must perform an exorcism of sorts. We must eradicate this evil from Phage's body, cast it out. We have our words to speak, words you must not know, but then the ritual will continue through the night and you must be present. You must draw her back, Soph."

"Of course, of course. Thank you for calling me. She needs me here. I wish I could do more."

"There is one more thing."

"Name it."

"Jen must bear witness. She must be here by your side."

"No, absolutely not. I'm not about to let a seven-year-old watch as maybe her mother dies. No."

"You must. She must. This is dangerous. We will do all we can, but she requires a reason to return. She must sense you calling her back. Your power is as a family. Do you understand what I am telling you?"

"If we aren't here, she will die," I whispered, knowing it was the truth.

"Yes. She will die. And your life, your family, my darling daughter, all will be obliterated. As dust."

"Just tell me when," I said, releasing Phage's hand and moving to stand.

My head swam, my vision clouded, everything went numb. Next thing I knew, I was smashing into the ground.

"Get him mended. We need him," ordered Peth, not an ounce of compassion in her voice.

Two witches came and helped me to my feet. I desperately wanted to see Jen, and for some stupid reason I kept thinking abut Bernard and that it would be nice to see him too, but I knew I couldn't go to Jen in this state. The witches would fix me up, I was sure. Then I'd see her. I half walked, half stumbled to the medical center aided by the two women, and once inside the very sterile, well-stocked room I lay on the bed covered in paper and let them get to work.

They stripped me down, said nothing about the fossilized scars or the size of my penis, which was nice, then got busy with conventional meds. They cleaned me, they injected me, they stitched me. Applied creams, gauze, and bandages, then gave me something to drink that cleared my sluggish mind instantly, leaving me on a bit of a short-lived high. Unfortunately, I soon crashed down to being boring, angry Soph again.

In an hour I was in new clothes from my pack, bandaged like a mummy, and feeling about as well as could be expected considering my chest was half-cleaved open. I had multiple puncture wounds, my side was infected and pulsed with heat, my wife was dying, my child was being baby sat by a grumpy lion, her new pet dragon had the taste for human flesh, and could now shape shift, and I'd just banished a rogue elf who may or may not have signed my death warrant as I definitely now knew more than I was meant to. Maybe more than anyone else still alive in this realm.

I could really do with a cup of tea.

As if they read my mind, the witches vanished then returned several minutes later with a cuppa and some cold cuts.

"Eat. Drink. Then see Jen," said a lovely young lass called Elsie.

I was about to protest but knew better. I had to look my best for Jen. She mustn't be scared when she saw me. I slurped the scalding, sweet tea, wolfed the food, and then handed everything back to Elsie. "Thank you. Thank you both. You fixed me up great. How are you two doing? You okay?"

"We're fine. A bit scary, that woman doing what she did. We never thought any of us would be marked on a note, but I guess it's part of the game." She smiled and shrugged.

"Yeah, all part of the game," I grumbled, then slid my legs over the side of the bed and dropped to the tiles. I composed myself, nodded my thanks, smiled at the two young witches, and went to see my daughter.

A Girl, A Lion

The door eased open silently and I crept into the gloom of the matriarch's living room. Lamps cast a warm glow, the fire crackled both for comfort and because Oz liked it hot. On the rug in front of the stove, Jen had curled up into a tight ball against the downy belly of the lion.

He opened an eye as I moved closer, his growl cut off when he realized it was me. One meaty paw lay gently over Jen's shoulder. A father's instinct told me to panic, to freak out, but years of such oddities meant I relaxed at the sight of her and her protector. I nodded to Oz and he rumbled deep in his belly as he closed his eyes and returned to sleep.

A witch snored on the sofa where she'd fallen asleep watching Mary Poppins of all things, the sound muted.

I crept over, bent and placed a kiss as light as a feather on Jen's head, then left and closed the door gently behind me. She needed the sleep; I'd wake her when the time came.

The witches were out en masse where Phage lay by the fire. Unsure what to do, hurting like I couldn't believe as the meds wore off, I wandered over and watched as they lay assorted rocks, crystals, and various trinkets around her still body. The fire roared. The woman were solemn as several bent and tended to Phage, moving her limbs a little, arranging her just so. Finished, they stepped back and Peth took over.

"This has been a terrible night for the sisters. We have lost one of our own, and I will not lose another. I will not lose my daughter. We will save her. As sisters, we have the skill, the strength, the power. We shall bring her back. Whisper your words, each in turn, and then join together as we revive her. Soph, leave us now. You shall be summoned when you are needed. Bring my granddaughter with you. Don't forget, this is as important as anything we do." I nodded, then left, and sat alone at the community hut while they began their ritual.

Nobody was allowed to hear what the witches whispered. It was how all the covens worked, how many individuals used their power. Over the years, the words became ripe with meaning as practitioners honed their skills, until the words became the catalyst for their magic. Some never uttered a word out loud, other covens, like Peth's, used a whisper, believing it carried more potency. Truth on the wind, made real in the world of humans, drawing on the Necroverse as it echoed silently through the cosmos.

The private, intimate words held their essence, and were taboo for outsiders. They would cut you like a knife, cause untold harm if heard, and the intent they channeled would become warped, lose its focus. So I sat out of earshot, not really understanding their ways, how this worked. This was not my world, not my place. Beyond my understanding.

"Fucking magic," I muttered to myself. Unable to stop it, my shoulders racked, my vision blurred, and I put my face in my hands and cried. I would not lose her. Of all the loves I'd had, all the children, the deaths, the untold heartache of living a protracted life, nothing had touched me quite like Phage and Jen. Was it wrong to the other children, other lovers and wives, that I had favorites? Was I deluding myself? Had I felt as deeply about them? It was so hard to know; so much time had lapsed. Until Phage, I had been alone for so very long, but I didn't think so. Yet I knew I couldn't trust my mind or heart, as time inflicts so much damage to both. All I knew was I loved them with all my heart.

"Christ, it's gonna be murder watching Jen grow up. Bloody dragons and unicorns and smug cats. Bloody notes. Bloody, fucking, bastard, fucking god-damn notes!" I slammed my hand onto the table in utter frustration. Why had I done this? No child should have to live such a life. I was a monster. But then she would have never been born. I'd argued this very thing with Phage so many times. No, she deserved a life, but could I bear to see it end?

I ambled over to see Bernard, but he was fast asleep in the straw so I let him be. Time enough for re-unions in the morning. Maybe the witches had done something to make him sleep. Last thing they'd want is a dumb unicorn pining over his mistress. I smiled as I thought about the daft guy. He sure was a handful.

Everyone busy but me, I returned to the communal area and sat back down. My mind replayed recent events over and over, the elf's words and actions on re-peat. The smell of the ship's interior, the smell of him. Of his magic. His essence. But mostly his words. I shouldn't know, didn't want to know. The risk was too high. And what now? Nothing, that was what. There was nothing I could do, not a thing I dared to do. I cer-tainly wouldn't tell Phage. The Necronotes, were they theirs? Did the elves do all of this? Play with us, keep us guessing, keep us under control? Nothing but a cull, to keep this world mostly free of magic, but enough for them to use, to visit and know they could return home? I wasn't sure what it all meant, even if it was true, but somehow I knew I was getting close. Damn, it had been years since I tried to get answers, and it had been better not knowing anything. But my note had sent me to him, meaning those behind them knew of his potential risk.

What did that mean for me? How much did they hear? Was I now being added to someone's note? An-other Constable visit?

Screw them all. They didn't know anything. If they did, then they knew me, understood my motivation, my yearning for peace and quiet. We were fine, we were safe. We just had to survive the night.

"It's time," said Peth. She stared down at me, face expressionless, hair plastered to her face. Beads of sweat glistened like tears on her fine cheeks.

I nodded. "I'll go wake Jen."

A Long Night

"Hey, honey, Daddy's here," I whispered, as I rubbed Jen's arm gently.

She mumbled in her sleep then reached out and grasped my hand. She was fast asleep. I tried again several times until finally she stirred and I got the mother of all hugs.

"Daddy! I missed you. How's Mummy?"

"She's fine, angel, just resting. Come on, we can go visit her now. How you doing? I hear you've been a very brave girl."

"She's incredibly brave indeed," said Oz, as he stood and stretched.

"Thank you, Oz." Jen rubbed his magnificent mane like it was entirely natural.

"I appreciate you caring for her," I told the lion as I picked Jen up and cuddled her tight. Poor thing was shattered. She fought to remain awake but was asleep again in a flash. Ah, the joy of youth and innocence.

I carried her outside and she woke as the fresh air hit.

"You doing okay?"

"I'm fine. It was scary earlier, Mummy got hurt, but then Granny helped her go to sleep. They're going to make her all better. Did you have a nice trip? Was it for work? I forget."

"Yes, just some work. All done now. Right, let me put you down. You're getting so big and heavy."

Jen smiled at me and we walked hand-in-hand over to the witches as they sat silently around the fire and sent waves of energy at my wife. Peth sat beside Phage, looking thoroughly exhausted and not much better than her daughter. I dreaded to think how I looked.

"Now, don't be scared, but we have to sit with Mummy now until she wakes up. Okay?"

"Okay." Jen yawned deeply and rubbed at her eyes. She was half asleep and I hoped she'd remain that way. Time enough for a million questions once we were through this.

Peth nodded to me and we sat beside her. Jen was instructed to hold her mother's hand and I took the other. Peth moved to the other women. I felt the power. Rolling energy gathered around us, cocooned us in a private bubble that sealed us together as an unbreakable unit.

Jen yawned again and curled up next to her mum, then fell asleep holding her hand tight.

I sat there with the witches all through the night, the hurt in my heart and my body so intense I wondered if I'd ever feel whole again.

Guess I nodded off close to dawn, as I awoke with a start to realize I was no longer holding Phage's hand. Panicked, I looked up only to find my wife and daughter sat at the communal table off a ways with Peth and several senior women, drinking coffee and tea and something usually off the list judging by the way Jen was grinning and gulping her drink.

Getting up was a major problem, but I made it without too much complaint, then wandered over hardly able to contain my excitement. I stopped before they saw me and stared at my wife, aghast.

"What have you done to your eyes?" I asked. Why's your hair a different color? And your face, it looks different somehow. What is this?"

"Soph!" Phage jumped up and ran to me.

Confused, I hugged her tight, but couldn't understand what had happened to her. She smelled like her, felt like her, but her body was different too. Fuller, rounder. Just different.

"You okay? You're up, and you look so... Ugh, is something wrong with me? You seem so different."

"No, it's still me, and you're not seeing things. It's the healing, the whispering. They gave a little of themselves to fix me. It'll wear off in a few hours, don't worry. I'll always be your Phage."

"Phew, that's a relief. Although," I stared down at her much heavier cleavage.

"Hey, don't even say it." Phage grinned. How amazing to see her smile.

"Wasn't going to. But, you know, if there's an option?"

"There isn't. Come on, there's coffee."

"Oh boy, that sounds divine." We exchanged another tight hug, no need to say much more, knowing we had all the time in the world now. My fractured world was whole again, now it was only me that remained broken.

"Daddy! Mummy's all better. Look at her eyes! They're like Grandma's. Can I get eyes like that too?"

"Not right now, maybe after breakfast?"

"Really?" Jen's eyes widened.

"No. Absolutely not," laughed Phage.

"Thank you," I told Peth. "You did it. All of you. Thank you all."

"You played your part. You brought her back." Peth's face was sunken, the other women were the same. Several witches were ambling about the enclave, all of them in a similar sorry state.

"Damn, Phage is the only one looking well."

"It takes its toll, as you well know," said Peth. "It will pass, and my daughter will return to her normal form soon enough." She turned to Phage. "Now I must rest, you should too. And you, Soph, you must recover." She walked off after kissing Phage and Jen, then came back. "Oh, you had some visitors last night. They were stuck quite a ways off, but I shall send word all is well and you may meet them on the trail when you leave. We will not allow them entry." She left, back straight, head held high, but obviously on her last legs.

Jen skipped off to go see Bernard. Phage and I were alone.

"Are you really okay?" I asked her.

"I can't say I feel amazing, but I feel good. Like a bad hangover. That red witch nearly killed me. I felt her words squirm inside me, and I thought it was over. But I stopped her, and I guess you know that."

"Yes, you had no choice."

"No, I didn't. But I thought I'd lose you and Jen, and I never want that."

"Me neither. So, you really are okay?"

"Stop asking me that. I should be asking you. You look awful."

"Do I? Is it the hair?" I ran a hand through knotted locks.

"No, it's the limp, that massive cut across your chest you're hiding but I was told about, and the stabs and—"

I kissed my wife.

I'd never felt better in my life.

"Come on, let's go home."

"Absolutely."

"Oh, one thing, we have a new addition to the zoo. He's a... I'll tell you later. And um, you know Tyr?"

"Of course I know Tyr. Stop stalling and just tell me."

"Well, okay. He's um, he killed a guy and drank his blood and now he's a shapeshifter and can breath massive flames and he's twice the size."

"What!?"

"And, er, yeah, he can puke acid which dissolves flesh, and, er, probably anything else it touches. That's my news." I gave her a wicked smile.

"Haha, you nearly got me there." Phage's strange eyes sparkled as she stared into mine. "Tell me you're joking. You are, you're joking, right?"

"Um, only if you want me to be."

"I do, I absolutely do."

"I'm not joking."

"Oh boy. And this is Jen's future partner when she's of age. We better get a grip on him or he'll be wild."

"Tell me about it. Anyway, it'll be fun."

"Fun?"

"Yeah, you know, we can get him to dissolve twats that annoy us at parties. Who wouldn't want that?"

"True. He might come in handy."

I knew I was jesting, not so sure about my wife.

Leaving Bitch Town

Normally, we'd have stayed longer to be polite, and to recover from recent horrors, but Peth would rest for at least a day or two, so would the rest of the witches. They were also in mourning, had things to arrange, and we would be in the way. But more importantly, Phage insisted. It had shaken her and Jen, and home was the best place for them. And definitely for me. So we gave our thanks to everyone and packed up and got out of dodge without seeming too ungrateful.

By the time we met up with Tyr and Stripe, Phage was almost her old self again. Her body was back, her hair was chestnut again, and her eyes were almost normal.

I made introductions, which took a while as Stripe morphed between goblin then badger, which led to a lot of explaining. Jen thought it was brilliant, although she took it in her stride, which goes to show how rounded she was as an individual, or she'd seen too much weird shit already. Tyr's increased girth didn't go unnoticed. He and Jen acted like they'd been apart for years—the bond grew daily between them and there was no escaping that.

Bernard almost impaled Stripe as he went in for a sniff, forgetting he had a massive horn on his head.

Then the team headed home. Shaken, bruised, but not quite beaten.

Halfway, I remembered something I'd promised to do. I snuck off, made a phone call, then returned, smiling. I had Bernard take a rather large detour, much as he complained. Everyone asked repeatedly what we were doing and why couldn't we go straight home.

I told them they'd have to wait and see, and as we drew closer so Jen's excitement grew until she was fit to burst.

"Jen, calm down," Phage told her, as she jumped from the cart into Stripe's arms. A new game they'd devised to keep themselves entertained.

"Where are we going?" she asked yet again as Stripe jogged beside us.

"Just wait and see. We are nearly there. Ah, just on the left here, Bernard," I said.

"I'm tired," he whined. "Can't we rest?"

"In five minutes you won't be thinking about resting," I told him cryptically.

"What are you up to?" whispered Phage, rubbing my leg in a lovely way. Her eyes sparkled with mischief.

"Oh no you don't," I warned. "You will have to wait too."

"Spoilsport." Her hand remained. We smiled. This was what we wanted, what life was all about.

"Horse sanctuary," Jen read as we passed the sign.

Bernard stopped dead in his tracks. I almost fell out of the cart.

He hung his head and mumbled something.

"What was that?" I asked.

"Soph, you aren't, are you?" asked Phage, full of concern.

"Aren't what?"

"You're sending me to the knacker's yard, aren't you?" said Bernard, turning to look at me with utter sadness mixed with terror in his eyes.

Jen shouted, "No," and hugged Bernard's neck. Everyone stared at me.

"You have it all wrong," I protested. "Bernard, I would never do that to you. You're family. All of you. We stick together no matter what. Until the very end. No, this is about as opposite to that as you can get."

"You're taking me away from the knacker's yard?" asked Bernard, confused.

"Um, no. Look, keep going, you'll find out soon enough. Come on, it'll be great." I smiled at everyone, getting excited myself.

Bernard moved on reluctantly. Stripe ran ahead with Jen to open and close the gate behind us.

We followed the track, went past a timeless stone cottage and various outbuildings, then stopped in a yard outside a long stable block. Horses poked their heads out of the stable doors to watch us, some even said hello.

"Are we getting a horse?" asked Jen.

"No, better than that."

"Two horses?"

"Nope."

"Three?" Jen clapped her hands together and ran over to the stables and began chattering excitedly with the nosy equines.

"Are we getting a horse?" asked Bernard.

"Nope, I just said. It's better than that. Look, here comes Pam."

I waved at Pam and she waved back as she came over. She wore riding gear her way. Meaning, tight breeches, riding boots, and a very clingy black vest. Her hair hung loose over her shoulders, and she sported a cowboy hat set at a jaunty angle.

Phage's hackles rose instantly. "Is this the surprise?" she hissed.

Confused, I turned to her. "What? No, that's Pam, from the smoke shop. I told you about her loads of times. Her dad saved the day, remember? Poor guy."

"Oh, yes, her. You never said she was so..."

"So what?"

"So buxom."

"Oh, can't say I'd noticed."

Okay, I got the daggers, and of course she knew I was lying. I mean, hello. Man standing here.

"Hey, Pam, how you doing? You sure it's okay to drop by now?"

"Of course. Timing couldn't be better." Pam held out her hand to Phage and said, "Hi, I'm Pam."

"Hi. Phage."

They shook and then it went quiet.

Awkward.

"Okay, Phage, yes, I have big tits. Yes, they are utterly awesome. Yes, he noticed." Pam pointed at me. "He's a man. But he talks about you and Jen all the time. And no, he has never tried anything on. And even if he did, I would slap him down so hard. I don't cheat with other women's men. I don't even go with men. So, yeah, they're awesome." Pam did a jiggle. I had to look away, it was too much. I may have taken a little peek though.

Phage laughed. "I like you. And sorry, that was very rude of me."

"Sure was. But I have that effect on women. Come on, let's go meet your new recruit."

Phage introduced everyone else now there was to be no catfight, and they all chatted for a few minutes while I removed Bernard's tack. I heard Phage say sorry about Pam's dad—I already knew she hadn't heard from him since. Guess he went through with it. When I was done, Pam led the way. Bernard followed along, morose.

"You're in so much trouble," hissed Phage.

"Why? What did I do?"

"You didn't tell me she was so nice. And so curvy."

"Didn't notice," I mumbled. "Love you." Page slapped my backside. We smiled at each other.

"Okay, everyone ready?" asked Pam, clearly amused by the sight of us gathered around. A man, a woman, a little girl with a fat dragon on her shoulder. A goblin, and a grumpy unicorn.

"Ready," I told her.

Pam opened the stable door. From the gloomy interior a pair of pale eyes caught the light.

Bernard sniffed the air cautiously, then groaned. He looked to me and I nodded.

"Happy life, Bernard, my old friend."

Pam stepped aside and waved Bernard forward. He eased into the stall cautiously. We waited outside and after several minutes of whispering from the interior, Bernard emerged. Behind him came his new friend.

"Everyone, meet Betty," announced Bernard with pride. His head was held high, his horn sparkled, and his coat glowed pink with heat.

The most beautiful unicorn you could ever imagine stepped shyly from behind Bernard and bowed her head. "Hello," she said cautiously.

"Hello," I said. I turned to Pam and Phage "She said hello."

"Wish I could talk to them like you do," sighed Pam. "She's not been herself here, needs company of her own kind. I saved her from something terrible, but that's her tale not mine. She hasn't settled. Figured she'd be better with you, Bernard."

"She will be," he said, utterly in awe.

"It's another unicorn. A girl. Hello, I'm Jen." Jen stepped forward and put a hand to Betty. The shy unicorn took a small step back, then got brave and moved forward and lowered her head. Jen stroked her horn gently and I knew that was it. She would fit right in.

Everyone else said hi and we took a few minutes to get to know each other then left Bernard and Betty—what a bloody pair they made, like a sitcom husband and wife—alone while Pam supplied drinks and a light lunch.

With the day wearing on, and with plenty of miles ahead, we left after saying our goodbyes and Pam and Phage had a short private conversation.

Bernard pulled the cart, but Betty remained steadfast by his side the entire time. They didn't stop talking, seemingly very interested in the utter mundane minutiae of each other's lives. Jen rode each in turn. Tyr soared high then decided to sleep, and Stripe did likewise, the two of them curled up in the back together.

One big, utterly dysfunctional, happy family.

By the time we arrived home and had sorted out everyone's food and lodgings, it was the middle of the night. But nobody cared. Everyone was happy to be home, nobody more than me.

Life Returns

We waited and waited, nerves jangling whenever the postman came or there was a knock at the door. My phone scared the life out of me most days when someone called, and the animals stressed me out until I seriously considered expanding my culinary skills and cooking the damn lot of them.

Phage was edgy, chasing shadows, not her usual chipper self, and she cost us a fortune in dropped crockery.

Days passed, then weeks, and still I heard nothing. No Constable, no freaky third note, which would have been unheard of, and over time, without us really noticing, our old sparkle returned. It started with a tickle, then a laugh, and then we were back, slotting into family life perfectly. School runs, play dates, trips out, bike rides, swimming lessons, even new swings in the garden.

We went about our day-to-day business like any other family, except we weren't any other family. We were chosen. Marked, watched, controlled from afar. Never truly at ease, always extreme with our laughter or our crying, our ups and downs.

None of us belonged, not really. We were pretenders. Desired and feared if our friends only knew the truth about us, what we were. The crimes we were not only capable of, but had committed.

Murderers. And we knew it.

But we played along, and slowly the everyday, mundane stuff you do became who we were.

There was always that edge, though. An underlying current of when. When would it all fall apart? When would there be an unruly mob surrounding us, the townsfolk brandishing pitchforks because they'd finally seen through the veil we hid behind and now they knew we were monsters?

Was this why the Necronotes existed? To keep us in fear, hunker down and play the game?

We did it, we tried our best. But behind closed doors, or out in the fields where nobody could see, that was where we ensured our family would survive. Without her noticing, we began Jen's training. She got better at climbing, at jumping, could swing from ropes and even do a pull up or three.

Her riding came on in leaps and bounds. Plus a lot of bruises. We played games with toy swords that she loved. All the while her reflexes sharpened, her aim improved, her knowledge expanded along with her gifts.

At times, Jen and Tyr were almost inseparable, then it would be days and she would hardly pay him a second thought. Such is the way with children; I hoped it would remain that way for years. Tyr was a wyrmling still, and Jen had plenty of time to be with him when she wanted, but I never pushed it. Tyr needed his own freedom, to grow as a dragon should, so he flew, and ate, and grew little by little in a normal fashion, just like my daughter.

Mr. Wonderful showed up now and then to scoff at my stupidity, or demand food before buggering off for another day, and I even got to put my feet up now and then.

And then, suddenly, I felt free. Nothing hurt more than usual, I was out of the long funk, and Bernard hadn't smashed a window for a month. I had the house to myself, so decided to celebrate.

"Time for some breakfast," I told Woofer, as we headed down the garden.

"Woofer love breakfast. It his favorite. And lunch. And dinner."

"I know, buddy. Good boy." I patted Woofer's head.

"Let's get eggs, and what else?" I mused.

He circled me in a frenzy, shouting, "Sausages."

"Haha, what was that? I can't hear you?" I sang, smiling at the daft loon as he dashed back and forth, shouting the same thing over and over again.

"So, you want sausages, eh?"

"Woofer love sausages. Woofer love Soph." He sat, panting, head up, looking deep into my eyes.

I rubbed his head and told him, "I love you too. You're a great dog. The best."

Woofer's tongue lolled. Drool dripped onto the green grass where it was shaded by several large oaks. We walked to the fenced area where we kept the chickens, a large enclosure so they could free range but not damage vegetable patches or eat all the fruit.

The sound greeted us long before we set eyes on the small flock.

"I laid an egg! I laid an egg. It's massive. Come and look," shouted one.

"I'm laying an egg. It's massive! Wow!" screeched another.

"It's morning, everyone get up. It's morning, rise and shine," shouted the rooster, perched on a large stump, neck stretched, eyes darting this way and that, on the lookout for anything untoward that might come and steal his ladies from him.

"Chickens dumb," said Woofer, shaking his head.

"About the dumbest you can get and still be alive," I agreed. He was right though. Chickens were not too smart, but I liked them, maybe because of their simplicity. They did the same thing every morning, surprised about the egg they laid, or that another day had dawned. It was nice, reliable.

"Hey, girls," I said, smiling as I opened the gate and went into their compound.

"Soph, I laid an egg," said one.

"Well done, Hen," I told her.

"I did one too," said another.

"Good girl. Well done, Hen."

They pecked about, content.

"It's morning, Soph. Time to wake up," called Rooster.

"Okay, will do," I told him with a hearty wave.

Yes, they'd named themselves. Yes, the girls were all called Hen. Yes, every single one I'd ever had was named the same. And yes, we ate our own birds. The boys. They were called Chicken. And no, they didn't mind. Not that I told them. But if you grabbed one in the evening, by the morning nobody was any the wiser. They had memories, but they went back all of five minutes if they were smart ones.

I grabbed the eggs, said thank you, and got out of there before they started complaining.

"Let's go make that breakfast, Woofer."

"Will there be sausages?"

"Yes, there will." I scratched behind his ears and skipped back up the garden. Now, I'm not saying Woofer was as dumb as a chicken, but you know, there were similarities.

Woofer stopped. His ears flattened to his head, huge sad eyes full of pain bored into my soul. "Do you really love Woofer?" He cocked his head to the side; I felt my heart melt.

"Of course I do, buddy. You're the best friend a man could ever have." I bent and whispered, "Not like that stupid, mean cat."

"Then can Woofer come with you next note? I can help. Keep Soph safe."

"We'll see, old friend. We'll see. I would worry so much about you, do you understand? If you came, I wouldn't be focused, just concerned about my best buddy."

"Woofer is strong and fierce. I will protect Soph." His back straightened and he bared his teeth for me to see.

"You are a great guard dog," I agreed.

"So Woofer can come?" he asked, so full of hope and longing I almost caved.

"We will see. Okay?"

"Okay."

He moped back to the house, but then I screamed, "Sausages!" and he ran around in circles, sniffing the ground then the air, tail wagging. "Haha. Gotcha. Come on, let's cook up a real treat."

It was a special morning, one I will hopefully never forget. Just a man and his dog hanging out, being almost normal. Sure, he was a dog that communicated with other animals, and yes, we talked to chickens, but no, it didn't seem weird. Not in the slightest.

Months after the events of my notes had become just another part of my back story, it was Phage's birthday.

"Well, here we go again," said Phage, refusing to cry as she opened her note and tapped the details into her phone. For once, there was no attack, no daemons, just the note. Maybe someone was watching over us for once?

She sighed, then smiled at me with such inner strength and fortitude. I was immensely proud of her, same as I was every day.

We celebrated when Jen got home from school. Just us three and a very excited Woofer.

"Don't forget to make a wish," chirped Jen.

"I always do," Phage said with a smile to our sweet daughter as she got up from the table and blew out the candles. "I always do."

And yet, they never seemed to come true.

"Come on," I told my family. "There's one more surprise for us all today."

Joy

"Come and see," I told Jen and Phage as I held out my hands and smiled at them.

"See what, Daddy?"

"What's this about? Soph, why are you grinning like that? What is it?" Phage looked at me quizzically but I just laughed and said, "Hold my hands, and come with me."

Each took a hand, excited and giggling even though they didn't know what the surprise was. We walked out of the house and to the bottom of the garden, through the gate into the paddocks, then around the hedges and to the stables. As we passed the sleeping quarters of the animals, our friends, they called out cheerily but none of them gave away the secret. The air vibrated with palpable tension. A happiness. Everyone smiled and jumped about excitedly, or stood with a wing, a leg, or an arm over their mouths, almost bursting at the seams to spill the beans.

"Come on, in here," I told them as I stood at the stable door to Bernard and Betty's quarters.

"Are we visiting Bernie and Betsie?" asked Jen. "Good horses."

"I am not a horse," said Bernard, sounding knackered.

"Sorry, Bernard. Good unicorn."

"Close your eyes, sweetie. You too, Phage." Phage raised an eyebrow but I shook my head. Jen clamped her eyes shut tight, so did Phage, and my little girl gripped my hand hard, trying to contain her excitement.

We walked forward onto the straw after I opened the door. The room smelled of animal dung, of sweaty unicorn, and something else. Something new. Something wonderful.

"Open your eyes," I told them.

Both my girls stared at the scene before them and gasped. They looked to me and I nodded. They stepped forward carefully. Bernard was beside them, cautious, aware of how accident-prone he was.

"She's beautiful," gasped Phage.

"It's a baby horse," called Jen with delight. "Um, sorry, baby unicorn."

"It sure is. Do you know, there hasn't been a new unicorn for over a hundred years. We are very privileged to be a part of this."

"How wonderful," said Phage. "Congratulations, Bernard. Congratulations, Betty."

Betty was standing stock still, head bowed with exhaustion, looking about as happy as any mother could be. The newborn stumbled over on her stilt-like legs, stiff and ungainly, trying to figure out this new world, how to move in it, then found a teat and began to suckle.

"Thank you," said Betty. "Isn't she amazing?"

"She is," I agreed. "Well done, mum, you should be proud. Both of you." I patted Bernard's rump and he grinned at me like the fool he was.

"We're both very proud, and Soph, if it's alright with you, we want to let Jen name our little girl."

"You don't want to wait, let her name herself? That's the norm for Necros, you know that."

"No, we, er, we..."

"What Bernard is trying to say, is that you know as well as we do that we might not be the smartest of animals and—"

"Oh, no, don't be silly," I protested, figuring it was polite.

"We know what we are," said Betty. "We know our limits. But this one, she's different. We can both feel it. So we want Jen to name her."

Jen stepped forward cautiously and stopped in front of Betty. The youngster finished feeding then nestled Jen's hand, making her giggle. "Her tongue's so rough, like Mr. Wonderful's," she laughed, then stroked the unicorn's head, before running her fingers over its fresh horn.

"Be gentle with the horn, honey," said Phage. "It's very delicate when a unicorn is new to the world. It will get as hard as diamond, but not for a few years."

"Sorry. I'll be careful." Jen traced the ridges on the baby's horn, her fingertips brushing it lightly. The young one rubbed its head against Jen's leg.

"She will always be there for you, Jen. Always," Betty told my daughter. "This will be your true friend, like Tyr, but for other things," she added, not wanting to suggest her child would replace Tyr. I nodded that I understood what she was saying.

"So," said Bernard. "We know we aren't the best at naming ourselves. We want Jen to give our foal her name. Jen, would you like that?"

Jen clapped her hands, startling the foal who ran to her mother and hid behind her flanks. She peeked out from under her belly and we all laughed.

"What's happening?" asked Phage.

"They want Jen to name their foal."

"Can I, Daddy? Can I really?"

"Sure, if Bernard and Betty say they want you to, then it's alright with us. Right, love?" I turned to get Phage's confirmation. She was so choked up she just nodded.

"What will it be then?" I asked.

Jen put a finger into the corner of her mouth and scrunched up her adorable face, deep in thought. "Kayin," she declared, with surprising finality.

The room became silent. Even baby "Kayin" was still.

"I haven't heard that word for centuries," said Bernard.

"It has been a long time," agreed Betty.

I bent down and took Jen's hands in mine. "Honey, why that name? Where did you hear it? You know there is power in names, don't you?"

"Uh-huh," she agreed, looking a little scared.

"There's nothing to be worried about, is there, Phage?"

Phage bent down too and patted our daughter's head affectionately. "Nothing at all. It's just a strange choice, is all. Normally you name your animals Big Brown, or Cheeky Chops, things like that. Kayin is an ancient word, a very grown-up name. What made you choose it? It's okay, we won't be mad."

"I don't think I heard it anywhere. I just knew it. Is that okay? Am I in trouble?"

"No, you aren't in trouble," I told her. "If that's the name, then that's the name. But it's the name of a warrior. More exactly, it's the name for a warrior. It's ancient Hebrew. Do you know what that is?" Jen shook her head. Course she bloody didn't. She was seven. "It means the shaft, maybe the head, of a lance. Now, the horn of a unicorn is like a lance, which is a long weapon, like a massive dart really, a bit like that. So a name like Kayin, well it will give your new friend a lot of power. She will grow up being named after a weapon, of something signifying strength, the ability to battle, to fight. Maybe even to kill. Is that okay with you?"

Jen thought for the longest time, and then she broke my heart when she said, "I will have to fight. I will have to kill. I am a Necro, and that is what we do. Kayin is my companion on earth, as Tyr, the Tyrant of the Sky, is my companion in the air. My aides must be as strong as I." Jen almost collapsed; I grabbed her then lifted her up. She flung her arms around my neck and began to cry.

"I'm sorry," I told the parents of Kayin. "It's your choice, but you know what it means if your foal is the companion of our daughter."

"We know, and we love her so," said Betty. "I haven't known her long, any of you, but Bernard has told me everything, and I have seen how you all are, how you act, the things you do. You are good people, and Jen will need protection. So will this little one. I knew it before I birthed her. She is a warrior, Soph, there is no escaping it. Now it is official. Kayin," she said, sounding out the word. "I like it." Betty smiled at us as her foal suckled.

Bernard looked at me with the saddest yet bravest expression I had ever seen on his face.

"A fighter. Soph, my daughter is a warrior. I am so proud. I am so scared."

"So am I, my dear friend. So am I."

Jen was asleep in my arms, exhausted after her long speech. It didn't need saying, but I had to say something anyway. "Her awakening has begun. That wasn't just her speaking, it was the damn witches down the ages. The sisters. She is one of them, there's no denying it."

"I'm so sorry, Soph." Phage refused to cry, but I knew she couldn't hold it back for long.

"It's not your fault. It's not our fault. She's beautiful, she's smart, she's got my looks, haha, and she will be like nothing this world has ever seen before. But she's so young. Too young. She shouldn't know that word. She doesn't know it. Damn, we've got our work cut out."

"It's because we went to my mother's," said Phage. "They bloody did something, started the process."

"For once, I am not going to blame your mother," I said, surprising myself. "It never happens at this age, you know that. It didn't for you and look where you grew up. No, this is because our daughter is special."

"Look after her," said Betty, utterly exhausted now.

"And you two look after your daughter. Thank you for the honor. Our family truly appreciates it. Try not to worry," I told them. "We have many years before our children will be true cause for concern."

"So you won't worry until then?" asked Bernard.

"Course I will. Bernard, you are about to learn that you worry about your kids every single day of your life. Doesn't matter how young or old they are, you will always worry."

"Oh."

I didn't mention how many I had, or the level of stress it brought with it. The sadness, the tears, the utter heartache when they died terrible deaths, or passed of old age. The mood had turned dark enough already.

On that happy note, I carried my daughter out of the stable. Jen closed the door; we walked in silence back to the house.

Would there ever be a happy ending for my family? I consoled myself with the thought that my daughter had years and years of growing up surrounded by dragons and unicorns. I mean, it was a fairytale come true, right?

Right?

THE END

Does Woofer get to tag along? Will Bernard ever get into Mensa? Will Soph cheer up? Will Mr. Wonderful ever stop licking his nethers? But more importantly, how is Jen coping as she grows? And will Soph ever stop swearing?

Find out some, or none, of this, in Book 2: DOG DAYS.

Where We Have a Chat

There's quite a lot I want to say, but this is new to me. Usually, I finish a book and don't do this sort of thing. I'm still not sure if I should or not. But, for once, I wanted to explain a little about where things are headed and hopefully you, most valued reader, will want to continue the journey.

I am well aware this may not be everyone's cup of tea. A lot of Urban Fantasy is continuous running around and there is little time for back story or family life. I have written, and will undoubtedly write again, fast-paced, non-stop action books, and I'm sure we'll have some entries in this series much more geared towards that.

And yet, at the heart of every good story there is an actual human being. Someone you can relate to, even understand, and I always feel let down when that's missing. A 2D cutout rather than a real person. The Necroverse may be a little different to the regular world, but not so much. Just folks coping best they can in extreme circumstance. But they still have to wash the dishes and water the garden. Do the recycling and get their hair cut. I hope it has worked. That you feel immersed in their life. Like they are part of the family. And that includes the animals.

I feel a connection to Soph, and to his family. Yes, he's bad in many ways, but the world he lives in has undoubtedly made him that way. He's a survivor, and a hard man, but soft as a kitten too.

My plan, and this depends on you, dear reader, is that each book will jump forward. Sometimes years, other times a matter of days or weeks, even hours. And as the books progress, so we will follow Soph and his extended family. I would like to see Jen come of age quite a few books into the future, as I think following her progress and that of her close companions will be fascinating. I don't want to rush this, and would love to write a very long series, but let's see how it goes. That's the joy of being a writer, and a reader—you just never know what will happen.

Soph will continue to get his notes, and we can tag along. But also see how the world changes, which is an important part of this story. At the time of writing, we have just come through lockdown. A strange, frightening, terribly sad time for so many people all around the world.

Being outside with next to zero cars on the road was a truly strange experience. Currently, there is a fuel shortage, there aren't enough heavy goods vehicle drivers, and supermarkets are running short of produce and products otherwise taken completely for granted. And that's here, in the UK. So the Necroverse really is closer to home than I would have believed only a year ago. No, I am not worried about my family starving, but if we've learned one thing these past few years, it's that our freedom, our chance to have a cuddle with a family member without it feeling dangerous, is ephemeral, not set in stone.

There will be no sudden hero-against-all-the-odds revelation, where Soph single-handedly uncovers the truth about the Necronotes and destroys those behind it. This isn't what the series is about. A slow, tortuous build is what we are all in for if this is popular enough to continue. Little by little, more will be revealed, but as to what we will eventually uncover, well, let's find out. Some things just are, and you never get answers. It's life, and sometimes it sucks.

So, that's me blabbering away about my own book and utter absence of problems compared to others, and probably overstepping, or maybe not. Maybe you want to hear more about what I think, get to know the person behind the cheap, dirty bluetooth keyboard. You can always drop me a line and let me know.

I guess if you are reading this, then the journey has already begun and there are other books available, or will be soon, so let's see what the Necroverse has in store for Soph and his tribe.

To the future,

Al

Al@alkline.co.uk

Continue the adventure in book 2: DOG DAYS.

Printed in Great Britain
by Amazon